The *Boke*
of the
DIVILL

Reggie Oliver

DarkRegions
P R E S S

THE BOKE OF THE DIVILL © 2017 by Reggie Oliver

Edited by Joe Morey
Copyedited and interior design by F.J. Bergmann
Cover and interior artwork by Santiago Caruso
Cover and interior design by Michael Bailey

Dark Regions Press, LLC
P.O. Box 31022
Portland, OR 97231
United States of America
DarkRegions.com

Campaign Exclusive Trade Paperback Edition
ISBN: 978-1-62641-272-9

DEDICATION

for Isobel and Oliver Pritchard

A book is a mirror; if an ape looks into it, an apostle is hardly likely to look out.

—GEORG CHRISTOPH LICHTENBERG (1742–1799)

LIST OF ILLUSTRATIONS

Morchester is a cathedral city in Morsetshire, England and the only city in the county. The city is located in the south-east of Morsetshire, near the edge of Bartonbury Moor. It is situated on the River Orr, which flows to the south coast and into the sea at Brighthaven, Morsetshire. Morchester railway station serves the city, and is the crossing point between the West of England Main Line and the Wessex Main Line, making it a regional interchange.

It boasts a fine cathedral, St. Anselm's, mostly in the Early English and Decorated styles, but it was founded as far back as 1108 by St. Anselm (1033–1109) when Archbishop of Canterbury. Though originally named after St. Michael and St. George the cathedral was renamed after its founder St. Anselm in 1498, shortly after Anselm's official canonisation in 1494.

In Roman times it was already a thriving settlement named Morgovaria, after the Brythonic word "Morg" meaning a "seer" or "shaman." Thus the name meant "place of the shamans." The Roman historian Tacitus (AD 56–120) in his *Agricola* describes the area as "a location regarded by the Britanni as full of the powers of many gods, and from its people come priests and sages noted for their terrible gifts, according to the superstition of their tribe."

By 860, the area around Morgovaria/Morgueir was dominated by the Saxons who referred to themselves as Morgaetas, "People of Morg". The town became known as Morgceaster or Morcester, combining the original name Mor/Morg from the Latin and Celtic languages with cester, Old English for walled town and changed over time to Morcester/Morceaster and, finally, Morchester.

It continues to be a thriving market town, and retains its reputation as a centre for all things numinous, rivalling that of Glastonbury. Hence the many legends and myths surrounding its landmarks which survive to this day. Many "ley lines" are said to converge upon the city, and Morchester with its surrounding countryside is particularly favoured by UFO enthusiasts.

The BOKE
of the
DIVILL

REGGIE OLIVER

THE BOKE OF THE DIVILL

Seeke not to finde by what device
Men climb from Hell to Paradise,
Nor understand why Satann Fell
From starrie Paradise to Hell.
For curs't thou art, if thou dost looke
To find it in the Divill's Booke

—Jeremiah Staveley, 1595

CHAPTER 1

And as he opened the book it was like opening the jaws of a great beast and from its ravening depths a thousand things flew out. Flies with human faces, and tortoises in bowler hats, tennis balls with legs, pieces of meat in ballet skirts and bottoms: soft young bottoms, bottoms no older than a baby's first smile, old and sagging bottoms, big comfortable bottoms, like his wife's, troubling boy bottoms, bottoms with wings that buzzed, bottoms with teeth—

"Geoffrey!"

"Yes, dear?" said the Very Reverend Geoffrey Tancock D.D., Dean of Morchester, waking with a start.

"You just said 'bottom'!"

"Did I, my love?" The Dean sat up in bed and opened his eyes. "I was asleep."

"That doesn't really make it any better, Geoffrey." Phyllis, the Dean's wife, was not a fierce woman, but she had a limited intellect and a natural dislike of all unusual things.

"At least I didn't say 'arse'," said the Dean sighing.

"It isn't funny, Geoffrey. I've been worried about you lately. What exactly were you dreaming about? It's all right. You can tell me. I'm your wife."

"Well, it's hard to say—"

"Bottoms?"

"No. Not exactly. Actually, I was dreaming about the book."

"That book! That wretched, wretched book! Why did you agree to that dreadful man and his television crew coming here and poking about after the book?"

"I've told you before. The Cathedral needed the money, dear. It's in the most lamentable state of repair. If you'd been up on the chancel roof and seen what I had seen—"

"Wasn't there any other way?"

"What? Coffee mornings? Bring-and-buy sales? They'd provide a few hundred, if that. This was a big offer. It could mean hundreds of thousands, perhaps millions if we find it. I could sleep happy in my bed knowing that the cathedral roof is safe for another generation."

"Well, quite obviously you're not sleeping happy in your bed at the moment. You're dreaming about bottoms."

Long experience had taught the Dean that there were times when it was futile to argue with his wife.

The ancient city of Morchester with its dreaming spires, its gently flowing river Orr, winding through water meadows, its fine old cathedral and close where the rooks caw in ancient elms as they have done for centuries ... Yet Morchester hides a grim secret that goes back to the founder of its cathedral, a secret so sinister that it was simply not spoken of for centuries, a secret which at last in the twenty-first century we are going to dare to investigate. That secret is nothing less than the ultimate evil contained in a book that has lain hidden for nigh on a thousand years. Dire consequences are alleged to await any who find and open it. Yet we are going to do just that. We are on a journey to discover THE BOKE OF THE DIVILL.

"And cut, and cue titles."

"Was that all right?"

"That was lovely, Dave darling. Okay, everyone? Sound okay?"

"Sorry, chaps, we got a slight interference on the tape. Aeroplane, or something. We'll have to go again."

"Oh, fuckety fuck!"

"Sorry, Dave. Not your fault. We'll have to go again. Can't be helped."

"Arseholes! Triple arseholes! Will someone get me a skinny latte?"

"Emma! Coffee please, my love. We could all do with a bevvy."

"And since we're going again, Veronica, I'm not a hundred percent happy with that 'nigh on a thousand years': sounds a bit, I don't know— and it's actually more like nine hundred."

"Dave, love, this is a TV programme, not one of your university lectures."

"I know, I know. But I don't think we should dumb down unnecessarily. And while we're at it, 'dreaming spires' is a bit of a cliché, isn't it?"

"It's not a cliché; it's Matthew Arnold."

"I know it's Matthew Arnold. I did go to Oxford, you know, Veronica darling."

"Don't call me darling, Dave. It's sexist."

"*You* call everyone darling."

"Coming from *you* it *sounds* sexist. You're an academic; I'm a film director, and a woman. Let's try the other bit to camera, darling. We'll do this shot with the cathedral in the background. Hang on! What are those black things behind Dave's head?"

"They're rooks, Veronica. Birds."

"Well, can you do something about them? They're making the most godawful noise."

"It's okay, Veronica. I can cope with the rooks. They're not intrusive. They'll add atmosphere."

"All righty! Are we ready to go? Ready, Dave?"

"Look, Veronica, love— I mean, sorry, Veronica. Would you mind calling me David, not Dave. I'm sorry, I just don't like Dave. Nobody calls me Dave. It— I don't know, it just makes me sound like a taxi driver or something."

"Oooh! Hark at the professor. All right, then, Day-vid. Are we ready to go, Day-vid?"

"Yes, I'm bloody ready, Veronica!"

"Okay, and cue Dave to camera, and action!"

The Cathedral was founded in 1107 by St. Anselm, then Archbishop of Canterbury. Legend has it that it was built over a site sacred, as the chronicler William of Morchester, has it "to the ancient gods." Paganism was still practised there and there were tales of a local landowner of Saxon origin, one Cutbirth of Bartonstone who had great power thereabouts and was also a wizard or shaman. He was said to possess an ancient book, the so-called BOKE OF THE DIVILL, which contained words and signs of great power. St. Anselm had Cutbirth brought before him and condemned him and his book to be buried beneath the foundations of the Cathedral, so that he and his power would be forever confined in the sacred building. In later centuries Cutbirth might have been burnt, but this was in the days when paganism was seen by men like Anselm as a rival power to be conquered by Christian imperialism, not as some kind of perverted aberration from the one true religion. I am Professor David Huntley, I am a medieval historian, and today I begin my search for Morchester's hidden pre-Christian past, for the resting place of Cutbirth of Bartonstone, and for the mysterious.

"And cut!"

"Was that all right?"

"Fine, Dave darling, just fine. Now all we have to do is find this damned 'boke'."

That September afternoon, rain clouds gathered over Morchester and there could be no more filming. The streets of Morchester still enjoyed remnants of their ancient charm. Of course, there was Boots, there were Tesco and Sainsbury's jamming their plate glass, steel and gaudily coloured frontages into the old rows of houses. There was even a shopping mall; but all these signs of corporate commercialism still looked like temporary barbarian raids on the sedate citadels of traditional shopkeeping. When Emma Hartley, personal assistant to Veronica Boyd, the film unit's director, walked along the main thoroughfare, St. Anselm's Street, she found plenty of old-fashioned establishments that seemed barely to have changed in a hundred years. There were tea shops, craft shops and haberdasheries, even an old-style gentlemen's outfitters which sold cardigans, striped flannel pyjamas, and cravats. Emma rejoiced in all of this, but would not have told anyone, let alone Veronica, that she did. She was twenty-three, fresh from a Media Studies degree at Wessex University, and this was her first job in television. She knew how lucky she was to get it and how she absolutely must not "blow it." That afternoon she was scouting for "visuals": images that would accompany Professor Huntley's recitations and prevent viewers with the attention span of a gnat from switching channels. And here in St. Anselm's Street was the very thing she had been looking for.

The sign above the shop front, in gold letters on a matte green background, read:

BASIL VALENTINE, ANTIQUARIAN BOOKS AND PRINTS

As she entered, an old-fashioned shop bell clanged. It gave her a cosy feeling. The atmosphere that surrounded her was still, almost timeless. The smell was clean, but not disinfected: a hint of wood shavings and old paper. Most of the shop was occupied by shelves of books, many in leather bindings, some in carefully preserved dust jackets. They were ordered neatly, almost obsessively. Against one wall were racks containing mounted topographical prints in acetate sleeves. Emma began a search for prints of Morchester Cathedral and its close. A faint shuffling sound behind her made her turn around.

Standing before her was a tall man immaculately turned out in an old-fashioned way, in cavalry twill trousers, check shirt and a cardigan, like a lieutenant colonel in mufti. He wore spectacles, and a full head of grey hair swept back in a mane from his high forehead. It was difficult to tell his age: he might have been an old-looking young man, or the other way around. Whichever way it was, there was a sense of his being not quite what he seemed.

"Are you all right there?" he said. The tone was gentle, rather over-modulated.

"Yes, thank you." Emma felt a slight unease, as one does when one is being looked at rather too closely by a stranger. "Are you Basil Valentine, the owner of this shop?"

"I answer to that name."

This was irritating. Was he hiding something?

"I'm Emma Hartley. I'm looking for old prints of the cathedral, and the town."

"You are looking in the right place."

"I'm with the film crew doing this programme about the cathedral and this ... book."

"*The.*"

"You know about it?"

"A little."

"Do you approve? I mean, do you think we should be investigating it or that we should leave well enough alone?"

"I have no opinion one way or another."

This was disappointing. Emma had begun to imagine that she had found someone who might make a valuable and interesting contribution to the programme—an interview which she might perhaps conduct herself. First jobs are nearly always exciting, but they are often vitiated by a sense of uselessness. All the same, Emma tried again.

"Would you like to be interviewed for our programme about this?"

"There is nothing I would like less," said Basil Valentine, then, seeing her disappointment, he said, "I'm so sorry."

It was now Emma's turn to be ashamed, mainly for letting her raven-ous ambition show.

"No, no! Please! Don't worry! It probably wouldn't have ..."

"Probably not." Valentine was smiling. He seemed amused, but he was not making fun of her. Emma selected a couple of old prints of the cathedral and the cathedral close.

"We'd like to make use of these, if we may. We'll pay you of course."

"How near are you to finding the book?"

"So you *are* interested. Well, Professor Huntley—"

"Huntley? David Huntley?"

"You know him?"

"I've heard of him."

"Well David thinks he's found this clue."

"In William of Morchester's *Gesta Anselmi*?"

"That's right. How did you know?"

"He may find the *Gesta* misleading."

"Why don't you tell him?"

"He may not welcome my advice."

"You know a lot more about this than you're letting on. I wish I knew—"

"What?"

"What you're up to."

There was a pause. Emma thought Valentine was going to take offence, but instead he laughed.

"My secret, if I have one," he said, "is that I'm up to absolutely nothing. By the way, does your Professor know about Aubrey?"

"No. What about him?"

"Some time in the 1680s he began to compile a book called *Reliques and Curiosities of Morsetshire*. Needless to say he never finished it. John Aubrey never finished anything. It was, in a way, part of his peculiar genius." He spoke of this seventeenth-century antiquarian as if he were an old friend. "The manuscript was found in the Bodleian in the 1960s and published in a limited edition by the Morsetshire Antiquarian Society as a chapbook. I happen to have a copy. It is rather rare, as you can imagine. Would you like to see it?"

He went to a shelf and plucked down a slender, paper-bound volume.

"Why?"

"Because it contains a reference to the book, the boke, I mean. Not many people know about it. Are you interested?"

"Yes." In spite of herself Emma's mouth was dry with excitement.

"I'll wrap it up. And those prints?"

"Thank you. Basil Valentine isn't your real name, is it?"

"It is now."

"But it wasn't."

"How did you know?"

"Because it's too good to be true. I mean, Basil Valentine is the name of a legendary alchemist or something, isn't it?" Emma had dragged this information out of something her father had once said. She was proud of the achievement.

Valentine nodded, as if to acknowledge it. "My real name is Night-fall. Basil Nightfall. Almost equally improbable, I know, but there it is. However, if I am going to help you, you will have to keep that information to yourself for the time being. Agreed?"

"Agreed."

"And while I remember, there is something else that might be of interest to you. It may help your understanding."

"Is it expensive?"

"It's a loan—no charge, but I should like it back. And it's something you may want to keep to yourself."

Valentine disappeared through a door into what Emma assumed were his private quarters. Left alone in the shop, she was seized with a quite irrational desire to take the two prints of Morchester she had chosen and the copy of Aubrey's *Reliques and Curiosities of Morsetshire*, and run from the shop. For a few moments the urge was so powerful that she thought she might do it, but just then Valentine returned. He was carrying a book with a faded cloth cover. He handed it to her. She opened it and read the title page:

Clerical Reminiscences
by
The Ven. Augustine Jedd

It had been printed by something called The Chapel Well Press in 1927. It was not a very well-made book; probably it was a private printing—perhaps even a vanity production.

"Yes," said Valentine, reading Emma's thoughts in a way that was beginning to irritate her. "It's mostly as dull as it looks, but you ought to look at Chapter 4, the one entitled *Quieta Non Movere*."

"Why?"

"Read it and see. It may enhance your understanding."

"Why should you want my understanding to be enhanced?"

Valentine smiled. "Remember. That book is just a loan," he said.

Some minutes later, having settled on a price for the Aubrey and the prints, Emma left the shop. A step had been taken from her own imagined status as "lowest form of life on the film set" towards something else. It was an exhilarating step, but one which also smelled of danger.

It was only after she had left the shop that Valentine wondered whether he should have warned Emma less obliquely.

"Praise the Lord! Oh, praise the Lord!" shouted the Reverend Gary Eastwood.

His wife, Marie, was beginning to wish he wouldn't say that every time he had an orgasm. In her opinion there was no need for one ejaculation to accompany another. It was also, she felt, something of an insult to her, as if the joys of the marriage bed were a matter between Gary and his God, and had nothing to do with his lawfully bedded wife. When it had first happened on their honeymoon (Torquay) she had been rather touched by the exclamation and had even, when appropriate, joined in, but now the novelty had worn thin, revealing the disturbing metaphysical implications behind it. Soon afterwards Gary was asleep, having slipped off her slim form while she lay awake pondering the imponderable mysteries of life. Would it be downhill from here: would the gilt of early glories be tarnished by the attritions of children and parish routine?

Gary, recently ordained, had got his own parish sooner than he expected. The church of St. Paul's in Morchester was one of the few in the city that had not been turned into a gymnasium or a wine bar. It survived mainly because it catered for a particular religious persuasion that rather despised the traditional Anglican religion as practiced in the cathedral. It was evangelical, charismatic and described by those who didn't like that sort of thing as "happy-clappy." Gary in turn described any other branch of the church which was not happy-clappy as "dead."

Marie had been in the choir of the first church at which Gary was a curate. It was not long before the two were going out together and marriage had become an inevitable end. Looking back on it, Marie found the swiftness of it all, the almost-immediately assumed foregone conclusion, a little troubling. She had fallen in love with him, yes: he was eager, gifted and good-looking, but she sometimes wondered whether he saw her as any more than the necessary adjunct of his career and the chaste repository of his powerful sexual needs. Marie fully shared in his beliefs and aspirations, but sometimes, she fancied, she could see beyond them. She had once been a science teacher, a good one, but all that was now abandoned—"for God", said Gary; but Marie often wondered if it was not for Gary.

These thoughts often came to her, particularly in post-coital wakefulness. The act seemed to have the opposite effect on them: Gary invariably fell asleep soon after giving his all; Marie usually lay awake, feeling vaguely guilty at her unfaithfulness to his abrupt passions. Some time after Gary had fallen unconscious, sleep overtook her, but it was always a dreamed sleep.

And as she opened the book it was as if she were drawn in, just as when she was drawn to open the book, without the possibility of resistance. And in a grey light she saw a corridor in which doors were set, and between them mirrors which reflected more doors and more mirrors so that she found herself in an infinite labyrinth of doors and mirrors. In order to escape from this she tried the handle of one of the doors, but the door was locked. She tried another, and another, but they were all locked. Then she saw something in one of the mirrors. Because it was being reflected, she did not know how many times, it was hard to know where it was and whether it was near to her or far away. Something grey and like a small squat human creature, naked but apparently sexless, was crawling along the corridor. Its bald head, sprinkled with sparse grey hairs, was lowered so that she could not see its face. It began to move, but towards or away from her? It was hard to tell. She stared around her to see if she could find the figure itself, unmirrored, but she could not. All sense of direction deserted her and she did not know which way to turn. She tried more doors. All were locked. Once more she looked in the mirror. The figure seemed closer to her. She thought she heard breathing behind her. Then she was seized, gripped by long sinuous arms that enfolded her and covered her eyes. She gasped for air.

"Are you all right, love?"

"What?" Marie battled upwards to the surface of consciousness and found that Gary had his arms around her.

"Bad dream, love?"

"I don't know … I suppose so."

"Those sort of dreams come from the evil one. Satan may be tempting you. We should pray for deliverance."

And Gary led a fervent extempore prayer for her deliverance from the evil, one which rather irritated Marie. It seemed to her an uncalled-for intrusion into her private world. It may have been Hell, but it was *her* Hell. Then Gary thought it appropriate to make love to her once more. Marie did not praise the Lord.

On the south side of Morchester Cathedral one may find the Chapter House, the library and the cloisters. The cloisters form part of the original monastery on the site of whose Minster church the cathedral was built and they are the oldest part of the cathedral complex. A covered walkway with an arcade of Norman arches surrounds a large square of green turf, the so-called "cloister garth", in the middle of which is an ancient stone well covered with an iron-bound wooden lid. It was on the greensward of the cloister garth that Professor Huntley stood the following day to deliver his next piece to camera.

"'When Anselm came to the Benedictine Priory at Morchester he saw the monks in much distress on account of their well. They had built their cloister around an ancient well that had been there for many centuries, and where in time past many foul and blasphemous ceremonies had been enacted to worship the ancient gods and demons of the pagans. For, it was said, in the depths of this ancient well were many caverns and paths beneath the earth, which connected with sea caverns on the southern shores. And it was also said that these demons came out of the sea and through the caverns to the well where they had been worshipped as gods in former times. Now certain of the monks, hoping to draw greater quantities of the sweet water to be found in the well, had descended into its depths to dig deeper and uncover new springs. But in so doing they had awakened the demons who had lain dormant in caverns beneath the well for many centuries. They had troubled their unholy sleep and awakened their anger. And these demons had arisen from the well to bring destruction on the monks and the people of Morchester. The monks were tormented by ill dreams and by odours as of fish putrefying. Women of the town began to give birth to all manner of abominations: infants with two heads, and mouths in their fundaments, horns upon their head, many arms but without hands; and one had the face of a great serpent. Such was their consternation that the whole people cried out to Anselm to deliver them from terrors by night and abominations by day.'

"So wrote the twelfth century Chronicler, William of Morchester in a manuscript to be found in the Morchester Cathedral archives. A fascinating legend, but did it conceal a more deadly secret? Would the well yield the truth behind the Legend of the Boke of the Divill? After extensive researches I have discovered the whereabouts of that well. This is the so-called Archbishop's Well here in the cathedral cloister, which has not been opened for nigh on a thousand years. Today, with the permission of the authorities, I am going to open up that well and lay bare its secret."

"And cut!"

"Was that okay?"

"That was fine, Dave."

"I'm still not happy about that 'nigh on a thousand years'."

"Dave, we've been through this before. Just say the bloody lines and think of your pay cheque. Right! Set up the next shot. The lifting of the lid of the well. Are the men ready to do that? Can we just—? I'm sorry, sir. We can't have members of the public in the cloisters at that moment. Dean, I thought I said the public were not to be allowed in this area during filming. Can you sort this out, please? ASAP?"

The Dean had been standing with the camera crew in the cloister garth watching the process of filming in a daze of astonishment. He had not been sleeping well. Besides, this had not been what he had expected when he had let the television company persuade him to allow them access. He had not expected this indifference to everything except sensationalism, this travesty of the truth. Now he was expected to be some sort of unofficial bouncer.

An elderly man in a rather strange assortment of clothes had entered the cloister garth and seemed to be shouting and gesticulating at the cameramen. The Dean felt a prick of recognition. The man had wild white hair and an unshaven face, but his jacket, trousers and waistcoat appeared to be the constituent parts of three separate tailor-made tweed suits which were (or, rather, had once been) good. He spoke in an upper-class accent, and loudly, in that way that people who expect deference do. By the time the Dean had crossed the lawn of the cloister garth, he had identified the wild stranger.

"Good morning, Sir Everard," he said.

"What the devil is going on here? Why was I not informed of this nonsense?"

"I saw no reason to inform you, Sir Everard."

"Don't you realise who I am, man?"

The Dean smiled. He was a plump, grey haired man in his fifties with one of those pink, fleshy, amiably meaningless faces that you often see on Anglican and Roman Catholic clergymen. Underneath, however, the Dean had humour and a certain steely serenity which sometimes showed itself. He had the strength of knowing how weak he was.

"I am Sir Everard Cutbirth. By rights I should be the owner of this land." He stamped on the turf to demonstrate his point. "We were until the damned Normans and their idiotic psalm-singing monks stole all my land and a lot of other things as well."

"But my dear Sir Everard, that was 'nigh on a thousand years ago'," said the Dean, delicately alluding to the commentary he had just heard.

"Not as far as I'm concerned. I'm a Cutbirth."

It was true. The Cutbirths had been a stain on the county of Morsetshire since before the Conquest. It might, in these politically correct days, be unwise to talk too loudly about "tainted blood," but that is what it looked like to the Dean. Over the centuries some of the Cutbirths had managed to acquire considerable wealth and influence, but always in an underhand way. In 1920 one of them even managed to buy a Baronetcy from Lloyd George via the notorious Maundy Gregory, an old friend of the family. From the purchaser Sir Everard was descended, but he was not undistinguished in his own right. He was a composer known to people interested in modern classical music, though, now in his seventies, his reputation, such as it was, was fading.

The Dean said, "Why don't you take this up with the director, Sir Everard? I'm sure she'd be most interested to meet you." With that, the Dean left. He knew he had created mischief, and a secret part of him was happy about it.

Emma saw the irascible-looking old man coming towards Veronica and knew that it was necessary to prevent them from meeting. She had gathered enough from his conversation with the Dean to know who he was.

"Sir Everard, how do you do? I'm Emma Hartley. Can I help you?"

"I doubt it, my dear. I would like, if I may, to speak to the organ grinder of this deplorable farrago, not her little monkey."

He was staring down at her cleavage with undisguised lust in his eyes. Emma was shocked—he was so disgustingly old!—but she knew she oughtn't have been.

"I'm afraid we are just setting up for the next shot. We are just about to open up the well, you see."

"That is precisely what I want to prevent, young lady."

"I'm afraid you can't do that. We've had permission from the Dean and chapter."

"Dean and chapter, my bloody arse! What have they got to do with it? There's a Cutbirth buried down there!"

"But this is fascinating, Sir Everard. You mean your ancestor Cutbirth is buried down there. With the book?"

"Idiots! I'm surrounded by idiots. So you and your half-wit Professor think Cutbirth and the 'boke' are down there? Rubbish! I mean my great-uncle Felix Cutbirth. He died down there just before the War. It's got nothing to do with the damned book."

"I see. This is important I'll just get hold of Veronica. Veronica!"

"Not now Emma dear, we're just about to do the shots of opening the well."

"But Veronica. This is Sir Everard Cutbirth. He's a direct descendant of Cutbirth of Bartonstone, the original owner of the book."

"Emma, darling I don't care if he's the pigging Pope. I have got a film to make."

By this time Sir Everard had approached and was standing over Veronica, her physical superior by at least a foot. A look of fury had concentrated his wild old visage into a single coherent aspect, like a theatrical mask. His white hair jutted up from his red face with a threat like a tidal wave.

"Listen to me, you vulgar little woman, you have no idea what you are doing. Moreover you have just made a dangerous enemy. I am Sir Everard Cutbirth. I happen to be a very great composer, not that I expect an ignoramus like you to have heard of me. You and your ghastly crew of T-shirted techies and pseudo-academic arseholes are trespassing on very dangerous territory. Not that you have a brain cell between you to recognise the fact. And when you find yourselves in the reeking shit-hole into which your folly will surely cast you, don't come whining and snivelling to me for help, because you won't get it. I will be looking down on your well-merited cancerous agony and laughing, to use a vulgar expression of which you would no doubt approve, like the proverbial bloody drain!"

There was a silence. All had heard. All had, reluctantly, been impressed. Eventually Veronica, to show herself unimpressed, said, "Fuck off!"

Sir Everard stood his ground for a withering few seconds, then said, "You won't find the book down there, you know." After that, he responded to Veronica's peremptory instruction and left.

"All right," said Veronica. "The fun's over. Let's get this little cantata on the road again, shall we?"

Emma had to admire her sang-froid.

The lid of the well had been prised away from its stone and mortar surround, and a couple of workmen were gently easing it off while Veronica directed the filming. Huntley, who had been keeping well in the background during the recent contretemps, stepped forward and said something to the camera. The lid was examined. It was found that a large silver crucifix, much tarnished by the years but in relatively good condition, had been nailed to the underside of the lid. At this Huntley showed real excitement and declared it to be possibly "of Norman manufacture and of the highest quality." He speculated that it had been put there to ward off evil spirits, "possibly the influence of the Boke itself." However when the inside of the well was examined, there was disappointment in store. It was filled almost to the top with rubble and mortar, quite modern in origin. The Dean was summoned.

"Oh, yes," said Dr. Tancock mildly. "I believe that it was filled in for safety's sake shortly before the Second World War."

"Then why the fuck—" began Veronica. "I'm sorry, Dean. Why didn't you tell us this before?"

"I'm sorry, I didn't want to interfere. What is that dreadful smell? It's like rotting fish or something. It seems to be coming from the well."

"Christ, yes! Sorry, Dean. Yes, thanks chaps. Could you close the well up now? I don't understand. How could it stink so much after all these years?"

"Just a minute," said Huntley. "Before we put the lid back on, do you think we could unfasten that crucifix, so that we can examine it?"

"Oh, should we? Must we?" said the Dean, his little pink jowls quivering.

"I think we should, Dean. This is a remarkable discovery. If, as I suspect, it is of Norman workmanship, it could be priceless. It should be examined. There may be inscriptions."

"Oh, well …"

"Has anyone got a chisel or something? We need to do this delicately."

"Oh, should we? Must we?" said the Dean again, but nobody was paying any attention.

By this time it was late afternoon and the extraction of the crucifix from the underside of the well cap took longer than expected. It had been affixed to the wood with long iron nails plated with gold, which with rust and the years had expanded somewhat. By the time the crucifix was free, grey clouds were sagging over the cathedral, and the world had become a dimmer and darker place.

The Dean bore away the crucifix to a safe place with Huntley in attendance fussing around him insisting that the temperature and atmosphere in which it was to be stored should be just so. Considering that the object had survived for nine hundred years in damp and unsuitable conditions, Emma thought that the professor's anxiety was misplaced.

It began to rain and everyone fled for shelter into the cloisters.

"Well," said Veronica looking out through the Norman Arcade at the rain beating down onto the churned and muddy turf of the cloister garth. "That's one place where we won't find the bloody book. God, I wish I'd never agreed to this ridiculous pantomime. I turned down another series of *Celebrity Makeover* for this crap, you know. This is going to be a damp squib. I just know it."

"I wouldn't despair just yet," said Emma.

"Oh, and what do you know about it, Madam?" Veronica turned on her a glance that was meant to be intimidating, but Emma returned her stare coolly.

Veronica revised her assessment of Emma Hartley. Could be useful; could pose a threat. Attractive girl, too full of herself.

"I may have found something that might help. An old book. I found it in a shop in St. Anselm's Street yesterday."

"Then give it here!"

"It's at my B & B. I need to check it over first. Perhaps we could meet for dinner?"

"Oh! That's the way it's going to be, is it, Madam? Very well. I'll meet you in the bar of my hotel, the White Lion. Seven o'clock. And don't tell that muppet Dave Huntley anything about it, do you hear? This is my project and I want it to stay that way."

CHAPTER 2

"Fuckin' rain. Fuckin' pissin' rain."
"Here, you coming to the club tonight, Kirst?"
"Nah."
"Why not?"
"Waiting for someone, en' I?"
"Bloke?"
"'Course it's a bloke. I'm not a fucking les, en' I?"
"It's not that Darren, is it?"
"No, Kel, it is not that Darren. Fucking wanker. He couldn't bloody organise a knees-up in a knocking shop."
"Who is it, then?"
"Secret fucking squirrel. You mind yours and I'll mind mine."
"Where you meeting then?"
"Down the cemetery at St. Paul's."
"You'll get fucking soaked, Kirst."
"Not where we're going."
"Spoo-kee!"
"I ain't afraid of nothing."
"See you at Uni tomorrow, then. You going to that lecture, Kirst?"
"What lecture?"
"Tomorrow. Dr. Craig. Anselm's Ontological Argument."
"Nah. It's crap, Kel. Anselm! Fucking wanker, if you ask me."

The Dean was officiating at choral evensong in the cathedral. It was his favourite service, his favourite task, one of the few occasions in life these days when he achieved ecstatic joy. The light of candles on the choir stalls shone in the vast grey depths of the cathedral like the glow of home on a cloudy evening. There he sat in his throne-like stall between choir and congregation, a master of ceremonies, grand, but only as an instrument. That was how he liked it. He was not a proud man.

The anthem was an old favourite: "Wash me throughly" by Samuel Wesley, with its treble solo opening.

Wash me throughly from my wickedness

The boy treble singing in the candlelight with his white surplice and ruffle and the red cassock beneath glowed like a young angel. His name was Aston: the Dean knew that because Matheson the Precentor and choir master had spoken several times in praise of him. He had pink cheeks with a delicate bloom of prepubescent white fur on them, like a peach.

I wonder if his bottom is like that too.

The Dean started. It was as if a voice had spoken inside his head, uninvited, unwanted. He blushed and looked around foolishly, half expecting others to have heard the voice as well. No. No one had noticed. In the congregation, his wife Phyllis looked as if she were half asleep.

I would like to pull up his little cassock and surplice and enter him savagely from behind. I want to feel his warm blood from the wound coursing down my bare legs; I want to hear him whimper with the pain and beg for mercy; I want to kiss away the tears of agony from his downy cheeks.

Dear God! There it was again! That alien voice, which he swears is nothing to do with him. Once more he stares around at the dim and somnolent congregation, the singing choir and their conducting Precentor. No one has noticed a thing. But wait! Someone has seen him; someone sitting in the stall opposite him on the North side of the Cathedral. Someone is in the Bishop's Stall.

It is not the Bishop. He looks nothing like Bishop Paul who, in any case, is in Malawi attending an Ecumenical Conference. Nevertheless the man opposite is dressed like a bishop, albeit in a rather antiquated style. He is in a white surplice with puffed lawn sleeves gathered at the wrist with red silk ribbon. His black stole has the episcopal arms of Morchester Cathedral embroidered on it, and he is looking at the Dean.

The Dean blinked his eyes several times and looked back in the direction of the Bishop's Stall.

The man dressed as a bishop is still there, but his outline is a little more vague. He is looking at him with a curious twisted smile as if he can read every thought that is passing through the Dean's fevered mind. He is about fifty, with a red-faced, raddled countenance and the remains of curly blond hair on his balding cranium. There is something utterly repellent about the man, as if every thought the man entertains has dirt and grease under its fingernails. Every thought is a cruel thought and pungent with sexuality, and he is sharing them with the Dean.

The Dean is sweating. Everything is blotted out except this wicked man opposite him dressed as a bishop. Suddenly he becomes aware of the silence. The anthem has finished and everyone is looking at him. He must read the prayers.

He scrabbles for his prayer book and for a moment the words swim and dance in front of him, mocking his efforts at self-control, like the man opposite. Everyone is looking at him; his wife too is in the congregation. At last he finds his place.

Lighten our darkness we beseech thee, O Lord, and by thy great mercy, defend us from all the perils and dangers of this night, for the love of thine only Son, Our Lord and Saviour, Jesus Christ …

"Amen!"

At last he has the courage to look again, but the strange bishop has gone. It was all an illusion. But who was he? Something tells the Dean he has seen him before. He announces the final hymn.

After the service his wife Phyllis fusses over him. "What was the matter just now?"

"Nothing, nothing, dear. Just a slight turn. The heat of the candles. Nothing to worry about."

"Wait. Where are you going? Aren't you coming back to the Deanery now?"

"In a moment, my dear, there is something I need to check briefly first. You go back to the Deanery. I won't be long."

"But don't you need a rest first? Come back to the Deanery now."

"Phyllis, will you do as I say!" The voice was raised in irritation. Several departing members of the congregation looked round. "I won't be long, dear," he added in more emollient tones.

Ten minutes later he found what he was looking for in the corridor that led to the diocesan offices. There was a half-length portrait by Millais of a seated man in the lawn sleeves and bands of a bishop. He recognised with a shock the red and raddled face, the sneer on the lips, the prying, cruel stare. The head, resting on the right hand, was slightly tilted, thus accentuating somehow the sinister intensity of that gaze. Below the portrait a label on the gilded frame proclaimed the subject.

The Rt. Reverend Herbert Hartley
Bishop of Morchester 1878–1882

Dear God! What was a long-dead Bishop doing in the cathedral? What was he doing turning the Dean's thoughts to filth: thoughts that had never before—hardly ever before—turned in that direction?

The Dean's mobile buzzed. It was his wife Phyllis.

Tell the fat old bitch to fuck off! Tell her to go to—

"Yes, dear. I'm coming." How much it had cost him to say just that in a quiet voice.

"Well," said Veronica, "now that I've bought you a drink, Miss Hartley, perhaps you could reveal your secret to me." They were sitting at a table in the bar of the White Lion Hotel, Morchester. Sales representatives and rising executives were talking to each other at the counter about their latest golf scores. An elderly American couple studied guide books and brochures, planning the next day's adventure. A couple of demure-looking prostitutes sat at tables waiting for one of the young men at the bar to join them. In the meanwhile they adjusted their makeup with discreet ostentation and occasionally texted their pimps.

"I've marked the passage," said Emma. "It's from a little-known work by John Aubrey—you know, Aubrey's *Brief Lives*."

"Thank you dear. I do know. I saw Roy Dotrice do it when I was a girl."

"Oh. Right!" Emma did not seem unduly put down.

> Among the curiose legends of this countye is that of the Divill's Boke. Manu Scriptum before, some saye, the Conquest of the Normans. Cutbirth of Bartonstone, a great Prince among the Britons and Count of the Saxon Shore did have it made, 'tis said, by certaine daemons and boggarts whom he had at his command, for he was accounted a greate conjurer and much learned in many depe arts. Then did Anselme come and take from him his boke and condemn him; and this said Cutbirth was buryed depe within the cathedrall and his boke buryed with him. But none knew where.
>
> Now there was in the reigne of Elizabeth a noted wise woman or witch, named Mother Durden, and many strove to have her condemned as such, for she had, they said, bewitched their cattel and some said they had spirited their children into regions beneathe the earth. And she was brought before the magistrates to be condemned and hanged

as a witch in the yeare of Our Lorde 1594. Yet before she was put to the torment and hanged she was saide to have sett downe many marvellous prophesies concerning the citie and its cathedrall. And this she thought might save her, yet it did nott and she laid a curse on all there.

And the paper she did write contained many wondrous things. My cousin Will Aubrey did see it once, but he did forget much of it and now 'tis burned. But one thing he did recall, and it concerned the Boke, for this he copyed as being a thing most curiose. Mother Durden gave certain signes whereby it may be found and did say that when found it shall be by a most ingeniose man, then Clerke of the cathedrall. He shall find it by the certaine indicacions which she gave. It shall bring him much power and gold, but in an evill manner. And he shall not profit long by it and will die most miserably. This person, it has for certaine been showne, was one Jeremiah Staveley, a Canon of Morchester Cathedral. Obiit anno 1595 and many curiose and dread legendes are told of him by the goodwifes and gossips of the citye. And the second time it shall be found by a certain noble cleric, by a stroke or accident of fortune, and he shall become Bishop of this Cathedrall thereby, but it shall not profitt him neither, for his wickewdness and fornications shall find him out. And the third time it will return to the house whence it came and this shall be its third evill guardian. And when it is once more discovered the verye gates of hell shall flye open and all shall not be well unless purity and courage shall close it once more and for evermore. But these things lie far beyond our mortall span and onlye darknesse is to be seene with but littel lights flickering within, some bright, some faint, some red with fire, some white as the colour of angell's wings.

And Mother Durden did conclude, my brother Will saide, with these verses which he could not forgett.

Seeke not the book for in it dwelleth Hell
The changeless agonie of fatall woundes
Old Adam's curse shall like a pustule swell
And through the eye of Satann breake its boundes
Yet those that may, may seek its secrets well

Who know no guile and broache the House of Lies
And find where four times thirty sorrowes dwell
In shelly cavern under starrie skies.

"Is that it?" said Veronica.

"Well, yes."

"So we're supposed to find this damned book through the maunderings of some mad old crone's prophesies. Come on, love! Get real!"

"Well, at the moment, Veronica, it's almost the only clue we've got. Unless you want to abandon this whole project. It's not as if we're making a scientific programme: it's just entertainment."

"Oh, is it? I'd like you to say that to Dave Huntley's face."

"I will if you like."

Veronica could not decide whether to hate Emma for being (as she put it to herself) such a damned smart-arse, or congratulate herself on hiring an extremely bright young P.A. She decided to suspend judgement.

"What exactly are you up to, young lady? What's your little secret?"

"My secret, if I have one," said Emma, "is that I'm up to absolutely nothing."

"Well, it's time you were and started earning your keep, young Emma. From tomorrow, you get cracking and chase up these references in Aubrey. I wouldn't trust Dave Huntley to research the piss in his own pants. If this effing Boke of the Divill is out there, Veronica Boyd is going to get it and put it on national TV and win a fucking BAFTA for it!"

Just then—and of course it was sheer coincidence—there was a flash from the street outside, closely followed by a crack of thunder. One of the prostitutes screamed and collapsed into giggles. This gave one of the smart young executives at the bar the courage to go over to her and proffer a restorative drink. And one thing led, as it usually does, to another.

Some of the Cutbirths are buried in the cemetery of St. Paul's, Morchester. Nobody quite knows why, because as a family they were not notably keen on consecrated ground. Nevertheless in the mid eighteenth century, one of the family, Sir Cuthbert Cutbirth had a mausoleum built in the churchyard, severely classical and rather grim in design, topped by a huge obelisk. It survives. Under its porch waited Kirsty in the rainy dark, her damp limbs trembling under the skimpy leather skirt she wore. Suddenly the sky split open with a flash and she saw him standing among the tombs.

"Fuck me! You took your time!"

The man ran towards her and the next moment he was in the porch and close to her. Their wet clothes scratched against each other. She felt his heat through the wet cloth and knew a dreadful excitement and forgot for a moment how quickly the fabulous thrill evaporated. Still, it was there.

"Hey, we're not going to do it out here, are we?"

"Of course not. I've got the key."

"I hope you've got a fucking torch."

"I've got everything. Let's get out of the rain."

When the bronze door creaked as it opened Kirsty giggled.

"Bloody hell! It's like all Dracula and that. Are there any bones? Skulls and that?"

"You'll see bones. This is my secret place. You and I are the only people who've been in here for hundreds of years."

"Fucking Hell!"

"You see that slab? That's the tomb of Sir Cuthbert Cutbirth."

"Fucking Hell!"

"Your conversation is becoming rather monotonous. Get down on that slab."

"Hey, don't push! Who the fuck do you think you are?"

"I am the Lord's Righteous punishment, and you are a piece of filth! Prepare to die!"

"Fucking Hell!"

CHAPTER 3

*L*ater that evening in her hotel room, Emma decided to look at the second book that Valentine had given her, the dreary-sounding *Clerical Reminiscences*, by the Venerable Augustine Jedd. She turned as instructed to the third chapter, entitled *Quieta Non Movere*. It had not occurred to her that she should share this particular source with Veronica, and almost as soon as she started to read she was very glad she had not.

CHAPTER THE THIRD: *QUIETA NON MOVERE*

It was in the year 1874 that I took up my first clerical position, that of a curate to a parish just outside the cathedral city of Morchester. Being of a naturally studious inclination, I devoted my spare time to researching the history of the district and, in particular, the cathedral. I even proposed to write a short monograph on some of the more curious funerary monuments to be found in that building. One in particular attracted my attention because of its strange inscription and carving. My enquiries about this particular monument elicited a story of some very shocking events connected with that tomb, which had happened some ten years prior to my arrival in Morchester. Despite the passing of a decade, the events were still very clear in the minds of those who witnessed them, and who were willing to speak to me. Their accounts are the foundations of the story I am about to tell.

Let me therefore remove you for a while to the ancient city of Morchester in the County of Morsetshire in the year 1863. Though the railway had arrived some fifteen years previously, it could be said that in all other respects time had stood still in the city for many decades. It had been, and remained, a prosperous market town; it boasted a fine cathedral, mostly in the Early English and Decorated styles. Rooks cawed among its towers and in the immemorial elms that punctuated the sward of its fine old close.

One cloudless afternoon in the July of that year the great bell of the Cathedral began to sound its bass note, summoning the city to the funeral of one of its servants. The Dean was dead. That ancient knell, that call to remembrance and reminder of mortality, would no doubt have seemed to Morchester's inhabitants no more than a slight eddy in the changeless flow of life and death which washed about its walls. Who could have foreseen that it tolled the commencement of a series of horribly inexplicable events?

In all conscience, the passing of The Very Rev. William Ainsley, Dean of Morchester was greeted with little sadness, and was the occasion, in some quarters, of no small relief. Dean Ainsley had for many years been infirm and fulfilled his decanal duties with a listlessness only just short of rank incompetence. When, on the day of his funeral, the Very Rev. Stephen Coombe acceded to the position and sat in his stall in the choir, there was much talk of new brooms sweeping clean. Even those who did not find such a metaphor entirely reassuring were compelled to admit that anything was preferable to the disarray of the previous regime.

Dean Coombe was a tall, lean man in his forties, heavily whiskered, as was the fashion in those days, and of High Church leanings. He was in possession of a wife and a daughter, almost as angular as he was. He was an upright man, but stiff and overbearing; he inspired respect perhaps, but no great affection. Being active and zealous in all his dealings, he very soon began to turn his attention to the fabric of Morchester Cathedral, which was indeed in a woeful state of disrepair.

The tenure of Dean Ainsley had been marked by neglect towards the great building he was appointed to maintain, so it was perhaps only just that this legacy of dereliction should be mitigated by his posthumous one. The late Dean had left his entire and considerable fortune to the cathedral, with the provision that a chapel, dedicated to the Virgin Mary, should be made in the North Transept as a permanent memorial to him. As the legacy more than amply provided for this, it was resolved by the new Dean and chapter to accept it. There had been murmurings from some of the more low-church canons that the building of a Lady Chapel might give rise to accusations of popery, but these were properly dismissed as old-fashioned. The new Dean was a forceful man and was used to carrying all before him.

An architect was engaged, and there needed only a decision to be made over the location of the chapel. The obvious place was an area closest to the crossing and facing east. This would entail the partial destruction of the eastern wall of the North Transept, an exercise which would require the relocation of a number of funereal plaques and stones, the most significant of which was a sixteenth-century memorial to a Canon of Morchester Cathedral, one Jeremiah Staveley. It was quite an elaborate affair in polished black basalt, about seven foot in height overall, set into the wall some three feet above the ground. It consisted of a slab topped with scroll-work, crudely classical in feel, with a niche in which was set a painted alabaster image of the Canon, standing upright in his clerical robes with his arms crossed over his chest. The figure was tall and narrow, the bearded face gaunt: a somewhat disconcerting image, which looked as if it portrayed the corpse rather than the living being. Beneath this on the polished slab an inscription had been incised, the lettering picked out in white. It read:

JEREMIAH STAVELEY Canonus Morcastriensis,
obiit anno 1595 aetat 52

It was followed by these verses in bold capital letters:

BEHINDE THESE SACRED STONES IN DEATH STAND I
FOR THAT IN LIFE MOST BASELY DID I LIE
IN WORD AND SINNE FORSAKING GOD HIS LAWE,
I DANCED MY SOULE IN SATANN'S VERIE MAWE.
WHEREFORE IN PENANCE I THIS VIGILL KEEPE
ENTOMBÉD UPRIGHT THUS WHERE I SHOULDE SLEEPE.

WHEN DEAD RISE UP I'LL READYE BE IN PLACE
TO MEET MY JUDGE AND MAKER FACE TO FACE.
STRANGER, REST NOT MY CORSE UNTIL THAT DAYE
LEST I TORMENT THEE WITH MY SORE DISMAYE.

The implication of these lines, that the body of Canon Staveley was actually entombed behind the slab, was borne out by
the Cathedral records and one of the old vergers whose family had been connected with the cathedral since time immemorial. Dean Coombe was disposed to be rather benevolent
towards this worthy, whose name was Wilby. The man was
a repository of cathedral history and lore, and the Dean was
content to listen politely to Wilby's ramblings, but he did
not expect his condescension to be rewarded by opposition
to his plans.

"Mr. Dean," said Wilby one afternoon, as they stood
before the memorial in the North transept. "You don't want
to go a moving of that there stone, begging your pardon, sir."

"My dear man, why ever not?"

"Don't it say so plain as brass on that there 'scription?
'Tis ill luck to move the bones of the wicked. So said my
granfer, and his before him."

"And who says this Canon Staveley was a wicked man?"

"Why, 'tis well known. There are tales that have passed
down about Jeremiah Staveley, which I might blush to tell
you, Mr. Dean. The poor women of this city were not safe
in their beds from him, they say. A harsh man too, to those
below him. But he was a fair man of music and when I were
a lad in the choir they still sang his setting to the Psalm one
hundred and thirty seven. 'By the waters of Babylon ...'—all
nine verses too. With the dashing of children agin the stones
and all. Some said he would have fain dinged his choir lads
agin the stones, too, when they were singing awry. Certain it
was, he spared not the rod among them. And there were tales
of meeting at night in the church with a man all in black, and
a gold treasure that he found under the earth in a field that
the black man took him to. But it weren't no good for him,
for soon as he was by way of enjoying his gold, the plague
fell on him and he wasted to a wraith of skin and bone, and

him as tall and narrow as may be already. And when at last he came to be in extreme, as you say, and within a hand's breadth of mortality, he summons the Dean, as it might be you, sir, a man with whom he had had some mighty quarrel, and begs him for forgiveness and to be shriven of his many sins. And all his treasure they say he left to the Dean and chapter, but saying he must be buried upright, to keep him awake, he says. Because in the last days he suffered terribly from dreams and was as mortally afeared of sleep as he was of death. So he begged to be buried upright that he might not sleep till the Last Judgement, even as a dead man. And when the Dean of that time, Dean Cantwell, as I think it was, came out from seeing Canon Staveley in his deathbed, they say the Dean's face was as white as a linen altar cloth and he spoke not a word to a mortal soul for seven days. This I had from my granfer, who had it from his, and it came down in the family with a warning, as my old father used to say. 'Don't you touch the Staveley stone, nor go nigh it at night, nor suffer his bones to be moved.' And that's what I say to you, begging your pardon, Mr. Dean."

"Well, well, Wilby," said Dean Coombe who was rather more shaken by this recitation than he cared to admit, "that is indeed a most fascinating legend. Most interesting. I must write some of it down."

"It weren't no legend, Mr. Dean," said old Wilby. "I had it from my granfer, and he—"

"Quite so, quite so, my dear man," said the Dean hurriedly. "Nevertheless, move this old monument we must. But make no mistake, we shall re-site it well, for it is certainly a curiosity, and if there are any human remains behind it we shall lay them to rest with all due respect. Goodness me! What was that noise?"

Both Wilby and Dean Coombe heard it, a sound like a long inhalation of breath, ragged and rattling, somewhat as if the breather—if such there was—was experiencing difficulty in drawing in air. It was magnified and distorted by the cathedral's echo, which was particularly reverberant in that part of the building. Dean Coombe was not a fanciful man, but he had been at his father's deathbed, and he knew the sound of a man's breathing as he nears the end. This sound was uncomfortably like it.

"Dear me," said the Dean. "I really must have that organ seen to."

Wilby gave the Dean a quizzical stare, then, bidding him a hurried "Good day, Mr. Dean" he began to shuffle off in the direction of the West Door with surprising swiftness. Dean Coombe remained behind, standing before the monument. A passerby was surprised to hear him mutter, "Hah! You won't affright me that easy, Master Staveley. We shall see!"

The following day the workmen moved in and began the demolition of the eastern wall of the North Transept. Dean Coombe had given explicit instructions that the memorial slabs were to be most carefully removed, and, towards evening, he was on hand when the dismantling of the Staveley Memorial began. Palmer, the head mason, had set up scaffolding and constructed a wooden cradle in which to take the stone.

Dean Coombe suggested that the painted alabaster effigy in the niche be removed first, but this proved unexpectedly troublesome. The statue had been very securely cemented to its base, and one of the workmen cut himself on one of the folds of the statue's long gown. The workmanship was unusually precise and unworn by time.

When the effigy was finally removed, Dean Coombe was intrigued to find that it had been carved all round and that the back of the figure, which had been unseen by any living soul since it had been placed in the niche over two hundred and fifty years ago, had been carved with as much care as the visible front. He noted with particular interest the minuteness with which the sculptor had represented every snaking strand of the subject's unusually long black hair. He had also taken care to represent a gold seal ring on the third finger of the left hand, even incising the seal with a strange geometrical figure.

The face too repaid closer inspection. As Dean Coombe remarked to a colleague the following day, in a rather striking phrase, it would seem to have been "done from the death rather than from life." The skin had been painted white, with a slight yellow tinge, the cheeks were sunken and gaunt and—a rather troubling detail—the mouth gaped slightly, revealing a tiny set of jagged greenish teeth. Then there were the eyes.

Dean Coombe did not care to dwell long on the eyes. There was, as he later remarked, something "not quite dead" about them. Under the heavy lids an area of creamy white showed punctuated by the pinpoint of a pupil in a cloudy, greyish iris. The impression given was of a last wild stare at life. The painter of the statue had somehow managed to convey the terror of the sinner at the very point of death.

Despite a certain distaste (as he chose to call it) Dean Coombe was impressed by the remarkably fine workmanship of the image. In the few moments of leisure that he allowed himself, he was something of an antiquarian, which was why one of his many projects for the Cathedral was the setting-up of a museum in the chapter house where some of the old plate and vestments of the cathedral could be displayed for the benefit of both the public and the cathedral which would take its sixpences.

"This is such fine work," said the Dean, in reality thinking aloud, but ostensibly addressing Palmer the mason. "I wonder if the craftsmanship could be Spanish, though they tended to carve in wood rather than alabaster. Certainly whoever did the painting—not necessarily the sculptor, for the painting of sculpture was a specialised art in those days, you know—looks to have been trained in the peninsula. Most unusual. I must get up something to one of the learned journals on the subject. Now then, Palmer, I want you to set this aside. Take great care of it. I shall have a plaster copy made. The replica we will put back in the niche, and we can display the original in my chapter house museum, in a glass case where it may be appreciated from all angles— Good gracious, what was that?"

There had been a cry of pain accompanied by— had it been an oath? Palmer and the Dean looked around much startled as they had been absorbed in the contemplation of the effigy. However they soon discovered the cause: it was one of the workmen, who had accidentally dropped a lump hammer on his foot. He was much rebuked both by Palmer for carelessness and by Dean Coombe for making an unseemly noise in a sacred building. The man protested that some mysterious force had knocked the hammer from his hand, but he was not listened to, for by this time the light was dimming, and it was decided to abandon work for the day.

And so Dean Coombe began to make his way home to the Deanery across the darkling close on that cool March evening. Picture him, if you will, as he takes this journey; a man, you might say, not much given to strange fears and frets. Here is a man who walks in life both inwardly and outwardly straight ahead, looking neither to left nor right, untroubled by fancy. This is what you would have said had you seen him stride out from the West Door to face a sun that is falling behind the ancient elms in an untidy wrack of clouds. Now he turns a little to his left and sets forth diagonally across the grass to where the Deanery is situated at the southwest corner of the great close that surrounds the edifice of St. Anselm's, Morchester.

Barely has he begun on this journey when a whole crowd of rooks, a "building" of them, if I may use the correct ornithological term, rises as one from the elms and begins to wheel about above the trees uttering their distinctive "kaa, kaa" sound. Dean Coombe must have witnessed this behaviour countless times, and yet he starts and stops for a moment to consider those birds. Their flappings across the ensanguined sky of evening appear to him more than usually agitated and chaotic, and their strange, forlorn cries, more desolate even than normal. But these thoughts occupy him for no longer than a few seconds, and then he is on his way once more.

He quickens his pace, now more resolved than ever to reach his destination. Yet once or twice we see him glance quickly behind him, so quickly that one wonders if he truly wants to see if anything follows. By the time he reaches the gate of the Deanery, passersby are amazed to see that this very sober divine is almost running. The housemaid is equally astonished to open the door to a breathless man.

We will pass over the Dean's next few hours. Let us say only that the Deanery, though spacious, is a chilly, damp old house, rather too near the river for comfort. Its physical atmosphere, moreover, is matched by that which exists among its inhabitants. Relations between the Dean and his wife have become distant over the years, and his daughter is a silent creature who longs to escape the Deanery but possesses neither the youth, nor the looks, nor the accomplishments to do so.

After dinner the Dean spends some time in his study before retiring to bed, writing letters and making notes for the forthcoming chapter meeting. His wife passes by his study door twice, bearing an oil lamp. She has taken to these nocturnal perambulations lately because she cannot sleep. On the second occasion, it being close on midnight, she looks in to remind her husband of the fact and finds him not writing, but staring dully at the dying embers of his fire. When he becomes aware of her presence, he starts violently and stares at her as if she were a stranger. Coolly, Mrs. Coombe reminds him of the hour, a remark which he dismisses with a perfunctory "Thank you, my dear." Soon afterwards she hears his heavy tread on the stairs as he goes to his bedroom.

Unlike his wife, Dean Coombe is accustomed to sleeping soundly, and it is one of the reasons why he sleeps apart from his wife. She would plague him far into the night with troublesome questions and admonitions if they still shared a bed. She has acquired a habit of discontent of late, and he lacks the imagination to supply the remedy.

His own bedroom is small, for Mrs. Coombe occupies the official matrimonial chamber, but it has a fine view over the close, and from the bed, if the curtains are open, you may just see the western front of St. Anselm's. Dean Coombe does not close the curtains because he likes to imagine himself the guardian of this great edifice, keeping watch over it day and night.

Once his nightshirt is on, the Dean feels suddenly exhausted, but still he kneels dutifully by the bed to say his prayers. When he has climbed into bed, he falls almost immediately into a heavy sleep from which two hours later he is awakened with almost equal suddenness.

The moon is up and shines across his bedchamber with a clear, cold light. Coombe thinks he has been awakened by a noise, but all is silence. Then he hears a sound. It is like wings fluttering in a confined space, a bird trapped in a box perhaps, but he cannot tell whether it comes from within the room or just outside the window. He chooses to believe the latter and sits up in bed to see out. There is not a cloud in the sky and the pitiless stars are out. The west front of the cathedral, whose details he can barely make out, looks to him like a hunched old man in rags, the dark rents in his clothing formed by the windows and niches of its elaborate facade. He is invaded by a feeling of infinite solitude, and in the silence that follows his ears become increasingly alert to any noise, but none comes. The stillness now seems to him unnatural.

As he continues to stare at the view beyond the window, screwing and unscrewing his eyes to get a better sight of it, he begins to be troubled by what he is looking at. For some moments he tries to find a rational explanation. At length his eyes become concentrated upon a dark bump or lump at the bottom of the window and beyond the glass. It looks to him as if he is staring at the top of a man's head, the greater part of which is below the window. He even thinks he can make out a few wayward strands of hair upon it.

"Nonsense!" he says to himself several times. "Ridiculous! Impossible!" But the fancy does not leave him. Then the head begins to move and lift itself up, as if to look at him.

With a great cry Coombe leaps out of bed and dashes to the window in time to see a rook, which had been perched on the sill, flap away towards its building among the elms. It was only a rook! But then, rooks are not in the habit of perching on windowsills in the dead of night.

Nothing more happened to the Dean that night, but he did not sleep. At breakfast the following morning his wife noted how pale and drawn he looked, but she offered no solicitude. That would have been to break the barrier that had arisen between them, and she could not do that. She felt safer behind it. The Dean would have been glad of some comfort, but he, like her, had passed the point of being able to ask for it.

That afternoon in the Cathedral, Dean Coombe was present when Palmer and his men began to ease away the memorial slab to Jeremiah Staveley. All had been prepared for the possibility of human remains being found in a recess behind the stone, but no one had anticipated the smell. As the slab, supported by ropes, came slowly away to be laid on a specially constructed wooden cradle, an overpowering odour pervaded not only the North transept but the whole cathedral. The organist stopped playing and several of the workmen took their hands off the stone slab to put handkerchiefs up to their noses. For a moment the memorial stone swung free on its ropes and threatened to crash into the wall and break into fragments, but just in time Palmer called his men to order and the object was laid to rest in its cradle on the scaffolding.

For almost half a minute after this had happened, nothing could be heard in that great cathedral but the sound of coughing and retching. One of the apprentice boys was violently ill into the font. Those who recalled the incident to me describe the odour as being one of mould, more vegetable than animal, "like," as one told me, "a heap of decaying cucumbers in a damp cellar." Others offered different similes, but all agreed that the scent stayed with them, on their clothes and in their nostrils for several days. Another told me that from that day forward he could never so much as look at a ripe cheese without feeling ill.

It was a while therefore before those present could bear to look at what the removal of the slab had revealed. When they did they found themselves looking at a figure that strikingly resembled the painted alabaster effigy that had been removed the previous day.

It was the body of a man in a black clerical gown, with his arms crossed over his chest. The skin was still present, but dark yellow, leathery and stretched tightly over the bones. The eyes had fallen into the skull, the nose was somewhat flattened, but otherwise the face was in a remarkable state of preservation. As with the alabaster effigy, the mouth gaped slightly to reveal a set of jagged and discoloured teeth. The hair and beard were an intense and almost lustrous black. Even the nails were still present on the digits of the skeletal hands and feet. A seal ring on the third finger of the left hand was of bright, untarnished gold incised with an unusually elaborate geometrical figure.

In silence the company wondered at this strange vision, and it occurred to several of them that it was astonishing that the corpse still remained upright. Then, as they looked the body began to collapse and disintegrate before their eyes. The first thing to go was the lower jaw which fell off the face and shattered into a thousand dusty fragments on the cathedral floor. Then, almost like a living thing, the corpse buckled at the knees, lurched slightly forward and plunged to the ground from its recess. A dreary sound, halfway between a rattle and a sigh, accompanied this final dissolution.

It was a shocking moment, but the Dean was the first to recover from it. He commanded that the remains should be gathered up and placed in the long deal box which had been provided for the purpose.

While this was being done the Dean suddenly uttered a sharp: "No, you don't, young man!" and sprang upon one of the apprentices who had been putting Canon Staveley's bones into the box. Dean Coombe thrust his hand into one of the boy's pockets and brought out a bright golden object. It was Staveley's seal ring.

When I interviewed that boy ten years later, he was by then a most respectable young man, and the owner of a thriving building business in Morchester. He told me honestly that he had intended to steal the ring and sell it to buy medicine for his sick mother. Nevertheless, he said, he came to be very glad that he had been caught out in the theft. He also told me that Dean Coombe had not returned the ring to the deal box but had placed it in his waistcoat pocket, muttering something about "the cathedral museum." I can testify that there is no sixteenth-century seal ring among the antiquities on display in the Morchester Cathedral Museum.

When he left the cathedral later that day, Dean Coombe seemed in more than usually good spirits. So we will leave him for a moment and return to the young apprentice whom I have mentioned. His name was Unsworth, and he told me that Palmer, the head mason, a strict but fair man, had spoken to him sharply about the attempted theft, but knowing his situation with a sick mother and no father, said he would not dismiss him. Nevertheless, as a punishment, he made the boy stay on in the cathedral to sweep and tidy up after the other workmen had gone. Never, Unsworth told me, had he performed a task with greater reluctance.

If there had not been a verger or somebody about—Unsworth heard footsteps occasionally and some fragments of dry, muttered conversation—the boy might have fled the scene and braved the consequences. As it was, he did his work conscientiously in spite of the smell, which was still all-pervasive.

One of his last tasks was to nail down the lid of the deal box that held the remains of Canon Staveley. Before the body was hidden forever from public gaze, Unsworth felt a compulsion to take a last look at the corpse. Much of it had turned to dust, but parts of the skull and the long thin limbs were intact, with shreds of parchment skin still clinging to the bone. Curiously, the black gown in which Staveley was clothed had suffered even more than the body from exposure to the air. It was now in rags and tatters, no longer recognisable as a cassock.

Unsworth covered the deal box with its lid and banged in the nails with a hammer to secure it. With each blow of the hammer Unsworth fancied he heard a cry, distant, perhaps coming from a dog or a cat outside the cathedral. He finished his work with reckless speed.

As he left the cathedral, Unsworth told me, some sort of choir practice was in progress. He remembers the groan of the organ and a piercingly high treble voice singing in a style that was unfamiliar to him. Nevertheless he remembered the words because he knew that they came from the end of the 137th Psalm:

"*Happy shall he be that taketh thy children and dasheth them against the stones.*"

As he stepped outside the cathedral, Unsworth saw that

the sun was low on the horizon, sinking through a yellow sky dappled with purple cloudlets. He breathed the untainted evening air with relief. There were not many people about in the close, and the noise of the day was hushed. The rooks had settled into their nests in the elms. It was a still evening with very little wind, perhaps even a trifle oppressive.

Unsworth had come out of the West Door of the cathedral, the only one open at that time of day, but his home lay to the east of it. His quickest route home took him around the northern side of the Cathedral, with the setting sun behind him. Unsworth remembers feeling a vague sense of apprehension as he set off.

Along the northern side of the close were a few private dwellings and a long low stretch of almshouses occupied by the poor pensioners of the diocese. Unsworth could see a few of their windows dimly glowing. In front of these almshouses were little gardens bordered by a low stone wall with gates in them for each dwelling. Most of these gates were wooden and painted white, which showed up against the grey stone houses and the deepening violet of the northern sky. As he rounded the North Transept of the cathedral Unsworth had to pass quite near to these gates and it was then that he saw a human figure silhouetted against one of them.

He took the figure to be that of a man because he could see the legs, which were unnaturally long and thin, almost stick-like in appearance. The arms were similarly emaciated and the head narrow and oblong. He could not see any clothes on the creature except for a few black rags, which fluttered faintly in the mild evening breeze.

He did not care to look too closely, but he took it to be some drunken vagrant, not simply because of the rags, but because of the way it moved. It was swaying uneasily from side to side and waving its arms about. Unsworth told me that he was reminded of some long-legged insect, perhaps a spider, that has become stuck in a pool of jam and is making frantic efforts to escape from its entrapment. The thinness of those writhing legs and arms appalled him.

Unsworth started to run, but was brought up short by the sound of a cry. It was perfectly expressive, but so high above a human pitch that it resembled a dog whistle. It pierced his brain and stopped him from moving. The noise spoke to him of desolation and rage, like that of a child that has been left to scream in its cot, except that the cry was even more shrill and had no innocence to it. It was the shrieking fury of an old, old man. Unsworth found that his legs could not move. Looking behind him he saw that the stick creature had begun to stagger stiffly towards him, still uncertain on its feet, but with growing confidence.

A succession of little screams accompanied these staggering steps, which seemed to indicate that movement was causing it pain, but that it was determined to stir. With its long attenuated legs it began to make strides towards him. It was coming on, but still, Unsworth told me, he could not stir, "like in those dreams, sir," he said, "when you want to fly but cannot."

Suddenly the great bell of the cathedral boomed out the hour of seven and Unsworth was released from his paralysis. He ran and ran until he reached the gatehouse at the Eastern end of the close where he stopped for breath and looked back. The creature was no longer coming towards him. He could see its starved outline clearly against the last of the setting sun. It had turned southwest and with long, slightly staggering strides was making its way, as Unsworth thought, towards the Deanery.

Let us now go there ourselves before whatever it was that Unsworth saw arrives.

Dean Coombe sups, as usual, with his wife and daughter. Conversation, even by Deanery standards, is not lively during this meal. It is plain to Mrs. Coombe and her daughter Leonora that their master is preoccupied and anxious to escape from them to his study. Perhaps he has a sermon to write, thinks Mrs. Coombe idly, half remembering a time when she interested herself passionately in his doings. Even the fact that her husband seems quite indifferent to her company no longer troubles her.

The Dean has barely taken his last mouthful when, with a muttered apology, he wipes his mouth with his napkin and excuses himself from the table. A few minutes later we find him in his study. A fire is glowing in the grate and an oil lamp illumines the desk on which it has been placed. Outside the uncurtained window dusk is falling rapidly over the cathedral close.

The Dean begins to take several volumes down from his shelves. One of those he needs is on the very topmost shelf, and to obtain it he makes use of a set of library steps. He plucks the book from its eyrie and, for some moments, he leafs through it rapidly on the top of the steps until we hear a little sigh of satisfaction. He descends the steps with his book, which he places beneath the lamp on his desk. The work is Barrett's *Magus*, and the page at which it is open has many sigils and diagrams printed on it. The Dean now takes the gold seal ring from his waistcoat pocket and begins to compare the design incised upon it with those in the book.

There is a rap at the door. The Dean looks up sharply and plunges the golden ring back into his pocket.

"Yes!" he says in a voice, half irritable, half fearful.

The door opens. It is his wife. She says, "Stephen, did you hear that dreadful noise just now?"

"What noise, my dear?"

"A sort of shrieking sound. From the close. Do you think it is those boys from the workhouse making a nuisance of themselves again? Hadn't you better see what is going on?"

"My dear, I heard nothing. Are you sure it wasn't a bird of some kind?"

"No, of course it wasn't a bird. It was nothing like a bird. I would have said if it was a bird. Are you sure you heard nothing?"

"Quite sure, my dear," says Dean Coombe in his mildest voice, though inwardly he seethes with impatience. The truth is, he has heard something, but he does not want to prolong the conversation with his wife. Mrs. Coombe expresses her incredulity with a pronounced sniff and leaves the room, shutting the door in a marked manner.

As soon as she is gone, the Dean takes the ring from his pocket once again and begins to pore over the designs in the book. So intent is he on his studies that at first he really does not hear the odd crackling noise that begins to manifest itself outside his window. It is a sound like the snapping of dry twigs. Slowly, however, he becomes vaguely aware of some mild irritant assaulting the outer reaches of his consciousness, but he applies himself all the more ferociously to his research. Then something taps on his window.

Startled, he looks up. What is it? The beak of a bird? There it is again! No, it is not a bird. Some sort of twig-like object or objects are rattling against the pane. Perhaps his wife had been right and it is those wretched workhouse boys up to their pranks. Dean Coombe goes to the window and opens it.

It was at this moment that a Mrs. Meggs happened to be passing the Deanery. She was the wife of a local corn merchant, and a woman of irreproachable respectability. I had the good fortune to interview her at some length about what she saw that evening, and, after some initial reluctance, she proved to be a most conscientious witness.

Despite the gathering dusk, she told me, there was still light enough to see by. What she saw first was something crouching in the flower bed below the window of the Dean's study. It appeared to be a man in rags, "though 'twas all skin and bone, and more like a scarecrow than a living being," she told me. The man's hands were raised above his head, and with his immensely long and narrow fingers he appeared to be rattling on the Dean's window. Then Mrs. Meggs saw the Dean open the window and look out, "very cross in the face," as she put it. Immediately the figure that had been crouched below the window sill reared up and appeared to embrace the Dean with its long thin arms. It might have looked like a gesture of affection except that for a moment Mrs. Meggs saw the expression on Dean Coombe's face which, she said, was one of "mortal terror."

"Next moment," Mrs. Meggs told me, "the thin fellow in rags had launched himself through the window after the Dean and I heard a crash inside. Then I heard some shouting and some words, not distinct, but I do remember hearing the Dean cry out. 'God curse you; take your ring back, you fiend!' And I remember thinking such were not the words that should be uttered by a Man of God, as you might say.

Then comes another crashing, and a cry such as I never hope to hear again as long as I live. It was agony and terror all in one. Well, by this time I was got to the door of the Deanery, and banging on it with my umbrella for dear life. The maid lets me in, all of a flutter, and when we come to the Dean's study, Mrs. Dean and Miss Leonora, the Dean's daughter, were there already, and Miss Leonora screaming fit to wake the dead. And who could blame her, poor mite? For I saw the Dean, and he was all stretched back in his chair, his head twisted, and his mouth open and black blood coming out of it. There was no expression in the eyes, for he had no eyes, but only black and scorched holes as if two burning twigs had been thrust into their sockets."

Only one thing remains to tell. At the Dean's funeral in the cathedral some weeks later, it was noticed that, though the widow was present, Dean Coombe's daughter, Leonora, was not. However, as the congregation were leaving the cathedral after the service, they heard a cry in the air above them. Looking up they saw a tiny figure on the south tower of the west front. It appeared to be that of a woman waving her arms in the air. Some of the more sharp-sighted among the crowd recognised the figure as that of Miss Leonora Coombe.

In horrified impotence they watched as Leonora mounted the battlements of the tower and hurled herself off it onto the flagstone path at the base of the cathedral. Her skirts billowed out during the fall but did nothing to break it, and as she descended all the rooks in the elms of the close seemed to rise as one and send up their hoarse cries of "kaa, kaa, kaa."

When Leonora hit the ground her head was shattered, and the only mercy of it was that she had died instantly.

Later, in recalling this final episode of the tragedy, several witnesses quoted to me, as if compelled by some inner voice, those final words of the 137th psalm:

"Happy shall he be that taketh thy children and dasheth them against the stones."

CHAPTER 4

The shop bell clanked. Emma couldn't help being delighted by such an innocent and inviting sound. It was one of those bright sparkling days that follows rain and she was feeling, as people in their twenties sometimes do, that the universe was on her side. She saw Basil Valentine sitting at a desk, writing in a ledger. His clothes, as before, were immaculate. He wore a bright yellow cardigan. Emma wondered how he managed to wear such conservative clothes with such panache.

"Ah, Emma," Valentine said without looking up. "Can I help you once more?"

"Are you still unwilling to be interviewed?"

"Nothing has changed."

"I looked you up, Mr. Nightfall. I Googled you. You have issues with Dave Huntley."

"The issues are no longer."

"You resigned from your Oxford Professorship because of a scandal."

"The Internet is a wonderful thing."

"It involved David Huntley. He accused you of plagiarism."

"Why are you telling me what I know?"

"Was it true?"

"I was supervising David Huntley in a thesis he was writing. I pointed him in the direction of a text necessary to his studies. He made this into a great discovery and when I published something also making use of that text and coming to roughly the same conclusions without acknowledging his work I was accused of plagiarism. Huntley was a coming man with powerful friends, and I was made to feel uncomfortable. I was beginning to be disillusioned with the academic world in any case, so I resigned. That is my version of events, but of course David may have his. Why not ask him?"

"You don't sound very bothered."

"I am sixty. Nothing bothers me, except the odd twinge of sciatica."

"Are you going to help me find this book?"

"You mean help David Huntley?"

"No. Me. I have to prove my worth on this shoot. I have a career to think of, even if you don't."

"Career. Yes. I remember those things."

"Please?" She smiled; he shrugged his shoulders. Something like a joke passed between them and she knew she had him on her side.

"I thought I'd helped you quite enough already."

"I just need a little point in the right direction."

"Very well. Come with me to the cathedral."

As they passed the churchyard of St. Paul's they saw the tapes of a police cordon, a tent, and a number of police, some in protective clothing. Just outside the cordon and close to where Basil and Emma were passing, three men were holding an animated discussion. A casual crowd of curious onlookers were watching the scene which added to its theatrical quality. *If only I had a camera*, thought Emma, and then repressed the thought with shame.

The three figures in the drama consisted of a choleric old gentleman with wild white hair who was addressing a man in a suit while a clergyman in a dog-collar with a bright blue vest stood by. Emma recognised Sir Everard Cutbirth.

"You realise that you are violating the tomb of my ancestor with all this rubbish," he was saying.

The man in the suit, who was a Detective Sergeant, said: "At the moment that is not our primary concern, sir—"

"Sir Everard!"

"Sir Everard. Unfortunately a young lady has been murdered in the mausoleum."

"I don't care if the Archbishop of Canterbury has been sodomised in there; get her out of it! It is still my family's property."

"I'm afraid we will have to continue to treat it as a scene of the crime for the moment, Sir Everard."

"Good God! Haven't you police better things to do than bother about the squalid end of some dirty, drug-addled tart?"

"The victim was nineteen years of age and a student at Morchester University."

"Reading 'media studies' no doubt, or some such feeble-witted excuse for an academic discipline!"

"I don't think this has a bearing on the issue, Sir Everard."

"But how in hell did she get into my family tomb in the first place? It should have been locked."

The Sergeant looked at the priest, the Reverend Gary Eastwood.

"Is that so, sir? Was the door to the tomb normally locked?"

"I suppose so," said Gary. "To be honest, I really don't know."

"Fine guardian of church premises you are!" said Sir Everard. "What is the point of your existing if you can't even protect the dead from having some wretched pervert spill a girl's guts all over them?"

"Do you have a key to the mausoleum, Sir Everard?"

"Of course I do!"

"Reverend?"

"We may do. I will have to check."

"In that case, Sir Everard, I will have to ask you where you were last night between the hours of seven thirty and midnight."

"I was at home, Bartonstone Hall, Bartonstone, ten miles away. And my housekeeper, Mrs. Milsom, can vouch for me. Satisfied?"

"For the moment, Sir Everard."

Sir Everard pointed at the Reverend Gary Eastwood. "And I'm holding you responsible for this revolting mess, you damned psalm-singing happy-clapper. Understand?"

He turned and began to walk away from the policeman and the priest. He was coming down the path towards where Emma and Valentine stood. When he saw Valentine he hesitated, then came on again.

"I think the comedy is over for the time being," said Valentine. "We had better go to the Cathedral."

The ancient library of Morchester Cathedral, formerly the monks' scriptorium, is on the first floor and runs the entire length of the south side of the cloister. Its guardian was a Mrs. Arabin, the widow of a Morsetshire rural dean, who on the death of her husband found herself quite without support and was given the post of cathedral archivist and librarian out of compassion. A combination of ignorance, stupidity and a strong feeling for the dignity of her office made her difficult to deal with. Emma had already had problems with her while negotiating to film in the library.

As Emma and Valentine climbed the wooden stairs to the library, the sun was streaming through the mullioned staircase window, throwing great dusty bars of light onto the lime-washed walls. At the top of the steps was a landing. A great gothic doorway led to the library. Valentine sat down on a wooden chair under the window, panting for breath. Emma was surprised that he was so apparently out of condition. She rapped the cast-iron ring of the door latch on the wood. There was a click of heels on the wooden boards on the other side of the door, which then opened. Mrs. Arabin was an elderly, chunky woman in tweeds.

"Ah. Miss Hartley, isn't it? I'm afraid I can't see you now. You should make an appointment— oh, Mr. Valentine! I didn't see you there at first."

Valentine had risen from the chair and ambled into the librarian's line of sight. Emma noticed an immediate softening in Mrs. Arabin's manner. The look she gave Valentine was proprietorial, almost amorous.

"I do beg your pardon for disturbing you, Mrs. Arabin," he said.

Emma could see that Valentine was using his charm in a quite calculated manner, but that did not make it less potent. She was conscious of the man's attractiveness in the abstract, even though she personally was not attracted. Twenty-three and sixty: of course it was ridiculous.

"Not at all, Mr. Valentine," said Mrs. Arabin, simpering. "We're in a little bit of a state here. I have just had a call from Miss Bhose at the Chapter House museum. Apparently a ring has gone missing from one of the glass cases in the exhibition there, and we don't quite know when it happened. We're wondering if we should alert the police. You see, we don't even have a proper description of the item, so I am trying to find any reference to it. Is there anything I can do for you ... both?"

"Well, Miss Hartley would like to look at any documents relating to Jeremiah Staveley, one of the canons of the cathedral. 1591. I believe he was a musician and composer."

Mrs. Arabin looked shocked: "Oh, that's most odd. Goodness me! You see—and it may be just a coincidence—the ring in question is known as the Staveley ring. That's all there was on the label. These things have been so carelessly done, I've always said ... But I suppose one must presume that the ring relates to the Canon Staveley whose memorial is in the cathedral."

"Then perhaps we can help each other, Mrs. Arabin."

"Yes. Yes. I suppose you might. Well, do come in, Mr. Valentine and Miss— er—"

Mrs. Arabin finally let them into the library. It was a long chamber vaulted in the perpendicular style, with tall bookcases at right angles to a central aisle that led to an oriel window at the end whose glass was decorated with the arms of former bishops of Morchester. It reminded Emma of Duke Humfrey's Library in the Bodleian at Oxford. For some reason she found this reassuring. There were tall windows to her left and right all the way to the end. On the right they looked down into the cloister garth, now a wicked, gleaming green in the sunlight. To her left the plain leaded panes of glass let in great bolts of dust-flecked sunlight.

"Ah, well," said Mrs. Arabin with an air of expertise. "I think I might start you off in the music section."

She brought them to a section of shelves from which there was a view onto the cloister garth. In the midst of the lawn by the well they could see David Huntley and Veronica having an animated discussion. Emma, seeing her two employers at a distance, absurd, puppet-like figures in a distant play, found herself beginning to grow out of the awe she had felt at her first job in television.

"I don't know why I am doing all this," she said to nobody in particular.

"Good!" said Valentine, smiling.

"Then why are you helping me?"

"Because it's begun. The cat is out of the bag, and so, it would seem, are the Ring and the Book."

They heard a scuffling sound, or was it suppressed laughter? The noise was strangely ambiguous. Mrs. Arabin said: "Excuse me?" and then "Oh!" She appeared round the corner.

"Did you see them?"

"Who?"

"Two men. Old gentlemen. In cassocks. I thought I saw them in here."

"I'm afraid we've seen nothing, Mrs. Arabin," said Valentine, smiling. Emma looked at him and he almost imperceptibly shook his head.

Mrs. Arabin stared at Valentine, temporarily at a loss. "Ah, well!" she said briskly. "Trick of the light. Sometimes it's like that in here." And she trotted off, her stout, sensible shoes making a clacking sound on the floorboards.

"What the hell was all that about?" Emma whispered.

"We shall see."

The music archives were gathered in a number of large box files. They were in a great state of confusion; it was obvious that few people had paid much attention to the past musical life of the cathedral.

In one of the boxes they found some of the oldest material, handwritten on parchment and fine, old linen paper. A few bore the signature of Jeremiah Staveley, a ragged, crooked hand that contrasted strikingly with the neatness with which he put down notes on the stave. Most of the music were quite simple settings of the psalms, characteristic of the reign of the Protestant Elizabeth I, but some pieces harked back to the more elaborate multi-part writing that prevailed in the reign of the Roman Catholic Bloody Mary. In particular there was one setting of Psalm 137, "By the Waters of Babylon," that could have rivalled Tallis's *Spem in Alium* in its complexity. On the top of this Staveley had written in his crabbed hand *non nobis gloria!* "Not unto us the glory!" Obviously he had been particularly proud of the work. Other scraps of paper in his hand contained fragments of musical phrases, evidently jotted down for future use. Against one such musical notation, only a few bars long, he had written:

> *Hearde an olde blinde fiddler playe a fine melodious tune (though somewhat melancholique) in a fielde, Midsummer's Eve Anno 1592. They that stoode bye called it the Dance of Damned Soules, and certaine, I did see some white figures in robes like grave cerements at the end of the field who did writhe and turne to his playing, but when I did approache they all vanish'd away like smoke in the summer dusk. And I did thinke, though t'was but my fancy and not to be regarded, that they were the dead or damned on holidaye for a brief sojourne from their infernall home.*

At the bottom of this random pile of papers was a parchment with some verses written on it in Staveley's hand and, pinned to it, another piece of paper, whiter and inscribed in a more modern hand.

The verses were as follows.

> *I wandered in ten thousand wayes*
> *Seeking the gates of Life and Death*
> *Through manye a desert, manye a maze*
> *I journeyed till I scarce had breath*
>
> *And when all hope had bene forsook*
> *I found deliv'rence in a booke.*

It open'd on a path that led
Unto two portals fasten'd well
Before which stood the countless dead:
The gates of Paradise and Hell.
And those who know whereon they look
Have found their answer in that booke

Both gates are heavy, rude and dark.
My booke hath said by what device
I might both open, learne and mark
The gates of Hell, and Paradise
So I a fearfull path have took
By reading of that curséd booke

Jeremiah Staveley anno 1595.

"1595. The year of his death," said Valentine.
"But what—"
"Wait! Let's see what this piece of paper has to say." He unpinned it
from the parchment. It was written in a steeply sloped Victorian hand.

The remaining papers relating to Jeremiah Staveley, Canon of
Morchester, have been removed on the command of The Right
Rev. Herbert Hartley, Bishop of Morchester August 6th 1880.

Then in another hand were written the words.

See Bp Hartley's Box (retained by order of the Dean and Chap-
ter May 1882.)

Both Emma and Valentine had been so absorbed by their research
that they had ceased to be aware how quiet everything had become.
It was a soft, preserved kind of silence, as untainted by the modern
world without as the motes of dust that continued to tumble whisper-
less through the bars of ancient sunlight. Then there was a noise, a dry
crackle, half laughter, half cough, as if whoever had made it had been
breathing in the dusty air for centuries. After that they heard Mrs. Arabin say, "What! Who?"
Valentine, followed by Emma, came out of the alcove of shelves and
saw Mrs. Arabin sitting very upright at her desk. Something in her pose,
seen from the back, gave them the impression that she had dozed off

and just woken with a start.

"Mrs. Arabin?" said Valentine.

"What! Who?" Mrs. Arabin turned round and seemed relieved to see them. "Oh, it's only you!"

"Who did you think it was, Mrs. Arabin?"

"Nothing! Nobody! I was concentrating so hard on my paperwork that I was quite startled." She smiled and nodded approvingly at her own meritorious labour. She even made a show of shuffling her papers as if she really had been at work. "Did you find out anything about this ring?"

"We may have done," said Valentine soothingly. "Mrs. Arabin, we need to take a look at Bishop Hartley's box."

Mrs. Arabin started so violently that her papers spilled out of her hand and onto the polished wooden floor. "What! No! Certainly not! No, please! Don't do that! I can manage."

Valentine had crouched down on the floor to recover her documents, but Mrs. Arabin was rejecting his help almost vehemently. She snatched some papers out of his hands.

"No! Thank you! Please don't try to help. You'll only disarrange things."

"Why not?"

"What?"

"Why may we not see Bishop Hartley's box?"

"I'm afraid you can't. It's forbidden. Not without the Dean's permission. It's locked away in a special place. No, no! As I told— It can't be done. Why do you want to see the bishop's box?"

"As you told whom, Mrs. Arabin?" Valentine spoke softly, almost insidiously, smiling at her the whole time as if half-amused. He appeared to be soothing and agitating her at the same time.

"Oh, nothing! Nobody! It's just odd … Well, a coincidence, if you like. But quite recently someone else was asking for it."

"Who?" said Emma. "David Huntley?"

"Huntley? Huntley? Good heavens, no! That man has not so much as been near the library. No, no!"

"Then who, Mrs. Arabin?"

"I am not in a position to say. I really can't. Now if you don't mind, this library will close-"

"Cutbirth, was it?" said Valentine.

"Good heavens! How did you—?"

"Did he say why he wanted it?"

"No, no. He just … Well, I told him that it was not in my authority, and that he had to talk to the Dean."

"And did he?"

"I don't know."

"What's so special about Bishop Hartley's box?" Emma asked.

"Hartley resigned his bishopric under something of a cloud," Valentine said.

"What sort of cloud?"

"I'll tell you later. It may have a bearing. Come along, Emma," said Valentine, "we must see the Dean."

As they descended the stairs from the library Emma tried to get the Dean on her mobile. "He's not answering," she said. "I think he's switched it off."

"In my experience the clergy have very troubled relationships with mobile phones," said Valentine.

"I bet you don't even have a mobile."

"You're quite right. I don't. There is a streak of asceticism in me which sometimes expresses itself in inconvenient ways."

They had by this time entered the cathedral cloister. To her relief Emma saw that Huntley and Veronica were no longer there. She looked up at the library. Through one of its windows she could see two faces looking down on her. Both were thin and angular and, though she was seeing them from a distance, their features were present to her in unpleasant clarity. Both faces were flattened against the glass, their old skin touching it. They were the faces of old men, one yellowish, the other a blotched red, except where their noses and cheeks touched the glass, and there they were a leprous white. The eyes appeared to her to be looking in her direction, but there was no expression of communication in their glances. They were inscrutably hungry. Emma remembered how once she had caught her father looking at the photo of a naked woman in a magazine; it was that look, dead and yet full of lust.

"Anything the matter?" Valentine asked.

"Up there in the library. Can't you see them?"

"For a moment I thought I saw something."

"Two faces. One red, one yellow."

"I see."

"What do you see?"

"Never mind that now. We have to move fast."

Something buzzed nearby.

"Oh, crap!" Emma said. "It's my mobile. Hello?"

"Emma," said a voice, "where the fuck are you?"

"Oh, hello, Veronica." She turned to Valentine. "It's Veronica. My director. Can we meet again later?"

"Come to my shop. There is something I should show you."

When Emma had gone, Valentine looked up again towards the library windows. The faces were gone.

CHAPTER 5

*I*t had been a hard day full of unexpected harassments for the Dean, of calls to architects and surveyors, of examining accounts, of dealing with difficult people. Then there had been the business of the missing ring from the Chapter House Museum which had finally been reported to him days after its absence had been spotted by Miss Bhose. He supposed he must inform the police, but he wasn't sure. He would decide later: another few days' delay would do no harm.

But that had not been the trouble. The trouble had been something that should not have been troublesome at all. In the panelled corridor outside his office was the Millais portrait of Bishop Hartley. He had averted his gaze from it ever since that evensong two days ago, but that day, as he went along the corridor from his own office to others, he had passed it frequently. The more he tried to stop himself from looking at it, the more he felt compelled to do so. It was absurd: the more he tried to deny its power, the more its power of fascination increased.

In his office was a bookshelf containing various books relating to the Cathedral. All were informative rather than interesting. He took down one volume, compiled by two clergymen and published in 1934, entitled *Historical Records of the Cathedral Diocese of Morchester*. The section that described the ministry of Bishop Hartley was notably terse and lifeless. It concluded with the following paragraph:

"Bishop Hartley was not a strong man, and the onerousness of his duties put physique and spirituality to the test. He never lost his diligence in administrative matters, but his life of prayer failed. In 1882 he sent in his resignation to the Archbishop and hurried abroad, where he died little more than a year later after much suffering, and a 'life of strict penitence'*. (*Private correspondence to the authors)"

The Dean pondered this paragraph. He read it several times as if he

expected the words to yield a deeper and more secret significance, but they did not. "Life of prayer"—what did that mean? It was a phrase, of course, with which the Dean was familiar; he had even made use of it himself in sermons and in seminars conducted with younger clergy, but did he have one? He said his prayers, yes, but this was part of his daily round. But was this "prayer life" an active and evolving component of his personality? He had never really thought about it. To his shame he could not say it was. It made him feel guilty. Bishop Hartley's "life of prayer" may have "failed," but at least he had had one. Perhaps the Dean had got it wrong and Hartley was someone who deserved his compassion. He went out into the panelled corridor to look again at the portrait.

There sat the Bishop in his lawn sleeves with an elaborately jew-elled pectoral cross hung about his neck; rather ostentatious for a period in which distrust for all forms of popery was still prevalent. The face was still rather hideous, but the look in the eyes, which the Dean had thought malign, seemed to him more pathetic, even pleading, as if his sympathy were being solicited.

The right arm, which supported the Bishop's drooping head, was in turn supported by a pile of books on a table. It was the first time the Dean had noticed this, but the books on which the Bishop's elbow leaned were rather unusual. There were three of them. Two were red leather with gilt tooling, the Bishop's coat of arms embossed on the sur-face of one of them, but the bottom book, which rested on the elaborate damask tablecloth, was black and unusually large. The artist had given no indication of any lettering stamped on its ribbed spine, only a single geometrical figure outlined in a reddish gold colour. It was hard to tell what it was meant to be; the painter Millais had only suggested it with a few deftly casual brushstrokes, but it looked to the Dean like an inverted pentacle. Yes, definitely a pentacle! The Dean thought it strange that he had not noticed it before. After all, he had been passing that painting almost every day for the last two years.

After these reflections, the Dean thought he had done his duty by the old Bishop. He felt relieved somehow. The oppression brought on by his deliberate avoidance of the painting was lifted. All the same, the Bishop's look stayed with him. Infinitely sad, it seemed to him, yet im-penetrable, like a soul peering out from the pit of Hell.

The bell began to ring for evensong. The Dean dismissed these thoughts and started to hurry towards the cathedral vestry. Usually he was in good time and well prepared for the evening service in the cathedral, but this evening he felt rushed and confused. When he entered the vestry the choir was already dressed and being talked to by Mr. Matheson , the Precentor, in that irritatingly authoritative way he had. The Dean noticed two boys giggling and whispering together as he put on his surplice. One of the boys, unusually cherubic, was Aston, the boy who had sung the solo at evensong the other night. The Dean's eyes were irresistibly drawn to his fresh complexion, pink with a coat of down on it, like a peach.

"Aston!" Matheson said. Aston looked up at the Precentor with a subtle impersonation of innocence. "Please bear in what you are pleased to call your mind that you are doing the solo part in our anthem this afternoon."

"I am aware, sir," said Aston with a hint of disdain in his voice. The accent was upper-middle-class, but whether this was assumed for effect the Dean could not decide. Matheson seemed baffled as well. Aston had gone to the very edge of being insolent without actually incriminating himself. The Dean, fascinated rather against some inner inclinations, wondered whether Aston's flirtation with danger was calculated or instinctive. His amusement betrayed itself in a smile which was noted by the Precentor and resented. He glanced at Aston and observed that the boy also had noticed. Thus a tiny bond had been forged between the Dean and this boy whom he had barely noticed before, or so he imagined. Wrenching his will away from this and to the matter in hand, he led the choir out into the chancel of Morchester Cathedral and began the service of choral evensong.

It went, as always, with the slow, timeless dignity that was, in the Dean's opinion, the Church of England at its best. The Dean loved this event in the life of the cathedral and his part in it. He took the service whenever he could, but ever since those strange incidents a few days ago, his pleasures had been tinged with apprehension. However, all went well until the anthem.

This was a setting of Psalm 137, "By the waters of Babylon," by, as the Dean gathered by looking at his service sheet, someone called Jeremiah Staveley. He had never heard of him, but the Dean knew enough to recognise the style to be akin to that of Byrd and Tallis, complex and polyphonic. It was somehow typical of Matheson, who prided himself on his musical scholarship, to have dug out an Elizabethan obscurity for the choir to sing. Nevertheless the Dean prepared himself to enjoy a new musical experience, but he could not. The music, ingenious and finely crafted though it was, shifted like a restless sleeper and would not settle in one key or mode. The Dean began to be reminded not so much of Tallis as of a motet of Gesualdo he had once heard, the same nightmare-like impression of a directionless voyage, of shifting sands. Gesualdo, he remembered, was that Prince of Venosa who had murdered his wife and her paramour in the act of love, and then spent the rest of his life immured in his own castle tormented by guilt and the fear of revenge. He dragged his mind back to the present tense where the anthem was still continuing. It seemed interminable. All nine verses of the psalms were being dwelt on with intense elaboration. Occasionally Aston's pure treble voice would soar above the others in this lament of exile.

He observed Aston's face. It seemed transfigured. Gone were the dizzy, silly thoughts of a boy on the verge of puberty: his whole being was taken up into this strange, tragic, horribly adult world of desolation.

How shall we sing the Lord's song in a strange land?

At that moment Aston's beauty was that of accidental selflessness; and it was disturbingly arousing. The Dean looked away from him. He did not want those thoughts to come again, but it was at that moment he saw them. Yes, there were two of them now.

The Bishop's Stall opposite him should have been empty; instead, he is there. As before, he is in a white surplice with puffed lawn sleeves gathered at the wrist with red silk ribbon. His black stole has the episcopal arms of Morchester Cathedral embroidered on it, and he is looking at the Dean as before. But this time he is leaning his head on his right hand, his elbow propped up on the arm of the stall. It is precisely the pose he adopted for the Millais portrait of him. The mockery in his eyes makes the Dean sure that this is deliberately done to torment him.

Next to him in a minor canon's stall sits another figure. His clerical garb is even more antique than Bishop Hartley's and his face is a yellowish colour as opposed to Hartley's livid pink. He is gaunt and his pale lips are parted just enough to allow the Dean to glimpse a set of irregular, greenish teeth. He too is staring at the Dean, but with the eyes of death rather than of malice. His face is slightly lifted as if he is trying to catch the scent as well as the sound of the music. Something about him seems familiar.

The Dean shook himself and blinked several times as if trying to wipe away the hallucination. He turned to look again at the choir. Still the anthem went on. Aston's voice once more raised itself above the others whose singing had descended to a pulsating drone. Dear God, thought the Dean, he is actually going to sing that terrible last verse.

Blessed is he that taketh their children and dasheth them against the stones.

Aston seemed oblivious of the genocidal implications of the psalmist's words. There was a kind of Satanic purity about him: he was invulnerable. Nothing the Dean could do or wanted to do to him would harm him. Pain and ecstasy, adoration and loathing would all be the same when the Dean had taken him. The Dean blinked again. Those were not his thoughts, he could swear to it, and yet they had formed themselves in his brain and would not let go.

At last the hideous psalm was over and he must attend to the prayers.

Lord grant us a quiet night and a perfect end, now in the time of this mortal life, for the love of thine only son Jesus Christ....

He spoke the words and, not for the first time, wondered what on earth they meant. It meant, at that moment, as far as he was concerned, that the ordeal of Evensong was over for another day.

In the vestry, as they were disrobing, Matheson approached the Dean. Matheson looked pleased with himself.

"So what did you think of the anthem this evening?"

"Oh, yes. Yes," said the Dean noncommittally.

"I thought you'd like it. Bit of a discovery really, though I say so myself. I've been rooting through the archives. By Jeremiah Staveley, Canon of Morchester in the Elizabethan period. Remarkable composer. Almost up there with Byrd and Orlando Gibbons in my view."

"I was thinking Gesualdo …"

"Funny you should say that. There are resemblances: the adventurous chromaticism for example. And Staveley was not unlike him in appearance, actually."

"What!?"

The Dean's obvious shock surprised and disconcerted Matheson. "Yes, his effigy's in the Cathedral. Didn't you know? It's that rather bizarre monument to him in the North Transept with a most peculiar inscription in verse. Something about—"

But the Dean was no longer listening. He had thrown off his surplice and cast aside his stole and was out of the vestry with a rapidity astonishing in a man of his build. Aston and his special friend Davies watched his departure with delight. Grown-ups, particularly clerical grown-ups, behaving oddly was always good for a snigger.

"That's enough, Aston and Davies, you horrid boys," said Matheson.

"By the way, Aston, well sung this evening. You seem by some miracle of osmosis to have managed to imbibe a modicum of my musical expertise."

Mr. Matheson's mock pedantry was also a source of amused contempt to the boys, but this time Aston and Davies kept it to themselves.

The Dean was standing in the North Transept, staring up at the painted alabaster effigy of Jeremiah Staveley. There was no doubt about it. It was the same figure that he had seen in the Canon's stall next to Bishop Hartley. He wore the same Elizabethan gown and bands; his face had the same gaunt and sallow complexion; even the little crooked teeth that peered through his parted lips were the same unpleasantly greenish hue. But what was he doing here, now?

He began to read the inscription below the effigy:

BEHINDE THESE SACRED STONES IN DEATH STAND I
FOR THAT IN LIFE MOST BASELY DID I LIE
IN WORD AND SINNE FORSAKING GOD HIS LAWE,
I DANCED MY SOULE IN SATANN'S VERIE MAWE....

Just then he heard a noise behind him like a suppressed cough, or a giggle. He turned round and saw Aston and Davies standing almost at the centre of the crossing, staring at him. They adjusted their expressions and assumed demeanours of exaggerated solemnity.

"Hello, sir. Goodnight, sir."

"Goodnight, boys."

He watched them turn and make towards the West Door, their heads together, once more conspiring some subversion or other. The Dean watched them carefully, then, treading lightly and concealing himself as much as possible behind the vast Early English gothic piers of the cathedral, he began to follow them.

Aston and Davies, heads still locked together, took the stone path which led diagonally across the green of the cathedral close. They were heading northwest towards the Deanery, but soon they would turn west again and pass through the medieval stone gate into the city of Morchester. The sun was setting behind a stand of elms where a parliament of rooks were circling round their nests and cawing in preparation for their nightly roost. Their black shapes against the yellow evening sky seemed oddly threatening, but the Dean gave them only a glance. He was intent on following the boys.

Why was he following them? The Dean did ask himself the question; he had retained that degree of objectivity. Yet, like the alcoholic about to take one drink too many, it seemed to him that the decision had been taken for him already. Besides, at present he was doing no harm, merely indulging his curiosity. He wanted to know about Aston and Davies, these boys whom he saw every day at services, but to whom he had barely even talked. What did they do when he could not see them? What did they read? What games engrossed them on their computers? Had they begun to masturbate?

Just then they reached the edge of the green. If he was going to follow them now the Dean could no longer pretend to himself that he was merely going back to the Deanery. He would have to walk past the Deanery and follow Aston and Davies into the city. He did so.

The Dean smiled to himself. He was just having a bit of fun; he wanted to know what boys got up to these days. As they passed under the dark arch of the medieval gateway, Aston and Davies started to jostle and push each other, trying to trip each other up. Then they began to run into Morchester's main thoroughfare, St. Anselm's Street.

A rook flew past the Dean, strangely low, cawing loudly with a troublingly human, minatory intonation. Dean Tancock did not run to catch up with his quarry—that would have been undignified—but he did make his pace brisker.

When he came into St. Anselm's Street he saw Aston and Davies not too far away, dawdling in front of a mobile-phone emporium. It reminded him of the peremptory ban he had imposed on any choirboy carrying a mobile in the cathedral precincts. He could not hear what they were saying, but he became convinced that, at this very moment, they were mocking his little rule. He crossed to the other side of the road and followed them cautiously as they idled and giggled their way down St. Anselm's. Probably what they were saying to each other was very silly indeed, but he would have loved to know. He wanted to enter their beautifully simple lives, be a part of them, possess them. Of course he knew it was impossible. They would never let him in. To possess them he would have to destroy them, and that too was impossible. All the same, he could still follow them.

Suddenly, they had turned off St. Anselm's and into St. Paul's Street. Where were they going now? The Dean followed them along the street at a distance until they came to a low wall which bordered the churchyard of St. Paul's. There was a gate in it which opened on a path to the church, but this was locked. Davies shook it while Aston straddled the low wall and urged Davies to follow him. The Dean approached cautiously.

Once they were in the graveyard and among the tombs the two boys became silent, almost reverential in their manner. Obviously they were aware that a murder had taken place there two nights before. An area around the Cutbirth Mausoleum was still taped off. They went right up to the tape and peered at the blank neo-classical monument. For almost ten seconds they stood still and silent, then Aston (the taller of the two) reared up over Davies, raising his hands above his head and howling like a wolf. Davies started violently and began to run. Then they were off, chasing each other around the gravestones, stifling their laughter, but occasionally letting out little whoops of mock terror. At last Aston had Davies pinned down beneath him on a table tomb. He gave his wolf imitation again while Davies giggled ecstatically.

"I am the Morchester murderer!" Aston said in his deepest voice, clutching at Davies's throat. For a moment Davies was silent, as if his friend had gone too far even for him. Then the laughter was redoubled.

The Dean, meanwhile, was crouched behind the wall, watching the two boys with fascination. There was something peculiarly arousing about their activity.

"I am the Morchester murderer!" Aston said again, attempting an even more sinister voice.

"Oh, no you're not!" hissed the Dean from behind the wall. The two boys sprang apart as if stung by an electric shock and ran wailing, now in genuine terror, round to the north side of St. Paul's Church, where they disappeared from view.

The Dean did not know why he had done that; indeed, he was scarcely conscious of his decision to do so, but he was rather pleased with the result. When he saw them next, Aston and Davies would be abject, ripe for moulding and manipulation. He straightened up.

"Geoff?"

This time it was the Dean's turn to start violently. But even in that moment his shock was mingled with a degree of indignation. Nobody called him "Geoff"; nobody, that is, whom he would call a friend or colleague. Even his wife called him "Geoffrey"—"Darling" had evaporated some years ago now—and those who had attempted the abbreviation were always jumped-up sort of people who wished to trespass on an unmerited familiarity. The Dean had always been adept at giving them a demonstration of polite frigidity which soon put them in their place. He turned and saw a fresh-faced young clergyman in a dog-collar and a rather smart black leather jacket. Immaculate blue jeans and an expensive pair of trainers rounded off the ensemble. It took a moment for him to recognise the man as the new rector of St. Paul's, the Reverend Gary Eastwood.

"Ah, hello, Eastwood," said the Dean in his stuffiest manner, immediately afterwards feeling a little ashamed of his hauteur.

"Did I see you crouching behind that wall just now, Geoff?"

"What? Ah! Yes! Just … doing up a shoelace." A brief prayer to God thanked Him that the Dean had put on a pair of brogues that morning.

"These kids," said Eastwood, with seeming irrelevance. "There's no discipline, is there? There's no sense of sin anymore. Sin has become a dirty word, hasn't it?"

"I always assumed that it was."

Eastwood scrutinised the Dean, smiling. "You know, Geoff, I've no doubt you think you're very clever and intellectual, but that doesn't cut much ice with me. More importantly, it doesn't cut much ice with God. I'm sure your kind of out-of-touch ivory-tower Anglicanism is going to sneer at this, but we're fighting a battle against Satan right here in Morchester, and it's because of you."

"I beg your pardon?"

"Yes, Geoff. It's about time a man of God who believes in the Bible told it to you straight." The Dean's unease was beginning to be mitigated by the fact that Eastwood was clearly enjoying himself. "For pure financial greed, you let in that film crew to look for a blasphemous book, just so you could line your coffers. Is it any wonder that the Devil is abroad in this city, that there has been a murder—the murder of a teenage harlot—and that others will happen? Is it any wonder that your cathedral services are dead? My friend, I am telling you for the sake of your salvation, you need to repent; you need to be washed in the blood of the risen Christ."

There were many stinging things that the Dean might have said at this point, and it would have been very satisfying to do so. But he did not. In the first place, he had no talent for off-the-cuff repartee; in the second place, there was at his heart a tiny steel core of humility which always prevented him from reacting too violently to criticism.

He said: "Very nice meeting you properly, Eastwood. You and your wife—Marie, isn't it?—must come and have tea with us one day at the

Deanery." He held out his hand which Eastwood shook as if it had been a leper's hand. The Dean turned and strolled away from him, controlling every footstep, forcibly preventing himself from breaking into a run.

He could not go home yet. That night he walked the streets of Morchester, trying to control the relentless turn of his thoughts, going over and over Eastwood's evangelical tirade and his own feebly magnanimous response. It was only when sheer exhaustion began to slow the carousel of his reflections that he turned his steps towards the Deanery at last.

In his perambulations about the old city he had barely noticed a thing. The projections of his own vivid mental cinema had blotted out all observations. Once, though, towards the end of his aimless trudge, he had spotted a car driving out of the city at speed. This was after midnight, when few other vehicles were about. In it the Dean was sure he had seen the Reverend Gary Eastwood, driving alone. What was he doing?

When the Dean finally returned to the Deanery the bell of the cathedral clock was chiming one. There was a note from his wife in the hall to say that there was some shepherd's pie in the microwave, and that she had gone to bed. The Dean had no love of shepherd's pie, especially not his wife's. He was neither hungry nor unhungry, but in one of those states of mind in which food seems like a vulgar irrelevance. He crept upstairs to his bedroom.

There was enough light from the street lamps in the cathedral close filtering through the thin net curtains for him to move without stumbling over furniture. He could see his wife's substantial bulk in the bed. She was turned away from him and snoring lightly. He undressed and, instead of putting on the pyjamas which, as usual, were neatly folded on his pillow, he got into his bed naked next to his wife's back.

Phyllis Tancock was wearing a white flannel nightgown decorated with tiny pink roses which looked exquisitely frivolous sprinkled over her substantial form. The Dean drew back the covers and lifted the nightgown gently off his wife's thighs so that he could see the whole of her backside from the waist down.

He had not hitherto taken much notice of his wife's bottom, and it was a revelation. Unlike her breasts, her buttocks had not withered with age. On the contrary, decades of biscuits and cakes at Women's Institute meetings had rounded them into two vast soft globes, delicately flattened where they met, tinged with the roseate blush of comfortable good health. They were an unexpected wonder to the Very Reverend Geoffrey Tancock D.D. *O, my America, my Newfoundland*, he thought, remembering the words of another Dean. He traced their silky contours with a sensitive finger.

"Geoffrey! What on earth are you doing?"

It was to be a night of the unexpected for Phyllis Tancock too.

CHAPTER 6

*I*t was evening. Emma and Valentine were in the shop.

Valentine said: "I have some papers that you ought to see. I'll shut up shop and you can come upstairs and look at them. I'll make us something to eat while you read."

Emma looked at him. Normally she would never have trusted such a suggestion, but Valentine was different. She was not sure that he was someone she liked, and certainly he was far too old to be remotely attractive, so she told herself, but she somehow knew that she was safe with him. Nothing needed to be said. He shut up shop, and she followed him through the door at the back of the shop and up a narrow, winding staircase, made narrower by the presence of crammed bookcases on both sides.

At the top of the stairs was a large room that was situated directly above the shop. It too was lined with books. A bay window looked out onto the street, and across the roofs opposite could be seen the spire of Morchester cathedral. The room seemed to combine comfortably the functions of dining room, sitting room and study. In the window stood a Pembroke table on which reposed a neat stack of photocopied documents. Emma had somehow expected Valentine's living quarters to show signs of bachelor slovenliness, but the almost Spartan neatness she encountered was obviously not simply contrived hastily for her benefit. Valentine, in any case, was not the sort of person to put on a show for anyone.

"You may as well know, Emma," said Valentine, showing her to a seat by the table in the window, "that my family has something of a connection with Morchester. In fact, my great-grandfather on my mother's side of the family was bishop here from 1882 until his death in 1909. It's not something I talk about for various reasons, one of them being that my great-grandfather would not have wanted it. That sounds like excessive family *pietas*, but it was rather more than that. My great-grandfather's dying words were succinct and enigmatic: 'No life.'"

"Well, I suppose he was dying."

"Yes, but he was a man whose belief in the afterlife was absolute. I'm told that the day he discovered that his illness was fatal, he was almost exultant because of it. Well, various interpretations have been put forward for his words. It was generally assumed, however, in the light of various remarks he had let fall in his declining years, that what he meant was that he wanted no one to write his biography. As the year of his death was 1909, a time when lives of Church of England bishops were a more marketable commodity than they are now, this was something of a disappointment to my family. But it was also a time when the wishes of the deceased were obeyed, to use the word appropriately for once, religiously. A few days after his death, my great-grandmother, a formidable lady by all accounts, assisted by her two sons, my grandfather Charles, a clergyman, and his elder brother Cyprian, organised a huge bonfire in the garden of the Bishop's Palace at Morton Episcopi. On it were burnt several forests' worth of papers belonging to my great-grandfather, the Bishop of Morchester: correspondence, diaries, even the manuscripts of sermons and his remarkably tedious theological works.

"The mystery of why there was to be 'no life' remained, but the legend of those last words was preserved. My grandfather died when I was eight, long before I would have had the urge to ask him about it. His daughter, my mother, told me that it probably had something to do with the circumstances in which my great-grandfather took over the see of Morchester, but that was all she knew. Curiosity was never a fault of hers.

"The only trace of a clue I could find was in an excessively dull book published in 1934 entitled *Historical Records of the Cathedral Diocese of Morchester*, compiled by two clergymen whose names I forget.

"After my great-grandmother's death in 1926, it was discovered that there was a black japanned tin box among her effects with my great-grandfather's initials painted in white on it. It was locked and the key was missing, but the weight and general feel of the thing suggested that it contained papers. It is somehow typical of my family that this item, known simply as 'The Bishop's Box,' should have been carefully preserved by my grandfather but never opened until 1976 when, unknown to my parents, I forced the lid with a chisel. I read the contents and put them in order. What you have in front of you are photocopies of the original documents. I think it forms a fairly coherent narrative. Whether you believe it or not is another matter. I'll leave you to it"

The next moment Valentine was gone. There was nothing for it but to read what was before her.

Letter from the Reverend Alfred Simms, Canon of Morchester Cathedral, to Miss Agnes Taitt, No. 2 The Close, Morchester, Wednesday 15th February 1882

My Dearest Agnes,

There are a hundred endearments with which I should begin this letter, but I fear you must take them as read, because there is something I must tell you. Even now, I see you blush at these words and put your fingers up to your lips in that charming way you have, and say "Oh, gracious, but what?" Be assured that it does not concern you, or, should I say, "us." I would say that my love for you is constant were it not for the fact that far from being constant it increases daily and swells in your absence, not that—God forbid!—it should diminish when we meet again! But enough of this! I see I have already done what I said I should not.

You will be surprised to learn that what I have to tell you is not something that has occurred to me in the course of my daily existence, but a dream. And yet it was such a dream that it burns into me in a way that no incident has done of late. I have had it more than once and its essentials remain the same. Its details are an accumulation of what I can remember over several nights.

What sets it apart from other dreams is that the location does not vary, nor the point of view from which it is observed. I am standing in the northwest corner of the Close and looking across the green at an angle of some forty-five degrees—you see how clear it is in my mind's eye!—to the great West Door of the Cathedral. It is a bright and cloudless day; the sun is pitilessly hot, and I am standing in a small crowd of people who are townspeople, not gentlefolk. All of them are sombrely dressed, as am I, for I am in my black cassock.

We are watching a funeral procession. It is headed by six

people carrying a coffin that seems to me unnaturally long. This is followed by twenty or thirty others mostly in single file. All are in black like the coffin, which is draped in black. It is too far away to see the mourners' faces, but, as far as I can tell, these also are black or obscured by black material. I ask one of those standing by me, a respectable-looking old gentleman with long white whiskers, whose funeral this might be.

"Why, do you not know, sir?" he replies. "'Tis Satan's funeral."

The others murmur their assent and I am filled with wonder—as well I should be! I see that the procession has not gone in by the West Door but is snaking around the Cathedral towards the little North Entrance. Suddenly my mind is filled with urgent necessity and purpose. I know that I must inform the Dean because only he—I believe—can prevent the cortège from entering the Cathedral, and it is of the utmost importance that it should not. So I set off towards the Dean's residence in the Close, but, as in a dream, I can move only slowly; it feels as if my boots are made of lead and that I am wading through treacle. My desperation grows, but, as it does, my mind slowly approaches waking consciousness. There is a point where I know that I am dreaming, but the urgency remains because I am certain that this vision from the realm of sleep is trying to communicate a message of importance to my woken self. On waking I am convinced that a message must be delivered: but what? You see my difficulty and my distress.

You may say I think too much about this strange dream, but only yesterday I came across this passage from a book I picked up in Archdeacon Bourne's library. (He tolerates my use of it from time to time in return for my accompanying his execrable violin playing on the pianoforte.) The book, entitled *Ancient Customs and Curious Legends of Morsetshire*, by the Rev. Augustine Willows, was published in 1843 and the passage runs as follows:

"The villagers of Morton Abbas and some surrounding hamlets have a curious custom. Whenever one of their number disappears and is presumed dead, though the body be not found, they hold what they call a 'devil's funeral.' An empty coffin covered with a black pall is brought to the church and the appropriate canonical rites are pronounced over it by a man in holy orders. Some years back, a clergyman of my acquaintance who was then Rector of Morton was asked by some of his parishioners to perform such a ceremony. The request was quite properly denied, but the consequences of his refusal, he tells me, were most disagreeable to himself, his wife and his five daughters. He has since moved to a more congenial living. I have heard also, but on somewhat dubious authority, that suicides are sometimes granted the same unorthodox exequies."

The village of Morton Abbas is not ten miles from Morchester, and when I tell you that until yesterday evening I had no notion of this "devil's funeral" being in the folklore of this or any other English county, you will imagine my confusion and consternation.

I tell you this, dearest one, not that you may offer any explanation, for it is beyond me, or, I suspect, any of us, but simply that you may know my state of mind. There should be no secrets between us, either now or in the bliss of marriage that awaits us.

I am, as always, your ever loving, Alfred

From the diary of the Very Reverend Montague Sykes Bennett, Dean of Morchester, Saturday 18th February 1882

A chill grey day. The new housemaid Jane had let the fire go out in my study, which added to my discomfort. I rebuked her gently and agreed not to tell my dear wife Lizzie of her offence. Received a visit from Canon Simms, an odd young man, tall and angular, with a very prominent Adam's apple and an earnest air about him. He teaches at the choir school and is, I believe, well thought of, both as pedagogue and musician. He often sings the responses at evensong, and his voice is pleasing. (Even Lizzie remarked on it with approval.) He told me that he was troubled by dreams, but when I pressed him he would not say what they were. Then he began to talk about Mr. Darwin and his theories. I told him firmly not to trouble his head about such matters. I said to him: "The truths of the Gospel are the truths of the Gospel; the truths of Mr. Darwin (if they be truths) are the truths of Science." Render unto Caesar, etc. I am not sure if he took in what I was trying to say. A most unsatisfactory interview. I am flattered, of course, that he should seek spiritual guidance from me, but I cannot fathom what he wants. Lizzie wishes to dismiss Cook, but I dissuade her. (For the time being.)

From a letter of Canon Simms to Miss Agnes Taitt, Monday 20ᵗʰ February 1882

I guess from your last dear letter that you do not greatly care for my dreams. Dearest, I do not blame you! I do not like them myself, but I must tell you of what I might call a "development" in my dream that I had last night. It is as before. I am standing at the northwest corner of the Close and witnessing the same mysterious event of the Devil's Funeral. The cathedral never looked lovelier to me: its immemorial stones and soaring pinnacles scintillated in the sharp sunlight. Never did it seem to my inward eye more like a great bastion of the spirit, a fragment of the Heavenly Jerusalem come down to earth. And yet to no avail! If the cortège were to enter the Cathedral by the North Door all would be lost! I look to the assembled company for someone to whom I can communicate my distress and, to my astonishment, whom should I see among the assembled townspeople but the Bishop, with his stout frame and his great long legs! He wears his frock coat and gaiters and is watching the proceedings with rapt attention. I call out to him, but I think my voice is faint and muffled in the hubbub. I try to move closer to him, and then I see that there is a boy standing next to him. It could be one of my boys at the choir school, but I cannot be sure. I watch with horror as the boy, unseen by all but myself, proceeds to pick the Bishop's pocket! He delicately draws aside the flap of His Grace's frock coat and reaches into the pocket of his black breeches, and the Bishop notices nothing. I try to cry out, but you know how it is in dreams; the sound that I make is barely audible, no more than a squeak. The boy withdraws his hand from the Bishop's breeches, and I see that in it is an oblong silvery object, a whistle perhaps, but curiously twisted and gnarled. He runs off and I stand there incapable of any action, and, at the same time, consumed by guilt for my incapacity. And still in my waking hours I feel the guilt. Dearest, you will tell me in your sweet, sensible way that it is only a dream, and so I know it to be, and yet "all's not well about my heart."

From the diary of the Very Reverend Montague Sykes Bennett, Dean of Morchester

Ash Wednesday 22nd February 1882

The bishop and I pay a pastoral visit to the choir school. Bishop Hartley has always taken the greatest interest in "my boys" as he calls them. His condescension shows an admirable sweetness and humility of spirit, but I cannot help feeling that he is at times a little over-familiar with the lads. We were in the main music room. Canon Simms was there, looking very pale and withdrawn. I approached him. He seemed nervous, but grateful for my conversation and company. As we spoke, though, his eyes kept darting towards the Bishop who was talking to some boys in the corner of the room. The Bishop had acquired a number of penny whistles and, besides demonstrating a surprising prowess on the instrument himself, was disseminating a number of them to the choristers. There came a moment when there was something of a clamour among the boys. One of them, Damer, a treble on the Cantoris side, was demanding one of the penny whistles that the others had been given. The Bishop said that he had one left for Damer; it was in the pocket of his breeches, but he would not get it for him: Damer must reach into the Bishop's pocket and fetch it for himself. At this such a look of horror passed over Canon Simms' face that I was quite taken aback. There was perhaps some impropriety, certainly over-familiarity, in the Bishop's conduct, but it was no doubt intended in a spirit of harmless fun. I did not think it warranted quite such a violent reaction from Simms. By way of conversation, I asked him if he had had any further dreams, but he looked at me aghast. He is a strange young man, somewhat alone in the world, and perhaps in need of fatherly guidance. I invited him to call on me at any time and he shook my hand warmly at that. On returning to the Deanery I found Lizzie with Mrs. Fogle, the Precentor's wife, taking tea in the parlour. I have noticed that whenever Lizzie is talking with Mrs. Fogle in a room and I enter it, they immediately fall silent. I am afraid Mrs. Fogle is an incorrigible gossip and a bad influence on dear Lizzie. I must speak to her on the subject. Lizzie said: "Have you been with the Bishop?" And Mrs. Fogle said: "And how is the dear Bishop?" I cannot be certain, but there was something about their tone which I did not like, a sort of knowingness. Have they been gossiping about the Bishop? I must speak to Lizzie.

From a letter of Canon Simms to Miss Agnes Taitt Wednesday 1ˢᵗ March 1882

As I told you, dearest one, I have not been having the dream of late, or, if I have, I have forgotten it. (But if you forget a dream, can you truly say that you have had one?) Then yesterday I was giving a scripture lesson to the choir-school boys. We were reading the passage in the gospels about the Temptation in the Wilderness, when suddenly one of the boys, Wilkins it was, a fair boy with the face of an angel, asked: "If God is all-powerful, why doesn't he kill the Devil?" I confess it "knocked me all of a heap," to use the vernacular expression. Given the dreams I have been having, his question seemed to pierce my very soul. ("Foolish man!" I hear you saying in that sweet voice of yours.) I think I acquitted myself well, though. I pointed out that the Devil was a spirit and therefore immortal by nature and that God had decreed it so. "Why?" asked the indefatigable Wilkins, but I passed on to my second point, which was that God had granted all beings, angels and devils included, free will, and that this was a sign of His love. I concluded by saying that, by the death and resurrection of Jesus Christ, the Devil had been defeated because Salvation had been granted freely to all who accept Christ. This seemed to satisfy them, even the inquisitive Wilkins, though, I confess to you, it did not entirely satisfy me. I know that it is the teaching of the Church, my love, and I do accept it in my heart, but as I spoke the words, they seemed to mean nothing to me. That afternoon I went a-walking by the River Orr, which winds through tranquil meadows beside the Cathedral. It was a dull day, but it did not appear to threaten rain. You know, dearest, how I often walk there and think of you, because of that day when you came and we walked in the water meadows and talked of the time when we would be together for always. Do you remember the bench where we sat down and I held your hand? Dear Heaven, I feel your hand now, soft and cool in my own! I often go to that bench and remember all the things that we said to one another, and it consoles me for the time when we must be apart before the Blessed Sacrament conjoins us and sanctifies our union in spirit and in body. I sat down on that bench, but my thoughts did not at once fly to you. Restlessly I went over what I had said to the boys about God and the Devil and why God had not killed the Devil, and my dream of the Devil's Funeral. You remember, my love, how that bench looks onto the slowly winding stream of the Orr, and beyond it to the cathedral itself: solitary, majestic, its high spire pointing heavenwards. You remember how I told you, as we looked at it, that we too were going to heaven, and that our heaven would begin on earth when we were together. Well, as I sat there before that sublime scene I began to feel calmer, and I think I must have fallen into a kind of trance or reverie. That is the only way I can explain it. The sky was darkening and I wondered whether I should move before it began to rain, but I did not want to break the spell of the stillness. As I watched the flowing river I began to notice something. It troubled me a little perhaps, but, at first, it did no more than excite my curiosity. The current, which flows from left to right as you see it from the bench, was beginning to slow down. It was as if the water were changing its natural constituency into something lazy and sluggish like mud or treacle. I wondered whether this had been caused by some obstruction in the stream farther up river. The height of the water remained the same but its surface became smoother, glassier. I also noticed that the birds, whose song is an added delight in that meadow, had fallen silent. The whole world seemed suddenly to be thick and soundless. Wonder and bewilderment began to be replaced by horror as I saw that the river now was slowing to a standstill. In its mirror-like surface I could see an exact reflection of the great dirty bellies of cloud that now hung over the spot. Then the stream of the Orr gave what I can only describe as a kind of lurch and began to flow backwards. [These words are heavily underlined three times.] At this, I lost all restraint, I screamed, I roared aloud, and then I think I must have fainted. The next thing I knew I was being helped to my feet and then onto the bench by an elderly man and his wife, both respectable folk. The man had long white whiskers and looked not unlike the man in my dream who told me it was the Devil's funeral. I tell you this, my love, not to frighten you, but to say that today the sun is shining and that all my fears have gone. I have been trying to find out a cause of all these aberrations and the only explanation I can think of is that you, my love, are the utterly innocent agent of my afflictions. Or rather it is my longing for you that torments me, to see you, to touch you, to hold you in my arms and lay my tired head on your soft breast. No, do not blame yourself, or your good father for his inflexibility. It is life, it is fate: we are on the Calvary side of the grave.

From the diary of Dean Bennett

Sunday March 5th 1882

A most curious thing happened at evensong today. I had just given out the Psalm—"Lord, who shall dwell in thy Tabernacle?"—and was looking down at my prayer book which was opened at the psalm, when I saw what looked to me at first like a file of black ants crawling across the page. I was disgusted and appalled. I brushed them hastily off the page, but somehow they could not be moved. Or were they just specks of dust that had become ingrained on the page? No, they were most definitely moving. I did not have my spectacles on, so I could not be sure, but they looked to be less like ants than tiny figures in procession, carrying a longish object, almost like a funeral cortège. Nonsense, of course. I blinked several times in case the specks were in my eyes rather than on the page, then I looked across the choir to the stalls opposite me. I noticed that Canon Simms from his stall was staring at me intently, as if he were trying to communicate some thought to me. I frowned back and looked down again at my prayer book. The ants or specks or whatever they were, were gone. Lizzie told me afterwards that I read the lesson very badly this evening. The strange thing is that I couldn't remember anything about it. I had to look it up in the order of service. It was from Matthew 18, "But whoso shall offend one of these little ones …" etc. We should not pay too much attention to these occurrences. God in his Infinite Mercy knows what they mean, but we may not.

From a letter of Canon Simms to Miss Agnes Taitt, Tuesday 7ᵗʰ March 1882

I cannot begin, my love, to express to you the pain I feel in having caused you pain. If, in my last letter, I have been, as you say, "over-familiar" and presumed too much on our future union, then I most abjectly beg your forgiveness. If I was "improper" then it was only through an excess of the very proper feeling of love. It was regrettable that you should have been so careless as to allow my letter to fall into your father's hands. I cannot think how this could have happened. Do you not keep my letters as safe and close as I do yours? But I do not blame you, my love. I will only say this: that it pains and surprises me that your father, whom I revere, should have chosen to read what was quite obviously a private communication. Nevertheless, I have caused distress and that I humbly regret.

You say that he has forbidden all correspondence between us. That cannot be! I have therefore written to your sister enclosing this letter, hoping that she and her good husband will have pity on me and pass it on to you. I have always understood that they live not far from you and that you visit them frequently.

If this action seems presumptuous, I cannot help it. I have no life without you. No life at all. You may say, but what of your life of prayer, what of God? Well, if I cannot have you, I will not have God. You are all the God I want, the only God I need and He is no substitute. There, I have said it, and it may be blasphemy, but God will forgive me because I have told you the truth, and God loves the truth.

I admit freely that there have been too many gloomy things in my letters of late, so let me try to be cheerful and amusing instead. It is perhaps not my natural bent, as you know well, but I will try, just as you must try to accept me as I am.

I visited old Archdeacon Bourne yesterday to play music with him. What a funny old fellow he is, with his patriarch's white beard, his quips and quotations and his great house full of servants who are all looking after him alone. They say he is as rich as Croesus and goes every year with his manservant James to the Royal Academy, where he buys an oil painting and James is allowed to select a water-colour or a small bronze. He is the very devil for punctuality, and if I am even so much as a minute late by his watch I have to stand for a full quarter of an hour before he will speak to me, and then not before I have said *"mea culpa, mea maxima culpa"* seven times! On this occasion I was most punctual, and he was in high good humour. After we had played our music, he on the violin, I on the piano—he will have a dash at the Beethoven sonatas for which he is quite "o'er-parted"!—we had some general conversation. He was remembering his time as fellow and tutor at Oriel which was quite thirty years ago.

He told me that during his time there Bishop Hartley had been up at Oriel as an undergraduate. "He was in those days what was called 'a heavy swell'," said the Archdeacon. "The younger son of a Baronet, you know, which is sometimes an invidious position to be in, so my friends tell me. The Hartleys were a military family, I believe, and he was by no means destined for the Church. He had money, went around with the fast set, joined the Grid, kept a couple of hunters at Abingdon. He was known as 'Beau Hartley,' you know. You've seen that portrait by Maclise above the fireplace at Morton Episcopi. That's Bishop Hartley as I first knew him."

I had of course observed the picture of an exquisitely beautiful young man with the high stock and the tight-fitting embroidered waistcoat of an 1850s dandy, but I had never associated it with the Bishop. Bishop Hartley is a commanding figure, as you know, but somewhat stout, with a red, raddled face and receding hair. But what has most changed is the facial expression. The man in the portrait looks out boldly; impudently, you might say: the Bishop, for all his air of authority and command, has always to me had something furtive about him. He rarely looks you in the eye, and if he does it is always sidelong, half over a shoulder. I said to the Archdeacon that it was a wonder that he had never remarked to me or to anyone in my presence that the picture was of him.

"You and I, my dear Canon, have never been beautiful," said the Archdeacon, "and so we have had longer to become used to our imperfections. Those who come to ugliness later in life feel both pride and shame about their former condition. I don't know when Hartley decided on the church. It is a mystery to me. I did not see signs of a vocation when I knew him at Oriel. Not that he was exactly a miscreant; he did not miss his prescribed attendances at College Chapel, but—" For a moment the Archdeacon was lost in thought, as if contemplating an unfathomable and somewhat painful mystery. Finally he rallied with that characteristic low, breathy chuckle of his, like an old badger snouting for worms in a wood. "No one could accuse Hartley of having been the model for Mr. Verdant Green," said the Archdeacon. He laughed at his witticism which he thought so good that he repeated it several times. You remember, my love, "Mr. Verdant Green" was that most amusing book I told you of, about the innocent Oxford undergraduate who is led into some awful scrapes. Some fellows used to call me "Verdant" when I was at Corpus Christi.

And now to somewhat gloomier topics, I am afraid. I cannot forbear to mention that I have had that dream again last night, but events have moved on! I am standing in the Close where I was in my last dream, or perhaps a little further to the north, because I can see that the transept's North

Door is open and the funeral cortège is moving into the Cathedral. I am frantic because I know I should be inside. I can hear the choir singing; only the boys, though: the tenors and basses are absent. The chant they are singing is unfamiliar to me and quite beautiful, I think. I was able to write down the notation roughly when I awoke; but it was some of the words that struck me most forcibly. Most of them were indistinct because the whole choir was singing, but then there was a solo by one of the trebles, Damer or Wilkins, I think, and I could distinctly hear what was sung. Just these words: "Where is my Enemy now? Who is my Enemy now? Where is my Enemy now?" They seemed to me to be the most vital and terrible questions; I cannot quite understand why. I suppose the meaning is that if the Devil were dead, who would be the Enemy? But this is mere foolishness. You will tell me to dismiss it all from my mind, and so I shall.

If you can, will you convey my sincere regrets and best regards to the Professor, your father? How goes his great work on the Refutation of Darwinism? I am sure we all wish him a speedy completion to his labours.

From the diary of Dean Bennett

Tuesday 14th March 1882

Last night something very strange occurred. I was reading late in my study, as is my wont these days, when there came a banging at the door. It was about a quarter after eleven and, as I had dismissed all the servants for the night, I answered the door myself. It was the massive, dignified form of Skulpitt, the Head Verger, and he was in a great taking. He said there were lights coming from the Cathedral "where there didn't ought to be." He had happened to look out of his rooms in the close and seen them. Why he could not have investigated on his own, or with a Sub-Verger, I do not know. Perhaps something about it frightened him. He certainly appeared to be much relieved when I agreed to join him in his investigations.

As we approached the Cathedral, I thought I could detect a faint flicker once or twice from behind the seven lancet windows (called for some unknown reason "The Seven Sleepers") at the end of the South Transept. The first thing to determine was how the intruder had got in, so we carefully tried the doors, beginning with the South Entrance, until we came to the North Door, which was ajar. If Skulpitt had not had his lantern we would have seen nothing within, for there was no other light source. The lamp as he moved it threw fantastic dancing shadows onto the great ribbed vault of the nave. I commanded Skulpitt to stand still. If there was nothing to see, at least we might hear something. Presently we did hear a noise, a faint whispering and scraping sound. "It's coming from the crypt, Dean!" said Skulpitt. Sure enough, it was. When we came to the top of the steps to the crypt we saw a light faintly dappling the wall at their foot. At Skulpitt's earnest request, I took the lantern from him and led the way down the stairs. I do not know what I expected to find, but what I saw when we entered the crypt astonished me a good deal.

A lighted candle in a pewter stick had been placed on the crypt's floor, which is largely composed of massive funereal slabs commemorating long dead ecclesiastical worthies. Upon one of these a man in a cassock was crouched on all fours. He appeared to be minutely inspecting the cracks in the stone and was whispering the whole time: "Where is he? Where is he? Where is he?" It was young Canon Simms. I called to him several times but he took no notice. Eventually I went over and shook him quite roughly. This broke whatever trance he was in and he came to his senses. Such a look of shame and horror passed over his face when he became fully aware of his situation that I fully forgot all the words of reproof I had been preparing to deliver. "I must have been sleepwalking," was his only explanation. I had no reason to doubt this, but it is a strange kind of sleepwalking indeed that can take a man from his lodgings fully dressed, find a key, light a candle and deliver him into the bowels of a sacred edifice! Skulpitt and I escorted him back to his rooms and I told him to come and see me the following morning.

When he came today he seemed to remember last night's

events very imperfectly. Perhaps it is just as well, so I did not
seek to remind him. He talked of his dreams, which he appears to think foretell some great calamity coming to the
Cathedral. I told him to dismiss these fears and to pray earnestly for a deliverance from his dreams because they were
assuredly the work of the Evil One. At this he looked at me
sharply and said: "But who is the Evil One?" "My dear man,"
I said severely, "you know quite as well as I do who the Evil
One is."

I do believe, however, that I have discovered the root
cause of Simms' spiritual trouble. He is engaged to the
daughter of Professor Taitt, a thoroughly suitable match
in every way. Unfortunately, the Professor, with perhaps a
greater sense of propriety than of sympathy, has forbidden
the union for over a year. Canon Simms is a good young
man, but he needs the steadying and chastening influence
that marriage with a sensible, virtuous woman can offer. He
is evidently very much in love.

I consulted Lizzie who, ever practical, suggested that
Canon Simms, like many men in his situation, was not eating properly. She wrote out for him a strict regimen of nour-
ishment and insisted that he should dine with us at least
once a week. I thoroughly approved this course, which settles
at least some of his bodily needs.

From a letter of Canon Simms to Miss Agnes Taitt Thursday 16th March 1882

I cannot express the joy I felt at receiving your dear letter and
still more the relief I had at the news that your father has
relented. We are allowed to write to one another once more!
I am fully sensible that the possibility of a union between us
cannot be contemplated until your twenty-first birthday, and
I will contain myself in patience. A year and twenty-six days!
You must excuse me if I count the days, even the hours!

To receive your letters is a blessing, to be able to write to
you is almost as great a consolation to my spirit. I feel better
today, though my sleep is still disturbed. Monday night was
the worst, and though the memory of my dreams is more
confused than before, some parts of them stand out with aw-

ful vividness. The only relief I have is in writing them down and communicating them to a reader who will neither judge nor scold.

I told you before that my last dream of the Devil's funeral was a progression from the first ones that I had had; well, in this one again time had moved on. I was now hurrying to follow the cortège through the North Door and this I did. Imagine my confusion when, on entering the Cathedral, not only could I see no sign of the funeral procession, I could barely see anything else. The Cathedral was plunged in darkness as if the daylight from outside had suddenly been blotted out. Somehow a lighted candle came to my hand and with its aid I began my search for the mourners and the coffin.

I could see nothing, but occasionally I heard sounds, little scraps of that choral chant that I had heard in my previous dream. "Where is my Enemy now? Who is my Enemy now? Where is my Enemy now?" Presently I was able to locate the source of the singing. It was coming from the crypt. So I walked down into it, bearing my candle.

The crypt was deserted but the coffin was there. It lay on the floor across the memorial stone to Archdeacon Haynes. I approached and stood above it. The coffin was open.

I believe I told you that the coffin was an unnaturally long one. It was indeed horribly long, far longer than I had reckoned from a distant sight of it. Within was a body, of a sort. The top half it was covered in a black cloth, but the legs and feet from the thighs downwards were not. Besides being hideously long and thin they were not like human legs at all. With their knotted joints and callused, scaly skin, they were more like the legs of some monstrous bird, except that the feet and toes had a vaguely anthropoid aspect. The nails, though, were black and curled like talons, while the colour of the skin was a rough, leprous white, like the skin of a plucked chicken. Ask me why I was drawn to stoop down and pull aside the black cloth, and I cannot answer you. This was a dream. But I did. I will not describe to you the body: that must be my private torment until the day I die, but the face, I will, if briefly. I must. It was the face of Bishop Hartley, red

and raddled as in life, but dead, the eyes squeezed shut. Yet, though dead, the face did move, for a million agents of decay undulated and crawled beneath the skin, rolling his lips into a snarl and baring his blackened teeth. Some dark and rotten worm began industriously to lift the lid of his right eye, but before it could fully open I had somehow torn myself into the sweating, waking darkness of my bedroom in the Close. The Cathedral clock was tolling midnight. Yet this was not the end, for I found that I was not in bed, but standing at my window and fully clothed in my cassock! I had a vague impression that I had been somehow conveyed by an unknown agency from the Cathedral to my room.

You must comfort yourself with the thought that I am not quite alone in my difficulties here. Yesterday I went to see Dean Bennett who seems to understand more of my trouble than I thought, though he does not know the whole of it by any means. He and his wife have been most kind and sympathetic towards me. I do not deserve it. "Mrs. Dean," as we call her, whom he calls "Lizzie," is a lively, active little woman with a very imperious manner at times. But the Dean is more than a match for her. If she exceeds what he understands to be the natural prerogatives of her sex, he will simply say "No, Lizzie!" and lo, she desists! I think she reveres him as she reveres no one else in the entire world, not even His Grace the Bishop. I do not suppose that theirs is a great love, as ours is, my dearest, but it is a good one: "'t will serve".

From the diary of Dean Bennett

Palm Sunday 1st April 1882

Charlie and Cyprian are back from Temple Grove School for Easter. I have high hopes of a Winchester scholarship for Cyprian; Charlie's intellectual gifts are not, alas, of a high order, but he tells me that he has a great aptitude for cricket. Canon Simms dined again with us this evening. He is much improved; thanks to Lizzie's regime, less pale and gaunt, and though he will never, I think, be lively company, he is pleasant enough. He started to tell the boys about some old customs and superstitions of the county, and appears to be quite the antiquary. He was talking about a custom that prevailed at Morton Abbas, when I said that we would be passing that way tomorrow, for I was taking the boys in the dogcart to see the Bishop at Morton Episcopi a few miles farther on. At this he looked up at me very startled and anxious and said: "Really? Is that wise?" I thought this somewhat impertinent, but I let it pass, calmly telling him that His Grace had kindly expressed a particular desire to meet my boys. I could be wrong, but it seemed to me that, at this moment, a look passed between Simms and Lizzie, almost as though they knew something that I did not. Lizzie then said: "It is quite all right. I am accompanying them to Morton Episcopi." "Indeed you are not, Lizzie dear," said I. "His Grace did not extend the invitation to you as well." "Nevertheless, Monty dearest, I am coming," said Lizzie. I was so taken aback by the firmness of her tone that I could find no words to gainsay her. The moment had passed for objection and so, I suppose she is coming with us to Morton Episcopi. No doubt she has her reasons: it is most odd.

From a letter of Canon Simms to Miss Agnes Taitt Easter Saturday, 8th April 1882

Shortly I must go in to choir practice for the Easter Sunday Service, but before that I must put down these words. God knows, you are the only one who will understand. I am not mad, but I may be going mad. There is a difference, you know! I am being taken to a place, I do not know what it is, or where it is, but I think it is possibly Hell. But not there yet! Only you can help me. Hear me out. We had our Good Friday service in the Cathedral, and the Bishop was there. Bishops, as you know, only attend their cathedral services, as a rule, on special occasions. It was a long service. Archdeacon Bourne spoke on the Seven Last Words from the Cross. At the end of it all I think we were all exhausted. In the vestry afterwards I saw young Damer, one of the trebles, crying in a corner. I went to put a fatherly arm around him, but he shook me off quite violently. He is a dark-eyed, serious boy, eleven years old, and reminds me of the lad I was at his age. I asked him what was the matter, but he would only say that the Bishop had been watching him all through the service. I am sure that this was an exaggeration, but I knew what the boy meant. On the rare occasions when the Bishop does look at you, it is not easily forgotten: that sidelong glance, sly and, somehow, greedy.

Later I had to go back to the Cathedral to fetch some music from the organ loft that I had left. It was deserted and gloomy in the fading light. I remember how I made as much noise as possible walking over the flagstones and tramping up to the loft, just to keep myself company.

The music was not there, and then I remembered that I had left it in my stall. The Silence was gathering all the while and the more noise I made the more it seemed to hold me in its grip, in its great soft cold hands. I came down from the loft and went to my stall, where I found the music. I had noticed in passing that the cross, which is covered by a bag of purple cloth from Good Friday till Easter Sunday morning, had gone from the High Altar. I wondered about this: could it have been stolen? And, if it had been stolen, should I report the fact? As I was leaving my stall with the music, I looked up again at the altar to ensure that I had not been mistaken. Upon the altar stood a man, naked: a beautiful young man with long legs, his arms outstretched, palms outward, such as you see in the old crucifixes of Christ Pantocrator, but not clothed or crowned. He was utterly naked and, though well-proportioned, appeared to be over ten feet high. I am having a vision. The eyes are looking through me; sweat glistens on his chest. I am waiting for him to speak. He says to me: "I too am resurrected, though not as one but as many." Then his face becomes contorted and he shrieks aloud as his glistening belly begins to swell. It bursts with a great roar and out of its red and mangled fissure pours a great host that fills the cathedral: flies and flying things that buzz and soldiers with dead metal faces, and men and half-men and singing, whining heads with wings for ears. That is what I saw and you may call me mad. I say I am not; I am just going mad. Read this and pity me. I fled the Cathedral and staggered back the few hundred yards to my rooms in the Close. I sat up half the night waiting for my head to fall off or for the crowd to come for me. Maybe if I hold myself very still I can survive long enough for you to catch me in your arms.

From the diary of the Very Reverend Montague Sykes Bennett, Dean of Morchester

Easter Saturday 8th April 1882

Canon Simms collapsed on the steps of the altar after choir practice today. He was taken to his lodgings in a state of semi-consciousness. I have sent over my man Fisher to look after him as best he can. Dr. Pendlebury was summoned, but he could do no more than utter some rigmarole about "brain fever" and "neurasthenia" and prescribe a tonic.

Easter Monday, 10th April 1882

I heard this morning from my friend Ames that Mr. Rossetti, the poet and painter, died yesterday. I sincerely trust that the creator of *The Blessed Damozel* made a better death on that sacred day than he made a life. Providence had decreed him many prodigious gifts.

In the afternoon went to Morton Episcopi to the Bishop's, where he holds his Easter Monday gathering for the cathedral clergy and choir. It was a bright and cloudless day, and His Grace was in high good humour. There was fruit cup, and tea for the ladies, and all manner of delicacies to eat. The Bishop was very convivial and gracious with everyone and had a particular word with all the boys, for whom there were games on the lawn. Bishop Hartley, like many a confirmed bachelor, is full of queer eccentricities and fancies. He can carry off the grave side of his office with great dignity, but he has a sportive, at times almost childlike disposition. He is a great collector, having inherited the wealth wherewith to indulge himself, and one of the rooms in his Palace is devoted to an exhibition of ancient classical statuary, some of it not altogether decent. (This he excused to me by saying that they were the product of his voyages through Italy and

Greece in his youth.) In another he has amassed a most re-markable collection of painted lead model soldiers, no doubt in honour of the military side of his family. He has them laid out in dioramas to illustrate some of the notable battles of this century. Throughout the afternoon he was forever invit-ing the choir boys, often singly, occasionally in pairs, into the room to view "my military scenes," as he put it. I am afraid that what with all the games, the fruit cup (which was unconscionably potent), the food and other novelties, many of the boys became thoroughly over-tired by the end of the proceedings. I saw one being led away in tears by Mrs. Fogle, the Precentor's wife, and two of them were violently sick into His Grace's fish-pond.

On our return from Morton, my man Fisher came to me in great distress, saying to me that Canon Simms had disap-peared from his lodgings. I made enquiries, but no clue as to his whereabouts could be ascertained. In addition, Lizzie has scolded me for allowing Charlie and Cyprian to have too much fruit cup. I replied, rather too sharply I am afraid, that if she had spent more time looking after her sons and less tattling over the teacups with Mrs. Fogle, the boys might be in a less disordered state. A most exhausting and unsatisfac-tory day.

Tuesday, 11th April 1882

A gusty day of rain and oppression. No news yet of Canon Simms. Truly the bard was right when he said, "When sor-rows come, they come not single spies, but in battalions." This morning I heard of the most dreadful tragedy: the drowning of one of our choirboys, young Damer, in the Orr. He was found floating in some reed beds yesterday evening and would appear to have been dead for about six hours. No foul play is suspected, but accident, I fear, is equally improb-able: his pockets were full of stones.

Wednesday, 12th April 1882

A wire from Birchington-on-Sea that Canon Simms is found, but in a most dreadful state. He is in good hands, though, being looked after by his intended, Miss Taitt, who lives with her father, Professor Taitt, at Birchington. No doubt that was why he had fled there. He was found in a boarding house on the sea front, having attempted, it would appear, to take his own life by a most extraordinary method. He had swallowed one, or possibly several—the wire was too terse to be entirely clear about this matter—lead model soldiers. He has made some sort of recovery, but I fear his internal organs will be irreparably damaged, and the poisoning from the lead must take its toll. I would have gone at once to Birchington had not an even more dreadful occurrence intervened.

At about noon I was called upon at the Deanery by Mr. and Mrs. Wilkins together with their son Joseph, who is a cathedral chorister. They begged for a private interview with me, to which I consented, and they came into my study, leaving young Wilkins on a chair outside my study door. They then proceeded to tell me the most shocking story about the Bishop and their son. I might have dismissed them angrily and at once, were it not for the fact that Wilkins is a most respectable man. He owns the draper's in Milsom Street, has served on the Town Council and he and his wife are regular in their attendance at divine service in the Cathedral. Naturally the allegations had originated from young Joseph, but Mrs. Wilkins told me that she had seen physical evidence on the boy which supported his claims. I summoned Joseph into my study and interviewed him minutely. He answered all my questions carefully and without equivocation. He is a somewhat slow-witted youth, but this makes it all the more certain that he has fabricated nothing. I am quite sure that he was perfectly truthful. What he told me has darkened my outlook on life in a way that nothing hitherto has ever done. Mr. and Mrs. Wilkins then began to suggest that responsibility for the tragic death of young Damer can also be laid at the Bishop's door. This I angrily dismissed as mere supposition. I am afraid I may have been rather too harsh with them on this point, but, I must admit, I was not wholly in command of myself by this time.

As soon as the interview was over, I summoned the dog-cart and set off for Morton Episcopi. His Grace was taking a post-prandial nap when I arrived and seemed reluctant to have me admitted, but I forced myself into his presence.

I cannot possibly bring myself to give the full details of that interview. It is too inexpressibly painful to me. It would appear that His Grace is utterly lost to all decent feeling, let alone a consciousness of the peril to his immortal soul. He made very little effort to deny the allegations, but instead asked if the silence of the Wilkins family might be bought with money. I replied indignantly that I had with difficulty persuaded them not to put the whole matter before the proper authorities, and that it was only on condition of His Grace's immediate resignation from the see that they had agreed to relent. He replied in high choler that it was "devilish presumptuous," but whether he meant of me or of Mr. and Mrs. Wilkins I could not tell. The subject of young Damer was broached—I forget whether it was the Bishop or I who brought it up—and he assured me that there had been nothing in his conduct towards that boy with which he could reproach himself. He spoke so earnestly that I was forced to take him at his word. He said that ill health, due to the pressure of his labours and responsibilities, would have forced him to "lay down" his "burden" (as he put it) very soon in any case, and that he would write his letters of resignation that very evening.

Bishop Hartley then said that if I could keep all quiet and stop idle tongues wagging, he would speak to certain people that he knew about the suitability of my elevation to the see of Morchester. He reminded me that his brother, Sir Herbert, was in the Cabinet and spoke very warmly of my abilities. I replied that I had no personal ambitions whatsoever, but that it was in the greater interests of God's Church that this matter should be handled with the utmost discretion. Hartley nodded several times, then looked at me with that sidelong glance of his and smiled in a way that I did not care for at all. With that I left him.

On my return from Morton Episcopi, I asked Lizzie whether she had learned anything about Hartley's conduct from her conversations with Mrs. Fogle. She replied that she had, and I asked her severely why she had not informed me about such a grave matter. She replied, "Because, Monty dear, you would only have told me that I had no business listening to malicious gossip." I am forced to acknowledge that there may be some justice in her remark.

Letter to the Very Reverend Montague Sykes Bennett, Dean of Morchester

Manor Lodge, Birchington-on-Sea, Kent, Friday April 28th 1882

Dear Dean Bennett,

I received your message of condolence by wire this morning, for which I thank you. You will find in this packet such of the letters I received from Alfred as may throw light on the mystery that surrounds his terrible end. I do not wish them returned, for they are too painful to me; you may dispose of them as you deem fit. You and I are the only persons, I think, who concerned ourselves with him at the last. Both his parents are dead, and his uncle, who was largely instrumental in his upbringing, is in India. I have notified him of the tragedy.

This much you already know: that I found Alfred in a boarding house here in a most dreadful state and prevailed upon my father to let me look after him at home. My father is not a man without compassion, but he was very reluctant to admit Alfred to Manor Lodge. However, in the end he submitted with a good grace, knowing perhaps that poor Alfred's stay would not be a long one.

And so it proved. I nursed my darling with devoted care, but it was clear, almost from the outset, that he had not long to live. Moreover, and it pains me to write it, I think that, despite everything, he did not wish to continue in this world. Some heavy burden of guilt was weighing upon Alfred's soul, but with what cause I could not ascertain. Several times he said: "I had eyes, but could not see. I had visions, but would not speak." Much of his talk was delirious, and as time went on the lucid intervals grew rarer.

Last Saturday morning—it was his last Saturday—my father came into the room where he was. My father rarely visited Alfred and was uneasy in his company when he did, but on this occasion he was too preoccupied to be awkward. He said that he had just had news from one of his academic colleagues that Mr. Charles Darwin had died on the Wednesday (the 19th of this month). At this, Alfred, who had been in a torpor, became very agitated. He addressed my father directly, saying: "Where is the enemy now?" My father, taken aback, laughed—rather harshly, I thought—then rapidly left the room to cover his embarrassment.

It was shortly after this that my poor Alfred took a decided turn for the worse. Despite my father's earnest objections Alfred and I were united through a special licence by a good man in holy orders on the Monday. The ceremony took place in Alfred's room. On his insistence and at great personal cost, he rose from his bed and was dressed for this occasion. He had to return to bed soon afterwards, and I was with him almost without interruption until the end. Our union seemed to afford him great consolation, and he ceased to fret, but by Wednesday morning his condition was beyond all hope. I was holding his hand as my beloved husband took the final journey, in tranquillity at last, from this world to the next.

I understand from my father that your name is being spoken of in the highest quarters as a candidate for the now-vacant see of Morchester. In the midst of all these distressing events, that, at least, to all those who know you and who care for the good name of the Church of England, is encouraging news. May I extend to you and to your wife Elizabeth my most heartfelt good wishes.

I remain yours very sincerely,
Agnes Simms

"Well?" said Valentine.

Emma started. He had come into the room and had seated himself in an armchair without her noticing.

"I don't know ... Morchester would appear to be a dangerous place."

"It is a battlefield. A spiritual battlefield. Some places are, and no one knows why. I've made a little supper: would you care for some?"

CHAPTER 7

I am standing on Cutberrow Hill, just outside Morchester. And we are looking across the valley to Bartonstone Hall, the family seat of the Cutbirths since before the Norman Conquest. Unfortunately the present owner, Sir Everard Cutbirth, the composer, has not allowed us onto his land, but it was his ancestor, according to my researches, who was the first owner of … THE BOKE OF THE DIVILL. Are we at last approaching the heart of this intriguing mystery. or—

"I'm sorry," said the cameraman. "Cut!"

"What is it, Mick?"

"Sorry, Veronica, there's something moving behind Dave's left shoulder."

"It's David to you, Mick. And you apologise to me for interrupting my speech to camera, not to Veronica."

"Right. Look, they're waving, Veronica."

"Oh, Christ! It looks like the police. What the hell do they want? Go and see what the hell they want, Emma."

Two uniformed policemen were climbing Cutberrow Hill, the site chosen by Veronica for David Huntley's next "piece to camera." They appeared agitated, but as yet Emma, who was descending to meet them, could not tell what they were saying. It was a fine day, and to Emma's young mind this mysterious intervention was part of her strange adventure. Beyond them in the little combe bordering on Cutbirth land a tent was being set up and various scene-of-crime officers were wandering to and fro in white overalls to prevent contamination. Emma's heart began to beat faster. Somehow she knew what it meant.

The senior of the two policemen climbing the hill, a sergeant, could now be heard. He was overweight and sweating profusely as he struggled over the tussocky grass on which sheep usually grazed.

"I'm sorry, Miss. I'm going to have to ask your camera crew to clear the area."

"It's all right," said Emma. "We have permission from the farmer—the landowner, I mean."

"It's not that, miss. It's just we've found a body down there."

"Another?"

The sergeant looked confused, and the younger constable stared at him with the pleasurable indignation of one who has caught his superior out in an indiscretion.

"I'm afraid we're going to have to cordon off the area, Miss, and I'm afraid you're going to have to stop filming, permission or no permission."

"The body of a young woman, I suppose?" The constable nodded involuntarily and this time it was the sergeant's turn to look indignant.

"What makes you say that, Miss?" he asked.

"Well, it's a very odd coincidence—if it is a coincidence—that the body found two days ago was in a Cutbirth mausoleum, and today, if I'm not mistaken, 'the other' is on Cutbirth land."

"I'd rather you kept these speculations to yourself, Miss, and leave the detection to the detectives," said the Sergeant. "Meanwhile, could you clear your crew off Cutberrow Hill, please?"

Emma was secretly delighted by the reference to "your" crew. When she gave an abbreviated report to Veronica, she was expecting annoyance, even perhaps anger directed at her. Instead, Veronica was silent for a while, then said, "This is beginning to become interesting. The rest of you make a big show of clearing up. Mick, can you get your zoom lens onto that scene of crime down there and get me the best shots you can, but don't look as if you're doing it."

"And what about me? What about my piece to camera?"

"We'll do it as a voice-over, Dave. Saves people getting fed up with your mug, and we'll put in a new bit—it was while we were filming that a strange and sinister series of events began to unfold ...—something like that. Emma, can you draft something?"

"Do I get a say in any of this?"

"No, Dave darling, you do not. Not if you value the BAFTA award that is waiting for us at the end of it all."

At breakfast the following morning, the subject of what had happened two nights ago was still infecting the air of the Deanery. The Dean was placidly reading the Church Times with his mouth full of toast while his wife Phyllis was trying to engage his full attention.

"Geoffrey … Geoffrey! Will you please pay attention! I think this is serious. I need to know. I am searching for some sort of explanation for what came over you that night."

"Haven't you got it the wrong way round, Phyllis dear? If I remember correctly, it was I who 'came' over you." The worst of it was, there was amusement in the Dean's eyes, as he peered at his wife over the Church Times. "It says here," he said, looking at his Church Times through half-moon spectacles, "that Anselm's ontological argument is due for a revival. I wonder if that will have an effect on the church services here. We being Anselm's cathedral."

"Geoffrey! You do understand that what you … What you did to me that night was the sin of Sodom."

"Not really, Phyllis. In the first place, if you consult your Genesis, the crime of the Sodomites is a little obscure, but it appears to have been attempted homosexual gang rape of two angels: not a very common offence these days. In the second place, anal sex is nowhere mentioned in the Bible. The word 'sodomy' as applied to it would appear to be a medieval coinage. I am no expert, however, and will stand corrected if you find otherwise."

"You have been behaving very peculiarly lately. I'm very worried. Perhaps you should see a psychiatrist."

"What good would that do? How often have I told you that the science of psychology is in its infancy, and consequently its remedies are about as effective as those of Renaissance Alchemy. What use would it be to me if I went to a shrink only to be told that I was taken off my rocking horse too early?"

"Were you? You never told me that."

"Don't be silly, Phyllis."

"At the very least you ought to see a priest about it. What about Father Scruton, your spiritual director?"

"What goes on between Father Scruton and myself is strictly private."

"I'm sure it is, and I'm beginning to wonder why."

"I will ignore that frankly repulsive insinuation, Phyllis. I don't remember you making any objection that night to my advances."

"That is quite irrelevant, Geoffrey! Anyway I was half asleep at the time."

"That means you were also half awake—"

The doorbell rang and the uncomfortable conversation ended abruptly, much to the relief of both parties.

Phyllis opened the door to Emma and Valentine.

"We've come to see the Dean," said Basil Valentine.

The Dean ushered them both into his study in his most benign and condescending manner. Valentine noted it, as he noted Phyllis's flushed and agitated manner. She had offered them all coffee, a suggestion that the Dean had waved away with impatience. Something has come between them, thought Valentine involuntarily. He had recently become prone to these intuitions, though what they meant he was unable to guess.

"And how can I help you?" said the Dean, sitting behind his desk and putting his fingertips together in the approved clerical way.

When Valentine explained that they wanted permission to see Bishop Hartley's box, he noticed how the Dean's strained manner became even more distracted. He became pale. He got up and wandered to the window looking onto the deanery garden, which sloped down to a stream called the Wyven. It was a tributary of the great River Orr that snaked around Morchester. Between falling fronds of willow, the water flashed in the sunlight.

The Dean blinked. "May I ask why you wish to see the box?"

"It's part of our research for the programme," said Emma. "Basil is helping me."

The Dean searched Valentine's face for some clue, some weakness, but found only a mask. He felt strangely humiliated.

"The Bishop's Box," he said ponderously. "I have not looked at it myself, but I have it here. It's rather strange that …" And then he hesitated. He saw Valentine's questioning look. "I don't see why—"

"I think it's the right time, don't you?" Valentine said, smiling.

The Dean unlocked a section of dark wooden panelling between two bookcases to reveal a large space, in which stood a leather box as big as a small trunk, dark brown and frayed at the corners but otherwise in good condition. It was bound with stout leather straps, the brass buckles of which still gleamed faintly. There was a lock, but the key, an elaborate affair in silver surmounted by a replica of a bishop's mitre, hung from one of the straps by a purple silk ribbon. The Dean heaved it onto his desk.

"Funny," he said. "Seems much lighter than when I last … Well, there you have it. I think I'll … There's a photocopier there by the desk which you may use. Obviously, I must ask you not to remove any documents, or ... Well, I have a meeting, I must ... Do please ask Phyllis if you want any coffee or ..."The Dean left the room. He was not a man who usually failed to finish his sentences.

Out in the hall the Dean encountered the substantial bulk of his wife. The lights were not on and the only illumination came from a fanlight above the door. Phyllis seemed huger in this crepuscular atmosphere, but no less unexpectedly desirable.

"Geoffrey," she said, blocking his path. "I've been thinking."

"Good, good! Splendid, splendid! You just carry on doing that," said the Dean as he tried in vain to negotiate his way past his wife's body. "Must dash. I'm seeing Canon Ramsey about the windows."

"This is more important than windows."

"Then we must discuss it when I've more time." The Dean took her in his arms and bent down to kiss her forehead. Then, thrusting her aside with a tentative pat on her lower back, he made it to the door, to the fresh air of the cathedral close, to the rooks that cawed in their immemorial elms.

His wife Phyllis gave a half-suppressed little scream of frustration, but felt, in spite of herself, excited. She was just beginning to realise how dull it had been.

They had opened the box, which was half filled with papers of various kinds. There were manuscripts of sermons and some attempts at hymn-writing, which were of little value or interest, but there were some more unusual items.

There was a portfolio of etchings of naked adolescent boys. They were executed with exquisite skill: French and late-nineteenth-century by the markings. Most of the boys seemed in attitudes of pain or distress, so that Valentine and Emma instinctively recoiled from them. One showed a boy being seized from behind by a shadowy creature, half man, half bull; another lay disembowelled on a four-poster bed from whose heavily curtained canopy the leering face of an old man emerged. The boy's eyes stared at it in terror.

The prints were mounted and covered with a delicate film of tissue paper which had preserved their condition, as well as their shameless lechery. Sometimes, between the tissue and the print, little slips of paper had been inserted, written in the bishop's fine, sloping hand. They were verses, mostly fragmentary and incomplete.

One of them read:

Is it Love's shadow or itself I fear
If your moist limbs are wreathed in agony?
And when your plaintive cries of pain I hear
Is it an echo of true amorous melody?
Narcissus, was my damned soul made divine
When I had tasted blood from your sweet scars,
And when I touched your rose-leaf lips with mine,
Though dead, were we among the stars?

"It looks as if our Bishop was an imitator of Swinburne," said Valentine, "and a very poor imitator at that. Oh, dear; I was expecting better. Hang on, what's this?"

From the box he took an oblong package of dirty yellow vellum elaborately bound with a faded crimson ribbon. On it was scratched in sepia ink *J.S. Ob 1595.*

Valentine said: "I think at last we have our old friend Jeremiah Staveley."

Was it an illusion, or had the room become oddly silent, so that even the faint noise of Morchester beyond the windows of the Dean's study had been deadened?

"I think this is one for photocopying," he said, knowing that he said it only for the sake of making a sound, and testing whether he had gone deaf or not. When they had opened the package, they found several pages of vellum covered in a minute but legible sixteenth-century hand. They made two photocopies of the text, then both sat down to read it. It began:

Seeke not to finde by what device
Men climb from Hell to Paradise,
Nor understand why Satann Fell
From starrie Paradise to Hell.
For curs't thou art, if thou dost looke
To find it in the Divill's Booke.

CHAPTER 8

*I*t went on:

I, Jeremiah Staveley do here faithfully sette downe my tes-
ament and confessioun, knowing that my mortall body
approaches with dreadfull and unfaltering pace its finall dissolution, and my immortall soul stands on the very threshold
of the pit of everlastynge fire. I here sett downe that you may
knowe and praye for my soule, limed and ensnared as it is in
the net of sin, awaiting in terror the ravishment of that Great
Beaste which stands yet silent on the borders of my waking
minde and roars even now in my dreams, yet distant, as the
cry of the wolf is heard in a lonely forest at midnight, her-
alding the inevitable and frightfull feaste. Oh, Christe Jesu,
woulde that I had knowne! Yet knowe I did after a fashioun,
and in this manner as I shall tell without further ado.

In the yeare 1590, I was appointed Canon in Ordinary
to the Cathedrall of St. Anselme's in Morchester. Many
thought my preferment long overdue for I was knowne for
my skill and genius in Musick. Yet there were ever those who
murmured against me and did utter all manner of wicked
slander against my person, such as that my giftes were of the
Devill and not of God, and suchlike foolishness and damned
malice. Though my merits were conspicuous enough to
overcome such calumnies, yet these mutterings ceased not.
Notwithstanding, I applied myself most diligently and with
much rigour to improve the musickal capacity of the cathedrall choir, such that men and women did stand amazed at
my mastery of these arts.

Such being the way of the world, the more I excelled

at my art, the more did certain folk of inferiour genius carp and cavill and, seeking to bring me down from my exalted state above them, saw that only the most monstrous libels and slanders might effect it. Thus in deepe secrecy they did harbour dark designes against me, and I all unknowing stood in the light of innocence unsuspecting.

It was well known, for I made no secrett of it, that I was in the habit of wandering abroad in the countryside around Morchester, to visit the country folk and to extract from them memorialls of old tunes, songs and ditties that they, all unlearned in the higher arts, had taken from their rude fore-fathers before them. And many of these saide tunes, roundes, catches and rhymes were reliques, as I suspect, of ancient rit-uals and superstitions that went back even to Pagann times before yet the light of the most true Gospel of Christ did shine upon our green hills and fair-flowered meadows.

I sought these things, not merely for my owne curiose learning, but as a refreshment to my musickall genius and in-vencion. But being greene in the ways of the world, I heeded not that some of these songs were or might be seen as in-cantacions, summonings of the spirits or demons, spells, or yet curses and maledictions emanating from that prince of Demons, Satann no less.

There was one goodwyfe or beldame, Mother Durden was her name, from whom I acquired many of these cantrips and fancies. She dwelt in a hut in the woods below Cutber-row Hill, and many were the tales told of her. The country-folk round about would have it that she was possessed of demons, that a hare was her familiar; others told me that she could turn herself to a fox by anointing her body with the fat from a hanged man's corse. But for all their pratings these dolts would go to her for a salve if they had warts, or to cure a sick beast. In my prudence I would visit her in secret and had from her many ancient sayings and incantations, many wise saws and prophesies, so that I was many hours in her company. Yet, for all the benefit she did impart to me, I had to summon all my forbearance to stay in her company, for her person was most noisome and stinking, and her ancient face like an old misshapen rock that has stood too long in the rain, scored with deep lines of bitterness and hatred. Her hut, moreover, was dark and dank, o'er run with rats and other vermin; and when she spat into her fire—which was a habit of hers—it was green bile that sang in the embers and gave off a choking and most vile smoke.

This notwithstanding, I persisted with the old crone, for she had yet one secret, which she did call "the secret of her heart," which she would have me know but forebore to tell me, indicating that such a secret would be of great profit and encompass all desires. At length, seeing me growe impatient, she did impart it to me. She told me that from her mother she was of the ancient family of Cutbirth, of great note hereabouts since before the Conqueror, yet of ill repute to some. This mother of hers, she says, was gently born, but most ill-favoured, so that no gentleman would have her to wife, for all her fortune, and she would be condemned to live and die a maid. But one day a common ploughboy spied and wooed her and they lay together in the grass on Cutberrow Hill at Midsummer's Eve, so that by Michaelmas she was seen to be big with child. Then the family of Cutbirth, which to this day remains over-mindful of the lustre of its ancient lineage, was incensed with her and cast her out. For a while she lived with her rustick swaine in a hut in the woods—the same still occupied by Mother Durden—but, after the birth of their daughter, he wearied of her and deserted the unfortunate mother.

Mother Durden's parent, thus bereft, made strenuous effortes to reconcile herself with her family, but they would have none of it. They left her to rot in the utmost poverty. It was in these unhappy circumstances that her child (who bore the name Durden from her father) was brought up, schooled by her mother in many secret arts and in great bitterness against the family of Cutbirth. Her mother taught her many strange things about the family of Cutbirth, for they were a family long steeped in ancient lore.

One thing especially Mother Durden was told by her own mother and this concerned a certain booke. This volume has been called by many names, such as *Booke of Shadowes, Mysterium Arcanum, Booke of Secret Keyes,* but it has been most vulgarly called *The Boke of the Divill.* This booke, according to the most ancient tradition of the Cutbirth family, was taken or stolen from them by none other than Holy Anselme, founder of our Cathedrall and buried certaine fathoms deepe in the earthe where lay also her ancestor Cutbirth of Bartonstone.

It was Mother Durden's most earnest wish, and that of her mother also before her, to recover this saide booke, for she felte it hers by right, as 'twere, of disinheritance. In recovering the booke, she would gaine power over her enemies, and especially over the family that had blighted her life.

She knew for certaine that this booke was buried in the cathedral, somewhere in the crypte, and that she knew by what signes on the stone flags, one might finde the booke. But she herself might not enter the cathedrall, knowing her movements watched and suspect, and so it was only by some second party or Intermediary, she sayde, that she might discover that booke.

Then she made me a bargaine, and would to Christe I had not accepted it, yet I did never, as some may secretlie believe, sign aught; nor make a mark in my bloode upon a pact; nor kisse the Devill's arse as a token of my allegiance; nor any suchlike foolish whim-wham. It was meerly this: I consented that I should endeavour to recover this saide booke for her, having access to the cathedrall, and that if I did so, Mother Durden would grante me a share in the marvellous wisdome which, she assured me, it contained.

This I consented unto, yet for many dayes gave it no further thought. It seemed to me an idle plot, impossible of execution. Yet in my mind, the thought was never absent from me, for to tell truth, I received at that time many slights from my fellow clerks, and my great skills in musick were ever contemned by lesser minds. Some malicious worme of a Precentor reported me to the Dean for drunkennesse in a low alehouse which, when I came before him, I most vigorously denied, yet was I not believed and I was shamefully rebuked. My merits were despised, and my imagined vices bruited abroad by green-eyed jealousie. Such things festered in my hearte, so that I longed to strike down my unrighteous oppressors.

One evening, I had, to console myself, gone to a Maying at Great Bartonstone to observe the dances and take some note of the viol and hautboy tunes that were played. It was a fair evening, cloudless and still, as fine as any I have known, yet all was not well about my hearte. There was dancing about the maypole and I saw some fine rumps of beef being roasted on spits. The laughter of children was all about me.

Then I saw one mother gather her two daughters into her skirts and hurry them indoors. I wondered what was to do until I saw at the edge of the village green a solitary figure in black looking upon the scene. It was Mother Durden. Some men who saw her were for taking up cudgels and driving her by force from the spot. But I restrained them, saying that I would see her on her way, and they, out of reverence for the clerical garb I had on, held back.

Mother Durden met my gaze as I advanced on her, but said nothing. Together and in silence we walked from the village and, as we did so, the villagers who had opened their doors to welcome in the evening sun, closed them as we passed by. At length when we were on the open cart track beyond the bounds of Great Bartonstone, Mother Durden spoke.

"Where is my booke?"

I tolde her of the many and various obstacles which stood in the way of my achieving the volume, that I would consider a strategy and bring it to her in good time, but that at present I saw no chance of its fulfillment. In such like manner I excused my tardiness, talking in a most politic manner and with great subtletie, but she would heare none of it. Straightway she led me to her hut and, having no inke, penne, or paper to hand, she tooke an old dried calfskin, and cutting her arm with a paring knife, she dipped one of her long fingernails in her blood and with it wrote upon the skin. In truth, her writing was very ill, for she was all but unlettered and her hands, withered and curled with age, with their great nails for all the world like the talons of some monstrous antique bird, except she grasped one hand with the other to be steady, shook with the palsye.

Talking all the while, she drew upon the skin certain signes whereby the floor stones of the crypte were marked, and, in short, showed me where the booke had been laid to rest. Upon which I made many complaintes, videlicet: what if the booke were lost, or taken, or had rotted away in the damp of that ancient charnel house? But she would have none of it and told me to bring her the book by the next full moon.

Fool that I was, I now felt compelled to carry out her wishes: whether because of the vellum scratched with her blood, or the baleful glance of her eye, or by my own secret desire, I know not. Yet still I delayed, letting I dare not wait upon I would, till my dreams denied me rest. For in them I saw Mother Durden seated in a vast cave, yet like her hut, dark and noisome, illumined only by the red embers of her fire, and surrounded by a vast concourse of foul things: demons, boggarts, sprites, chimaeras, headless men who spake through their bellies and other suchlike terrors. And all of them did crye with one voice: delay not! Hesitate and you are lost!

And so at last I did summon up my courage, if courage it may be called, and, one night, concealed myself in the organ loft after evening prayer with pick, spade and lantern. Then, the great doores of the cathedrall being locked, I betooke myself down into the crypte, using all carefullie, and there lit my lantern.

The crypte is at all times and in all seasons a most dismall place, and at night, lit only by a lantern it is very dreadfull. Some blast, damp and noisome, blew through it from I knew not where. Now and then my eare caught a faint scuttering, as it might be of rats, but I sawe none. Then, taking Mother Durden's hide from my coat, I began to search among the tombs for the signs she had drawn in her blood. Many times I had to sweep away the dust to see what was scratched on the floore slabs, and it was long before I had satisfied myselfe that I had the very stone under which the booke was buryed.

It was a long stone of some whitish marble layed against the South wall in the far eastern corner of the crypt. I divined this to be the one, for it was carved very faintly with the head of a bearded man with hair all around him, like the image of the Sun God, Blad, in ancient Aquae Sulis, and this was also the blazon on the arms of Cutbirth to this day. And there were certain other carvings in ancient runic letters upon the stone by which, Mother Durden told me, I might know this was the stone to lift.

I had much to do, and yet I was assisted in that the mortar which bound the slab to its fellows was very old and had crumbled away in parts. At length I found my pick pierced through into a space beneath and, by dint of much leverage, I was able to lift out the stone slab and put my lamp in to see the space I had discovered.

There I found a pit, deeper than I had expected, about the height of a growne person, and at its bottom lay a man—or rather, his skeleton—armed and richly bedight with gold and jewels, yet very strangely, not like the knights we see on tombs, but more resembling the barbarians on Roman monuments. His helmet was a mask of bronze, gilded, and the face of the mask was of a wild man, like the Green Man of the country folk. Through the gaps for its eyes and mouth, I could see the eye sockets of the skull, dark as Hell's night, and a set of teeth that grinned at his owne fallen pomp. The bone hands were clasped across the breast and they held in their grip a dark thing like a boxe or bag of black leather: and this was the booke.

Then my heart rose and I was seized with a wild delight. Taking my lanterne I leapt into the grave, yet in my falle I let go the lanterne so that it smashed and fell, and in no way could I find it, nor could I discover tinder and flint to ignite once more a flame. Now all was black, blinde black, and no single thread of light. Yet I despaired not, and groping about with my hands I first put my fingers through the mouth of the dead man and felt his teeth. All at once I recoiled and felt down further until I came upon the skeleton hand that grasped that thing of leather. I seized it to prise it away from the dead man, thinking those ragged hands of bone too feeble to resist, yet something in the sinews held it fast, so that I must exert all my strength to take it. And when I did it was as if something gave a great sigh and all the tombe breathed.

But at length I had the booke in my hands, and still my

trouble was not over, for all was impenetrable night and I must climb out of the grave. And it seemed to me, doubtlesse in my terrour, that the walls of the grave were growne taller, higher than mine own heighte and that I was at the base of a deepe pitt, and indeed in the very pitt of death itself. Then I knew mortall fear and despaire, which was doubtlesse why I felt, or imagined that I felt, the dead and flesheless hands of that ancient warriour clawing at my feete in the grave, so that I began to trample underfoot his mouldering corse in my rage. Then, thinking at least to save the booke, I hurled it out of the pit and heard it fall with a great commotion onto the floore of the crypte, so that the whole vaulte echoed. Then I myself made a great leape and found my hands on the stone slab, which then began to slip towards me and so crush me by its weight in that hideous sepulchre. However, by some grace my other hand grasped the edge of the grave, and I let go the marble slab, which fell with a mighty crack into the tomb, missing my person by a bare inch.

Thus did I finde myself on the floore of the lightless crypte. I felt for and founde the booke, and with it made my way, crawling and not upright lest I fall againe, until at length I found the steps and the waye up into the dim Cathedrall where, through its vast windows, the first streakes of a grey dawne were beginning to anointe its sacred walles with light.

Finding a candle, I returned to the crypte where I took my pick and spade, and made all seem as though no man—or woman—had been there that night, and that the ruin of the tombe was but the naturall decadence of age and decay. I hidde the booke, with my spade and pick, in the loft of the pipe organ, and I thanked God that the zealots of Protestant faith (some, surelie, enemies of mine) had not succeeded in removing this noble instrument from the Cathedrall. Then, having a key to a side door of the cathedrall, I made my way secretly out of that holy house.

Never did blessed dawn come sweeter upon a troubled soule! I breathed free air; I had accomplished my purpose. Though I had known no sleepe that night I felt refreshed by the pure breezes of morning. Rooks were stirring in their parliament among the elms. I bethought myself to take a cup of ale at an Inn, then perhaps to my bedd. I had left the Cathedrall close and was come into the towne when of a sudden I heard a noise as of a great concourse of people which I greatly wondered at, it being barely past six of the clock, albeit in a bright summer morning.

As yet I saw no one in the bare streets of Morchester, and in my affrighted and exalted state, I thought that the Day of Judgement had come, and that the noise I heard was of all the dead rising from their graves to come before the Awful Throne of punishment and rewarde. In the next moment my wild apprehensions were put at rest.

I saw a great throng of men and women come up the main street and in their midst was a cart which some were drawing along the road. Upon the cart sat a figure muffled and bounde, but yet I saw her face, and it was Mother Durden. On the instant I concealed myself so that she would not knowe me, but I had seen in her eyes the dreadfull knowledge of her own doome and death.

Placing myself in the crowde behind the cart I asked my fellowes what was to do. They told me that they were bringing Mother Durden to the house of the Justice of the Peace, Sir Digby Fell, and were to lay before him most grave charges of witchcraft. I asked them on what groundes of evidence this charge was brought and they told me that she had brought a murraine on the cattle of Sir Everard Cutbirth, and that when Mother Durden had begged a cup of water off Goodwife Tebbitt, she being refused had bitten her thumb at her, and that very night Goodwife Tebbitt was seized with paines in her belly and did shitt in her bedd some small stones very like the balls of a muskett. I followed them to the house of Sir Digby Fell where she was arraigned before the said magistrate, and he still in his nightshirte and marvellously distempered that he should be roused from his slumbers. And when Mother Durden was unbounde and brought unto the magistrate she cried out with a loud voice that before God she was innocent of the charges brought.

I was standing at the back of Sir Digby's parlour and far removed from her, but yet she saw me, and called out for aid, but the crowd drowned out her speach with their shouting.

Even so, some who stood by me had guessed that she had called out to me, so that they did question me, saying: "did not Mother Durden call out to you for aid?" And I denied it. Then another came, saying: "Have I not seen you consort with that damned witch in the woods about Bartonstone?" And I told them I knew her not. And yet another, a most ill-favoured woman with but one eye and no teeth to her mouth, sayd: "Yea, I have seen him, and he has been into her hut in the woods to make the two-backed beast in foule and most unholy congress of lust with that limbe of Satann." And I said to her: "be silent you toothless turde! Have you no regarde to my priestly gowne! I tell you, I never sawe her before this day. Begone, foul lump of carrion!" And if any cock crew at that moment—for I had denied her thrice—I never hearde it, but Mother Durden was taken to a gaol where she was watched day and night and doubtless put to the question under torture, for three dayes later she did make a full confessioun and set her mark in blood to a document wherein it was written.

And therein she tolde how she met a man in black in the woods and did reverence to him as being the Lorde of this Worlde, and did kisse his excrements as a token thereof. And he in returne did give her five familiar spirits or imps, to wit: a boare-hounde with a calve's head named Cutbushe, a ram withoute any leggs at all called Farte-of-my-Arse, and three very small pigges, the size of ratts, named Hickitt, Hackitt, and Hockitt. But whether, even in the very extremity of her agonies, she mocked her tormentors, I dare not say.

And she said nothing of me, but the day she was to be brought before the assize she sent for me. And I did go, out of fear that if I did not she might betray me and say I had entered a pacte of Satann with her. I founde her in a most noisome cell, yet it was no fouler than her own hut in the woods, and she was crouched like a stricken beaste on a pile of filthy straw in the corner. And her eyes burned in their dark sockets and she seemed much stricken with terror and rage against all the world.

Bidding the gaoler go, saying that I would hear her penitence in private, I then asked her why she had summoned me. She asked me if I had the booke, and I tolde her that I had, yet I had not yet removed it from the organ loft where it lay concealed. She told me that I should take the book to a secret place under the starres and there consult it, for she saide, it must surelie containe her meanes of deliverance, but how she would not say, and I doubt that she knew. I told her that I was to do as she asked, but on strict condition that she was to say not a worde of me or of our doings with the booke. To this she did consent most readily.

There is a tower at St. Paul's church upon which, on certain nights, I and the Reverend Mr. Bowles, the Rector of that church, would sometimes come to contemplate the stars. He was my only friend, the only man in Morchester to match my wit and know my genius, a man of rare understanding far above the common herd. Yet even he proved unworthy in the end.

One evening I stole out of the cathedrall with the booke under my gowne, makyng my way to St. Paul's. There I told Mr. Bowles that I would have an hour of contemplation to myself, so, taking a lantern, I mounted the steps of the tower. The night was beauteous cleare and a full moon was out so that I could all but read the booke without the aid of a lampe. Below me lay the city, like a foul midden that teamed with little life. Up from below came the paltry cries of small lives as of a cloud of mayflies in an evening haze; small follies and the littel sinnes of fooles. Then to the East stood the great monstrous sentinel of St. Anselme's cathedrall looking down on us all below, but blindly as doth the church.

Then did I open the booke which is called *The Boke of the Divill* and looked within it. At first I was much amazed, for the first few pages seemed to be black, as black as night, and they were soft to the touch as if it were made from the hide of some beast; like a mole, but vast, for there were no sewings together of small peltes. And, as I looked, there were stirrings within the darknesse; but, not caring to see further, I pressed on and found many pages on which were written strange devices, and some words which were in the Latin tongue, and some in Greek and Hebrew, and some in what I took to be the Moorish script of the Heathen Mahometans, and some in a language I knew not but guessed to be, from some indicacions, to be the Saxon tongue of those in Britain before the coming of the Norman Kings into our island.

I will not say further what I read, for it is forbidden, but this I will say: that should any man or woman look in this book, let them beware, for they will see as 'twere in a glass, but darkly, the image of themselves, their desires and their fears, their longings and their hatreds. And I say this booke is forbidden, as the tree of the Knowledge of Good and Evil was to our first parents Adam and Eve, for to know Good and Evil is to know one's self truly, and no man nor woman will bear that much reality except he or she be pure of heart, and then, even then, at greate paine. But I was a man set aside from the Common Herd and I endured the blast of that booke. A man may finde great profit in this work, yet let him not wish too hard, for all that is wished for may be granted and therein lies immortall danger.

I believe that at the first much was saved me, as I sought the means of deliverence not for myselfe but for Mother Durden, for I had pledged to bring about her rescue from the profanum vulgus, and I feared her retribution, even from beyond the grave. And so I looked in these pages for some help to this end, and I came across this passage which was in Latin, or some other tongue of which I yet knew its meaning, and I read as here set downe:

> To make SOLOMON'S RING by which ye may passe unseen through crowdes and make your way unharmed to any place. Take unto you two ounces of pure gold and an ounce of silver and make thee a seal ring, and on the bezel thereof let there be engraved this signe or sigil.
>
> And thereupon that very signe was inscribed in the booke.
>
> And on taking this ring, let the wearer speake the wordes: Abrax Abraxas, and he shall pass safely on his way.

Then I removed the booke from the tower and concealed it in the church of St. Paul's without Mr. Bowles's knowing, for I dare not put it in my own rooms, knowing the mistress of my lodging house to be a prod-nose, a busy-legges, and a most arrant prattler and teller of tales. In the morning I took me to a jeweller, Master Gotobed in the towne whom I knew to be most discreet and greedy withall, so that I might stop his mouth with gold. And I had him make the ring according to my instructions.

Now the time for the assizes when Mother Durden was to be tried approached, whereupon she did send for me once more. And I went unto her very secretly, passing money to the gaoler to let me in unseen. And she lay in her cell on the foul straw and groaned, for she greatly feared the paines that awaited her in this life and, I doubt not, the next. And when she saw me, she crawled to me and grasped my gowne and asked me when was the hour of her deliverence. I told her a little of what had passed and said it would be soon, but yet I did not tell her by what contrivance it might be done.

The next day she was brought before Sir Digby Fell in the assizes, and I crepte into the assizes and saw her stricken face as she stood accused by that clamorous array of vermin that were her accusers. And ever and anon I saw her eyes, red with rage and distress, search among the crowd, doubtless for me, her supposed deliverer. And I stole away so as not to be seene by her. So I went to Master Gotobed, and he said he had made the ring and would know what it signified. I said that as I had paid him a fair price, what was it to him what it signified? But he said that there was much talk abroad of the Devill being loose in the land and of Mother Durden and her cursed imps, and he would not be seduced to being a party to some act of damned witchcraft in making the said ring. Then I said, what would you? And he asked for further recompense for endangering his immortall soule. Then I cursed him for a damned canting hypocrite, a whited sepulchre and a pharisaicall turde. And I picked up a moulding iron from his array of instruments and struck him over the mazzard that he fell down dead. Then, though I was seized with great terrour at what I had done, yet I still kepte my witts. So I fastened his house and took his body privily to feed it in pieces to the furnace in his cellar of work. And this business did take most of the night, so that when all was done and his body consumed it was the dawne of another day and I must creepe forth. When I looked out of Master

Gotobed's doore, I saw that there were already several folk about and one that I knew, Goodwife Samson, the mother of one of my choir boyes, she being a fat-guts, a prating lard-barrel, yet not without cunning. I watched her as she did look up in amaze at Master Gotobed's chimney which doubtless still belched most foule smoke, the dark and oily remnants of his unshriven body and soul.

Then I was once more afeared, so I did put on the ring, and saying the words Abrax Abraxas, I went forth boldly, albeit from the back doore of Master Gotobed's shoppe. And when I came into the streete Goodwife Samson did for a moment look upon me but yet she did not call out nor seem to heed my presence and so I passed away safely. But when I came to the market square I was greatly amazed, for I did see a vast pile of faggots amassed in its middle and within that mountain of wood a single stake upright and alone. Then I asked one standing by what might this signify, but he paid no heed to me, as if I truly were not there. So I removed my ring and asked him againe. And he saide to me: "Did not you know? Mother Durden was very swiftly condemned at the assize yester eve, and Sir Digby was most eager that this damned serpent of Satan be burned out of this world and into perdition with all haste, lest she foul the air with her curses and her wickednesse pollute us further."

At that my heart seemed to fall within me, and I knew I was as damned as she. Then began my descent to where I stand now, at the doorway of darkness, from which only the infinite Mercy of Christ may yet redeem me. At that moment I heard a murmuring sound and saw a great crowd begin to gather about the pyre. Then I saw Mother Durden being brought to the fire amid the howling of the common people and I saw in her eyes what I hope never to see either on this or on t'other side of the grave, a black despair, all hope abandoned. At that look everie mouth should have fallen silent but they roared and threw up their sweaty caps and rejoiced at their own cruel folly. And two strong men brought her to the post to bind her to it, but as they did so her eyes sought and found me and she began to struggle and cry out in a rage, so that the men, powerful as they were, had

much ado to bind her.

I thought then that all the world would turn to look at me for I knew it was at me she stared, but they did not. The common folk gathered there only thought this was some devilry of the old woman and laughed and rejoiced the more to see her agony redoubled by rage. I cowered into obscurity behind a butcher and his boy, for I had no more to do, and Mother Durden was beyond rescue. I saw the faggots lit and the smoke rise and Mother Durden's screams above the crowd whose hooting had now sunk to a low murmur. Now at last even these clods had been subdued by the prospect of a fellow human being in her death agony. I saw her skin turn black and erupt in blisters and pustules as in one last mute appeal she stretched her hand towards me over the flames. Then I could bear no more and left the scene. I went to the cathedrall to pray for Mother Durden's soul, but though words came from me, my thoughts remained below, as black as sinne itselfe.

For some days my spirit remained prostrate within me, while to the outward eye I continued to conduct myself as before. I did not neglect my duties with the choir and in making sacred musick. Then one night as I returned home to my lodgings, I chanced to see two of my colleagues walking in the town. One of them, Canon Costard; an idle fellow, but stiff and precise, a religious caterpillar, and it was he who had told malicious tales of me to the Dean. He said he had seen me in a low alehouse. I saw him then, but he and his companion had yet to see me. I shrank into a doorway and my hand felt in my purse for the ring which Master Gotobed had made for me at such cost, Solomon's ring. In the next instant I had it placed on the finger and uttered the words Abrax Abraxas. The two men passed me by as I stood in the doorway, and though Canon Costard's companion, the Verger, Master Cantwell, turned to look towards me, he did not seem to know my features, though I knew him.

When they had passed me I resolved to follow them and presently I saw them enter an alehouse, such an one as that canting shitt-breeches Costard had said I frequented. I did not follow them in but straightway went to my lodgings to secure me a stout cudgel that I kept among my effects. Returning to the alehouse I assured myself they were still there and waited till they came out, whereupon I struck them both down with my cudgel and ground their faces into the mud of the street and left them for dead, taking their purses with me.

The next day, I found that Masters Costard and Cantwell had lived but were sadly battered and disgraced for their pains. The Dean asked me if I knew aught of what had brought them to this pass, but I made a great show of innocence, though restraining any indignation I might have felt at these disgraced topers. Indeed I was much commended for my forbearance toward these fooles.

For all the shock and shame of what had gone before I began to feel rising within me a new spirit, as befitting a man who has at his command the powers of earth and air. Once more I went in secret to St. Paul's church where I had concealed my book behinde a panel in the belfry. There, once more avoiding the curiosity of my friend Mr. Bowles, I removed it and, lighting a candle, began to read.

I must not say much of what I saw, but I must observe that the book did not appear to be the one which I had first looked at. The pages made of some dark, softe substance like the skin of a mole had increased in number but what most astonished me was the sighte of myself. It was a portrait in miniature, most exquisitely done in the manner of Master Hilliard, prince of limners, painted in an oval upon a sheet of vellum in the book. It showed me in my clerke's gowne, head and shoulders, but standing against a sheet of burning flame as some lovers are now depicted by these limners. The eyes were marvellously executed and, though the picture was but some three inches wide, they stared out at me as if they were living and I were looking upon myself in a glasse. I wondered greatly at this and was filled with a fear which has not left me, and yet I cannot fully divine its root.

I turned the page and encountered these words:

To FINDE A TREASURE HIDDE IN A FIELD.

There then followed instructions which I may not repeate, but which I took down with the greatest care, and so, hiding my booke once more in the belfry, I hurried down into the church. There I founde my friend the Rev'd Mr. Bowles who looked upon me with much curiosity.

"Will you tarry with me and take a cup of sack?" sayd he. But I would not. "Whither away so fast?" sayd he, and I would not answer but straightway went out of the church and into the night.

The next morning I found myself in a field near Bartonstone on the margins of Sir Everard Cutbirth's land. At the very rising of the sunne, at the cold margins of the day, I made certain conjurations and uttered certain words I dare not mention, at which there rose out of the grounde like a black mist a very dark figure who in silence beckoned me forward.

I could not see if it were man or woman, for the thing had only thin legs, as 'twere of smoke, and the clothes were ragged and vaporous. I could not see the face which was veiled and turned from me. The creature led me towards a certain ancient oak in the woods of Sir Everard's park, then, with insisting gestures to the ground, it bade me dig in a certain place beneathe the oak. I had brought with me my pick and spade, and so I dug until I found a box of dear's hide studded with brasse. This I broke open with ease and founde therein the bones of a littel child wrapped in a white lace robe all stained with the amber colour of ancient bloud, and beneath this a greate store of jewels and gold coins. Then I looked up from my amazement at this sight to see the figure that had led me to the treasure, and within the blackness and smoke I saw the face of Mother Durden as I had last seen her in the hour of her immolation. Her face was all black and pumpled with blisterings and burnings, and the eyes were aflame with a hidden fire.

Yet had I no time to wonder in terror at this sight, for down the field and towards the oak came riding a man with a deer hound gambolling at his side and he was shouting out loud when he saw me as if I were any common trespasser. Then the black figure that was Mother Durden's hellish spirit made a sudden rush toward the rider, so that his horse reared up and he himself fell to the ground. Then I, without looking further, took the box of treasure and ran from the scene.

I later discovered that this rider was no less than Sir Everard Cutbirth and that he had broken his neck in a fall from his horse and died thereof. But I now found myself a rich man, though I showed caution and stelthe in display and disbursement. I bought myself a fine house in the city and gowns trimmed with furre, and I also gave almes to the poore and a gift to the cathedrall where I yet kept to my post. But for all that I was modest, yet open-handed towards lesser folk, still the murmurings against me would not cease. They said that my new founde wealth was from consorting with the Devill, though I told any who would listen that it was a legacy, but still I was dogged and found that the envy of my genius was compounded by envy at my wealth. So may a man never know content; for if he sinks low he is despised, and if he rises above, then is green-eyed jealousie ever at his heels.

I took to being alone, except when at the cathedrall in my work. If I went abroad it was at night, and then often wearing Solomon's ring to afford me protection from prying eyes. It seemed often as if I walked in a city of the dead when I did so, and many a time and oft I have glimpsed a shadow that looked like someone long dead, lurking in the grey streets of evening. My life became a half of what it was and my riches seemed to me but ashes, for the pleasures that they promised gave me no delight: neither wine, nor fine fabrics nor the purchased pleasures of the flesh.

And now I am growne sick so that I know death is near, and I must face myself and my deeds. Several nights ago, though weak, I took my walk abroad at night through dark and desert streets in Morchester. Though black and moonless yet methought I could see my way as through a thin grey mist, and all the town was soft and uncertain as if the very stones were made of dreams and smoke. The world was silent but for the faint sound of steps hurrying behind me. Once I turned and saw a creature like black smoke at the end of the street and it was the figure of Mother Durden who had guided me to the treasure and paved my way to Hell itself. The next night she was there also but nearer to me, so that now I dare not venture abroad even in daylight. I lie here in my chamber and write and look for some way to make myself right with my God before the hour of my judgement. Yet I have no hope of Paradise. Hell beckons and still I struggle. My candle gutters and I order fresh ones. Bring up the light, before the darkness comes to me! I am alone! Christ Jesu, deliver me hence! Have mercy! Begone from my chamber, foule witch!

Nothing followed except a scratched attempt at the signature of Jeremiah Staveley and some odd signs in a brownish ink which might have been blood.

Emma and Valentine finished reading almost simultaneously, and when they had done so they remained silent for some minutes, as if exhausted by the experience.

"Do you think the book is still there in the belfry of St. Paul's?"

"Oh, no. It's long gone from there."

"What makes you think that?"

"Because this document has been read by Bishop Hartley. It was found in his box, and the box looked as if it had contained something else."

"You mean—?"

At that moment the Dean's wife entered the room.

"Oh! Are you still here?" She made the words imply an unwarranted usurpation of her time and her husband's study.

"We were just going, Mrs. Dean," said Valentine smoothly. Phyllis simpered. She had an odd liking for being addressed as "Mrs. Dean": it implied a status.

"Have you found what you wanted?"

"I think so."

"Why this sudden interest in Bishop Hartley's box I can't imagine. He was a horrid man by all accounts."

"Interest? Have there been others wanting to see it?"

"Oh, yes. Well, only one really. It was a few weeks back that Sir Everard called on the Dean. Sir Everard Cutbirth, you know, the composer. Such a charming man."

"And the Dean let him see it?"

"Oh, yes. We left him to it. Sir Everard said it was something to do with documents concerning his family estate. It was strange. Such a charming man, yet when we looked into the study after an hour or so, Sir Everard was gone and the box was back in the cupboard. Just a scribbled note saying he had found what he had wanted."

Emma and Valentine exchanged glances.

"Thank you so much, Mrs. Dean. You've been most helpful."

"Oh, I do hope so. This is nothing to do with this wretched book everyone's talking about, is it, Mr. Valentine?"

"Only partly."

"It seems to have had a most unfortunate effect on my husband. I do wish these wretched television people would just go. I know they're paying the cathedral an awful lot of money, but it really is too absurd. It can't be good for anyone."

Valentine shook Phyllis's hands warmly and smiled; Emma merely smiled. When they were outside in the close, Emma said:

"So you think this Sir Everard stole the book from the Bishop's Box."

"I'm convinced of it. He may also have this ring."

"So what do we do about it? Report it to the police? Do we do anything?"

"Oh, yes. The time for doing has come."

"But why? I mean you don't really believe this book is really dangerous?"

"What matters is not what I believe, but what Sir Everard and the others believe."

"What others?"

"The living and the dead."

"And I still don't understand quite why Sir Everard is at the bottom of it all."

"There is one more thing that I think you should read," said Valentine.

CHAPTER 9

"My father," said Valentine when they were once again in the room above the shop, "was, like me, an academic, though I think he was made of sterner stuff than I. We had a curious relationship. It was not that we were different: we had the same academic bent, but there was a kind of reserve in him. He could never be close to me. My mother, whom, incidentally, he had first met when he was down here before the war, did her best to achieve some sort of contact, but it was no good.

"I always thought it was something to do with his war experiences, which I gather were pretty grim, but I now believe that it went back further than that.

"My father never spoke about his war experiences. That was to be expected, I suppose, but what is strange is that he hardly ever said anything to me about his life before it. I knew his academic career as a medieval historian had begun in the 1930s, and that was all. It was only after his death a decade ago that I discovered the diaries that he had kept during this period, and a sort of explanation for his reticence started to emerge.

"Reading them was an odd experience for me in many ways, chiefly because the person in these diaries was not at all like the one I knew. It was hard to reconcile this lively young man with my father, the dour, sarcastic Oxford don who seldom had any time for me. Only a few characteristic quirks and turns of phrase suggested that they were the same person at all.

"The journals begin in late 1936 when, at twenty-five, my father, Dr. Charles Nightfall, was appointed to a lectureship in Medieval History at the new University of Wessex. Its campus occupies land just outside the town of Bartonstone, some ten miles southwest of Morchester. My father's first years there seem to have been carefree and happy. He was a great giver and frequenter of sherry parties, then a popular form of

entertainment for those who were not quite smart enough for cocktails. By 1938, the year of the Munich Crisis, my father was beginning to be faintly aware that the world around him was darkening, but it was not until September that his own personal crisis began."

Once again, Valentine had arranged a neat pile of photocopied documents on the table by the window. Without another word, he indicated them to Emma and then left the room. They appeared to be the type-written entries of a diary.

September 2nd 1938

Bertie Winship drove down from Morchester in his old banger. I gave him dinner at the Crown, the only half-decent hostelry in Bartonstone, and we imbibed not a few glasses of Amontillado, followed by a bottle of the best claret mine host could provide. I have barely seen young Bertie since 'Varsity days, but he is the same cheery idiot who once introduced a python into the Master of Balliol's lodgings, causing much consternation and merriment thereby. It is strange to think of him now as a man of the cloth, a Canon of Morchester Cathedral, no less, and a master at the choir school. He regaled me with stories of Cathedral life, which seems to be by no means as dull as one might think. The Bishop, a gouty old sport called Bulstrode, is completely under the thumb of the Dean, who goes by the name of the Very Reverend Herbert Grice. Grice is, according to Bertie, a holy terror, all for change and doing what he calls "meeting the challenges of the modern world." Needless to say, this does not go down too well with some of his colleagues, who call him "Il Duce" behind his back because he is so fearfully keen on efficiency and making the cathedral services start and finish on time. His main opponent is the Venerable Thaddeus Hill, the Archdeacon, a white-bearded old patriarch who has been at Morchester since the Ark. All this would be very amusing but not worth recording, were it not for the business of the Archbishop's Well.

According to Bertie this well has stirred up a veritable hornet's nest. It's hard at first to conceive why. I have of course visited the Cathedral and seen it. It stands in the middle of the cloister garth, a patch of greensward on the south side of the cathedral. The cloisters that enclose it are the oldest part of the cathedral, dating back to the eleventh century, being the only surviving portion of the original Abbey Church of Morchester. The well, by all accounts, is even older, but it is extremely unimpressive to look at. It is a roughly circular enclosure of irregular stones, which have been frequently repaired over the years with ugly slatherings of mortar. The opening is capped with a heavy circular lid of oak, bound with elaborately arabesqued iron bands and attached to the stone surround by heavy iron rings and padlocks. No one knows quite why it is called the Archbishop's Well, except of course that the Cathedral itself is St. Anselm's, named after Anselm, the eleventh-century Archbishop of Canterbury and inventor of the celebrated Ontological Argument for the existence of God.

Well—the pun is purely accidental—the long and short of it is that Bishop Bulstrode, at Dean Grice's prompting, of course, wants to do away with this ancient relic and replace it with something useful and "up to date." A drinking fountain for the benefit of visitors to the cathedral has been suggested. A drinking fountain, forsooth! No doubt one of those polished granite monstrosities that rich "philanthropists" are in the habit of inflicting on our public parks. Oddly enough, says Bertie, the Bishop's proposal has met with quite a bit of support, but there is also some vehement opposition, most notably from old Archdeacon Hill. Bertie, to his credit, is with the old boy, but his voice counts for very little.

Bertie says there was a fearful row about it at the last meeting of the Dean and Chapter a couple of days ago. The Archdeacon said that the well went back quite possibly to pre-Christian times and that to remove it would be a sacrilege. To which Dean Grice smartly replies that if the well is pre-Christian it could not possibly count as sacrilege to dispose of it.

It was then that Bertie had what he is pleased to call his "brain wave." He proposed that an independent expert be called in to pronounce on the historic and architectural importance of said well. When asked, in sarcastic tones by the

Dean, where that expert might be found, Bertie replied that there was a just such a blighter with all the correct qualifications lecturing on things Medieval only up the road at the University of Wessex, to wit, yours truly.

I don't know whether to feel flattered or to knock young Bertie about the mazzard for being an infernal interfering pill. I expect nothing will come of it, though.

September 5th

A letter arrived this morning with the Morchester Cathedral crest embossed on the back of the envelope. Everything about it is stiff: the envelope, the notepaper within, and the wording typed thereon. It is from Dean Grice, inviting me over to Morchester to consult about the well and proposing a date for the meeting. The final paragraph reads as follows:

"I must earnestly entreat you to say nothing about this commission to friends or colleagues and on no account to inform the press. I cannot emphasise too strongly that the utmost confidentiality is essential. You will receive an adequate honorarium for the benefit of your expertise and any researches that might be required. However, should you breach the seal of discretion in any way, no such remuneration will be forthcoming."

It all seemed unnecessarily pedantic to me, perhaps even a little "neurotic," as the followers of Dr. Freud would say. What had got the wind up? Anyway, I wrote back agreeing to his terms as I must admit to being rather intrigued.

September 10th

This morning I took the train into Morchester, arriving shortly before ten. It was a fine, balmy day, so I walked the quarter mile to the Deanery, which is in the south west corner of the cathedral close. The Deanery is a pretty little three-storey Queen Anne house of mellow red brick with, over the front door, an elegant little pedimented portico made out of the local limestone. There is no bell push, but there is a bronze knocker on the door of curious design. I believe it to have been modelled from one of the gargoyles on the cathedral roof. (Morchester Cathedral, of course, is famous for its grotesque carvings.) It was in the shape of the head of some sort of beast. The eyes were large and saucer-like and there was little in the way of a nose, apart from a rather ugly cavity for a nostril. Where the mouth should have been there was a mass of strands or tentacles that seemed to writhe, snake-like, as if each one had a life of its own. It was a finely crafted piece, but all the more distasteful to handle because of it.

Nevertheless I grasped the thing and rapped on the door, which was opened by a tall, elderly, angular woman who looked as if her morning bath had had an iceberg in it. She scrutinised me with some disdain, then, pointing imperiously to her right, told me that all hawkers, vagrants and people seeking assistance from the diocese should apply at the tradesman's entrance.

I had on an old pair of grey flannel bags and a heavily patched tweed sports coat, but I didn't think that I looked that disreputable. Perhaps the fact that I had no tie on and wear sandals at all times of the year gave me a bohemian or even—O horror!—a Socialist look.

I explained that I was Dr. Nightfall and had an appointment to see the Dean. The lady still regarded me with suspicion.

"My husband is not unwell," she said indignantly.

Before I could explain to her that my doctorate was in History, not Medicine, she had disappeared into the dark bowels of the Deanery. After a while she re-emerged from the gloom to tell me that the Dean would see me now in his study, indicating the second door on the left of a dingy corridor that passed right through the house. I smiled and tried to thank her warmly but the frost on her upper slopes failed to thaw.

I knocked and was bidden to enter the Dean's study. The room I came into was lit only by the light from a window facing onto a back garden. At the bottom of the garden I could just see, through the willows, the glitter of a stream.

I have to say that Dean Grice's welcome was not much cheerier than his wife's. He greeted me by rising from behind his desk and favouring me with a handshake that felt like a long-dead haddock. He has a narrow face, parchment skin, and little round, silver rimmed spectacles that glinted in the dimness of the study, occasionally turning his eyes into blank discs of reflected light. Having obtained from me the solemn assurance that I had told no one about my visit, he suggested briskly that we should walk over together to the cathedral and take a look at the well.

As we stepped out of the deanery, a cool breeze blew up. The rooks, who inhabit a stand of elms at the west end of the cathedral close suddenly all flew as one from their "buildings" (as I believe their nests are called) in the trees and began to wheel around screeching, making their characteristic "kaa, kaa" sound. Once across the road and onto the green, the Dean and I took a diagonal paved path which leads directly to the West Door of the Cathedral. I stared in awe at the rooks as they circled and cried. I could not get it out of my head that they were, for purposes unknown, putting on a demonstration of some kind. The Dean, evidently well-accustomed to this curious animal behaviour, took no notice whatsoever.

While I was looking around me, I noticed that someone was on the path behind us and trying to attract our attention. It was a tallish man wearing a cloak and a battered sombrero hat. He appeared somewhat eccentric, but as he was a hundred and fifty yards away I could not make out his features. He waved a thin arm and said "Hi!" so I alerted the Dean to his presence. The Dean, without breaking his stride, turned round to look, then almost immediately turned back and began to walk even more determinedly towards the cathedral. I had seen a look of disgust, perhaps even of fear pass across his ascetic features.

"We wish to have no intercourse with that man," said the Dean.

"Who is he?"

"He is called Felix Cutbirth."

"Unusual surname."

"It is a variant of Cuthbert, an Anglo-Saxon name. He comes from a very old family, which has lived in Morsetshire since before the Norman Conquest. Unhappily, in his case, ancient lineage is no guarantee of respectability. The Cut-births have long had an evil reputation."

"What does he want with us?"

"I cannot possibly imagine," said the Dean dismissively. We were now at the West Door. "Come! Let us go into the Cathedral. He will not follow us in there, I fancy."

Once we were inside, I was conscious of a certain relaxation in the Dean. He became almost animated. Clearly he loved the place and his knowledge of medieval architecture was intelligent and extensive. My own complemented his, so we enjoyed each other's company as we walked down the great Early English nave, like an avenue of tall and stately trees. Weak sunlight filtered through the high windows and few people were about. I glanced quickly behind me. The Dean's surmise was correct: Cutbirth had not followed us into the cathedral. After this brief interlude the Dean took me out into the cloisters to survey the well.

Though I had seen it before, I had not examined it at close quarters because, as notices proclaimed, it was forbidden for ordinary mortals to tread the lawn of the cloister garth. The Dean led me boldly across it.

"There you see," he said. "Not a thing of beauty and a joy forever."

I had to admit he was right. The "thing" had been built, rebuilt and repaired over centuries. There was no unity in this strange circular wall. Some of the stones were large, some small, some rough-hewn, a few dressed. I noticed that there was a section at the base on the south side that was not made of stone at all, but brick, and Roman bricks at that. I recognised their flat shape and the excellent quality of the mortar. I mentioned my discovery to the Dean who merely nodded.

"Yes. That is known. Quite late Roman, I believe. Fourth or fifth century." He seemed unimpressed. I also noticed that some of the Roman bricks had a crude drawing of an eye scratched on them: a so-called "apotropaic eye" of the kind you see on the sides of Greek fishing vessels, designed to ward off evil. This I did not mention to the Dean.

When the Dean asked my opinion I told him that the well was of no architectural but of great archaeological interest. I said that there would need to be a thorough archaeological survey of the well before anything was done to it, and that to expedite matters I would, with his permission, discover all I could about the well from the Cathedral archives.

The Dean took all this in with a kind of weary resignation, as I suppose it was the answer he was expecting. The cloisters had been deserted when we entered them, but just as we were about to leave we heard a voice.

"I see you!" It said. The voice was a man's; the tone was mocking with a hint of menace about it.

We looked around. Finally we saw a face poking over the wall of one of the open gothic arcades. On the head was a battered sombrero. It was Cutbirth.

The Dean started violently when he saw him, executing a little involuntary jump which made Cutbirth laugh as he got up off his knees, lifted a long leg over the cloister wall and stepped through the arcade onto the cloister garth.

"You may not walk on this grass!" yapped the Dean.

"Why not? You do."

"What are you doing here?"

Cutbirth began to walk lazily towards us over the manicured lawn, removing his hat as he did so. He must have been about forty, but age with such a strange creature was hard to assess. He was long and loosely built, with abnormally large hands. His skin was a yellowish colour, coarse and porous in texture. His head was a large, virtually hairless oval, but the features were small, strangely caught together in the middle of his face, like those of a horrible baby. He was trying to exude an air of insouciant mockery, but the eyes—green, I think—were full of rage.

"I might ask you the same question," said Cutbirth. His accent was odd. He spoke with the languid drawl of the upper classes, but some of his vowels were pure rural Morsetshire.

"It is none of your business," said the Dean raising his voice and sounding petulant.

"I think it is. Mr. Dean. You do realise that this has been a sacred spot since long before your psalm-singing, milk-white Christians started erecting their pious monstrosities over it? I know what you want to do. You want to obliterate the sanctity of centuries. You want to banish the Old Gods forever. And for what? For some damned provincial little water trough to slake the putrid tongues of cheap charabanc tourists!"

"Who told you that?"

"Never you mind, Mr. Dean." Then turning to me, with disdainful a glance at my sandals, he said: "And what's your little game, my Communist friend?"

"Don't answer him!" said the Dean. To tell the truth, I was so shocked at being denounced as a Communist on account of my footwear that I was incapable of speech. "Will you kindly leave forthwith, or I shall be forced to summon assistance and have you thrown off."

Cutbirth laughed harshly: "I warn you, Dean Grice—" He pronounced it "grease." "—the House of Dagon will suffer wrong no more! The Old Gods are awaking from their long sleep and you would do well not to despise their help in the gathering storm. Soon the rivers of Europe will run with blood. You will bleat for the Nazarene to help you, but he will not come, and the tide of blood will advance till it engulfs even Morchester. I warn you, Grice!"

With that he turned and left us, jamming his sombrero down on his head as he did so. Despite this faintly ludicrous gesture, we were both stunned—I might almost say impressed—by his speech. For nearly a minute we stood there silent, motionless. Though objectively I have nothing but contempt for Cutbirth, I had been made aware of a certain power in him, or about him.

The Dean finally broke the silence. "Come, Dr. Nightfall. Let me show you the library where you will be conducting your researches."

"What was that about the House of Dagon?"

"Oh, just his usual nonsense," said the Dean irritably. Then he paused, hesitating whether to confide in me. At last he said: "Felix Cutbirth is by way of being an artist. I had the misfortune to see some of his paintings at an exhibition in Morchester not so long ago. They are vile things, vile ... but not without accomplishment. He studied at the

Slade in London, I believe. While there, he became involved with something called the Order of the Golden Dawn, an occult society. You remember: Yeats, Crowley, Machen, Mathers—?" I nodded. "Well, after a while he became dissatisfied with them and broke away to found his own little magical sect, called the Order of Dagon. I am happy to say it failed miserably. On his return to Morchester, Cutbirth tried to set up the Order here. He had a temple for a while at the back of a Turkish restaurant in Morchester High Street, but neither the temple nor the restaurant prospered. He still has a few devotees among the credulous of this city, but they may be counted on the fingers of one hand. That is all we need to know about Mr. Cutbirth!"

And with that we proceeded to the library.

September 13th

This is my second day in the library and I have made some progress. There is surprisingly little information to be had on the well, other than the rather surprising fact that it has not been used as such since the early twelfth century. A date of 1107 or 1108 is usually given for the closing of the well, but no explanation is given. I presume that it became contaminated in some way, but I could not understand why the whole structure was not destroyed.

Today, however, I have made a discovery. Of course the real story will, I suspect, remain hidden, but at least we have the legend. Legends are revealing in their own way.

One of the oldest volumes in the library is a kind of scrapbook, an untidy binding together of all sorts of early manuscripts to do with the Cathedral. Most of these are deeds and charters and inventories, not very interesting, but towards the end of the book I found what I recognised as a very early—perhaps even the original—manuscript of William of Morchester's *Gesta Anselmi*.

In the 1160s Archbishop Thomas Beckett was, no doubt for his own political purposes, pressing the Pope to make a former Archbishop of Canterbury, Anselm (1033–1109), a saint. To this end he commissioned William of Morchester to write a life of Anselm, praising him and listing all his miracles: a hagiography, in other words. This William called the *Gesta Anselmi* or "The Deeds of Anselm."

It is a typical work of the period with very little of historical value in it. It deals in the kind of absurd legends and miracles that the medievals loved: Anselm restores sight to a blind man; he revives a dead child; a barren woman prays at the tomb of Anselm and soon finds herself with child, and so on. I had seen copies of it before, but this manuscript seemed fuller and older than the others.

Towards the end of the MS I came across a passage that I had certainly never previously encountered. Several lines had been drawn through it, as if the scribe had deemed it unsuitable for further publication, but I was able to read it quite easily. It began:

Anselmus cum in Priorium Benedictinum Morcastri advenerat monachos valde perturbatos de puteo suo vidit …

"When Anselm came to the Benedictine Priory at Morchester he saw the monks in much distress on account of their well. For they had built their cloister around an ancient well which had been there for many centuries and where in time past many foul and blasphemous ceremonies had been enacted to worship the ancient Gods and Demons of the Pagans. For, it was said, in the depths of this ancient well were many caverns and paths beneath the earth which connected with sea caverns on the southern shores. [In the eleventh and twelfth centuries the sea was much closer to Morchester than it is now.] And it was said that these demons came out of the sea and through the caverns to the well where they had been worshipped as gods in former times.

"Now certain of the monks, hoping to draw greater quantities of the sweet water to be found in the well, had descended into its depths to dig deeper and uncover new springs. But in so doing they had awakened the demons who had lain dormant in caverns beneath the well for many centuries. They had troubled their unholy sleep and awakened their anger. And these demons had arisen from the well to bring destruction on the monks and the people of Morchester. The monks were tormented by ill dreams and by odours as of fish putrefying. Women of the town began to give birth to all manner of abominations: infants with two heads, mouths in their fundaments, horns upon their head, many arms but without hands; and one had the face of a great serpent. Such was their consternation that the whole people cried out to Anselm to deliver them from terrors by night and abominations by day.

"Then did the Blessed Anselm pronounce absolution for the sins of the whole people. Having done so, the Archbishop, taking his staff of office which contained a reliquary holding a fragment of the true cross and a thumbnail of St. Paul, ordered the monks to let him down into the depths of the well. There Blessed Anselm remained for seven days and seven nights alone wrestling with the spawn of Hell and in particularly the chief of these demons whose name was— [Here the manuscript has been corrected, scratched out and altered several times so that the name is unclear. My best guess is Dagonus.]

"After seven days and seven nights Blessed Anselm commanded that he be lifted out of the well, for he had vanquished the demons therein. Thereupon he commanded that a lid of oak bound with iron be placed over the well and that no person should thereafter remove it, and that new wells be dug to the North of the Abbey. And moreover Anselm blessed the waters of the Orr [the river that flows past Morchester] so that water might be drawn from it in safety. And he commanded that a great cathedral be erected in place of the Abbey Church for all the people, and that this cathedral be consecrated to St. Michael the Archangel, the vanquisher of demons, and St. George, the slayer of dragons."

It was only after Anselm's official canonisation in 1494 that the cathedral was rededicated to him. This not such a radical act as it might seem because it was simply sanctioning local practice. The building had long been known by the inhabitants of Morchester as "Anselm's Cathedral".

I suspect that there is a tiny core of truth in this absurd fable: namely that the well is very old indeed, which the presence of Roman brickwork confirms. It is just possible also that, as the text suggests, the well had at some stage become contaminated by sea water from an underground source. Hence also the stench of rotting fish?

I cannot help being intrigued by the coincidence—and it is only a coincidence!—that Cutbirth's little sect is called the Order of Dagon, and Anselm's main adversary in the well was Dagonus.

September 15th

I have given the Dean a précis of my findings and he has agreed that the well should be opened up and surveyed. Bertie is in a state of high excitement and jumping up and down at the prospect of what he insists on calling "an archaeological dig." I remind him that no digging will be involved, just the descent into a well which may, after all, be filled with rubbish, but nothing dampens Bertie. He clamours to be part of the "adventure."

A strange thing happened today. While I was in the cloister discussing the opening of the well with the Clerk of Works, a boy came up to me and handed me a letter. It was one of the town boys, I think, certainly very scruffy, and before I could speak to him he had run off.

Inside the envelope was a piece of stiff card, like an invitation. It had been expensively engraved with the heading *Ordo Templi Dagonis*—"Order of the Temple of Dagon." Below this was an elaborate design, rather well executed but curiously unpleasant. Within a fancy baroque cartouche was a drawing of a figure crouched on a throne. I say figure because it was not wholly human nor wholly bestial, but something in between. It seemed to be in an attitude of deep and trancelike thought but its outward appearance was savage. Curious tentacles drooped over its mouth parts. It reminded me somewhat of the Dean's knocker, but I did not study it long. Below it in capitals was written:

DO NOT MEDDLE WITH THE ANCIENT AND INFINITE. YOU HAVE BEEN WARNED.

The sender can only be Cutbirth.

September 21ˢᵗ

Troubling rumours from Europe. A cloudy day. The Clerk and his workmen set up equipment to raise the lid of the well and, if necessary, let me down into it. Bertie was there whenever he could to watch progress, which was painfully slow. In the first place, nobody could find the keys to the padlocks which secured the wooden lid to the wall, so they had to be smashed off by main force. It was beginning to get dark before the lid was raised.

The first of our surprises when the well was finally un-covered was the smell. A faint but still unpalatable odour, as of rotten fish, wafted up to us from the bottom of the well, which was so deep that my torch could not penetrate its abysses. I noticed, however, that the well was skilfully made, with dressed stone forming a perfect cylinder. The walls were virtually black and covered with a thin layer of darkish slime like the tracks of a thousand snails. We had not rope enough to let me down to the bottom, but I noticed that, some thirty feet below, steps had been built into the wall. They descended in an elegant spiral into the unseen depths and looked man-ageable.

Bertie, like the ass he is, dropped a stone down the well. No splash was heard. Instead there was a sort of cracking sound that reverberated in an odd way. Perhaps the *Gesta* was right, and there are caverns down there. That blighter Bertie then decided to try out the echo with his voice and sang what he assured me was an E flat above middle C. The echo lasted a good ten seconds after he had stopped sing-ing and was strange. Once it was over and I had started to tell Bertie off for his fat-headed behaviour, we both heard another sound come from the well, which was most certainly not Bertie's voice. It lasted only for a second or so, but it sounded distinctly as if some thing or things down there were scratching or fluttering about.

Bertie was all for investigating, but I told him not to be an idiot. It was late, it was getting dark and we had done enough for the day. I told the workmen to replace the lid over the well, and it was then that we received our last surprise of the day. On the underside of the lid I noticed that something black had been nailed to the wood. A quick examination showed it to be a crucifix of heavily tarnished silver, early twelfth century and of the finest Norman workmanship.

But what was it doing nailed to the wood, facing downwards into the blackness with nothing and no one to see it?

I decided to leave that and other questions till a later date. I am staying at the Dean's tonight, so as to start bright and early tomorrow. As I was walking back from the cathedral towards the Deanery, I noticed that the rooks were making more than their usual fuss. They were wheeling around their elms, cawing away, apparently quite unable to settle for the night. A few distant dogs seemed to have caught their mood and began to howl.

Dinner at the Deanery with the Grices was, as I had rather expected, not a lively occasion. Dean Grice is given to rather pontifical remarks on general subjects and sees himself as having very "up to date" opinions. He talked with some pride of his time as a chaplain in the trenches during the Great War and gave me his opinion that it had been "the war to end all wars" and that that sort of thing should on no account ever happen again. Then he asked me what I thought of "Mr. Hitler." It took me a second or two to understand whom he was referring to. He sounded as if he were talking about an erring member of his congregation.

Mrs. Dean has no conversation at all. Occasionally she will break her silence by simply repeating what her husband has just said. Needless to say I have retired early. I must try to get some sleep, but there seem to be an awful lot of barking or howling dogs about.

September 22nd

I passed a pretty restless night. In addition to the dogs, there were the cats. Everywhere they seemed to be out and about howling and screeching. One climbed up the sloping roof outside my window and started scrabbling at the window pane. I tried to shoo it away several times, but it was persistent and plaintive. Finally I let it in and it made straight for my bed. I tried to push it off, but it mewed pathetically and curled itself up in a crook of my arm. There it stayed all night and, apart from purring rather too loudly, caused me no further trouble.

But that was not the end of it. The next assault on my ears came from a most unexpected quarter. My bedroom is next to that of the Dean and his wife. It being an old house, the partition walls are quite thin, no more than lath and plaster sandwiched in between wooden panelling. At about two o'clock my fitful slumbers were disturbed by what I can only describe as a bout of amorous activity from the next room. I hesitate to write it down. I could barely believe my ears at the time. To judge from the cries made by the two contenders the event appeared to be violent and not wholly consensual on the part of Mrs. Grice. Neither can be less than sixty years of age.

At breakfast the following morning Mr. and Mrs. Dean were more than usually taciturn. I noticed that at different times they looked at me enquiringly. Mrs. Dean's hair was in quiet disarray. Fortunately I had an excellent excuse to leave as soon as possible. I needed to supervise the means whereby I was to be let down into the body of the well.

To cut a long story short, it was well into the afternoon before all was ready for the descent. A rope ladder had been found to let me down as far as the spiral steps. The idea was that, once I had reached the steps, further equipment, including a long rope, would be let down to me and I would attach the rope to the wall by means of a metal staple knocked into it. This rope would be there as a safeguard in case the steps proved treacherous. Then I was to walk down the steps into the unknown abyss. With me, in a knapsack, I had two electric torches, a tape measure, a notebook and pencils, and a small camera with flash bulb attachments.

Bertie, needless to say, was on hand and bursting with excited enthusiasm. I asked him if he had had a disturbed night, but he had apparently slept like a baby.

Before I began my descent, I was suddenly seized with apprehension. I checked everything was secure and told the Clerk of Works that at least two of his men should be on hand at the wellhead while I was conducting my investigations. A look was exchanged between the Clerk and his men that I did not understand, but he agreed.

The first part of the descent was made easily. I climbed down the rope ladder to the spiral steps, which were rather rough-hewn but not, as I had feared, very slippery. There the workmen let down some tools and the rope. I managed to drive a metal staple into the wall and secure a rope to it. Then, taking my electric torch, I began my descent.

I flashed my torch into the depths but could see no bottom, only the spiral staircase endlessly revolving into the depths. The masonry that clad the walls was smooth, and its composition was what is called "Cyclopean": that is, huge irregular slabs of stone had been dressed and fitted together, making the wall look like a gigantic piece of crazy paving on the vertical.

The whole, including the spiral steps, was an astonishing feat of construction and certainly not, in my view, Medieval. Anglo-Saxon, then? Even less likely. Roman? I had never seen Roman work that remotely resembled this.

Soon the top of the well had become a little white disc, no bigger than the moon. I trudged downwards, taking care not to touch the walls if I could avoid it. They were covered with a thin layer of something dark and glistening, sticky to the touch, that left a dark brown stain on the hands, like half-dried blood. My dear old tweed jacket was already ruined.

I had entered a world of silence, and if silence can be said to echo, then it did. I suppose what I am saying is that the slightest scrape of my feet on the stone steps came back to me in echoes a thousandfold. Once, I coughed, and it was like a fusillade of rifle shots. The scent of something decaying and fishlike was getting stronger.

Then I heard a faint pattering sound behind and above me. I look round and saw a light flickering and flashing, then further pattering, then what sounded like a stifled oath. I shone my torch upwards. Something was coming down the stairway towards me.

It was that infernal ass Bertie Winship! He was carrying a tiny little toy electric torch that was about as much use down there as a paper bag in a thunderstorm.

I gave the blighter a good piece of my mind and told him in no uncertain terms to go back up at once, but he was unrepentant.

"Sorry, old fellow," he said, "I simply couldn't resist it. Anyway, I thought you could do with the company."

I was barely able to admit it to myself, but he was right. The ancient solitude was beginning to oppress me. I told him sharply to put away his stupid little flashlight and take the other of my two torches. I also told him to remain silent as we made our way down.

I don't know how long we had been going, but the entrance to the well was only a pinpoint of light above us—no more than a distant star on a dark night—when we came across the carvings.

The first of them was a frieze carved into the stone, about a foot and a half in depth, that ran the whole of the way round the well, broken only by the run of the staircase. It was a continuous key pattern, or, if you like, a set of interlinked swastikas. Apart from anything else, it was astonishing to find workmanship like this at such a depth. What possible purpose could it serve?

I could only conjecture that its presence suggested that an early civilisation, probably of Aryan origin, had been at work here and created the descent for ritual purposes. I began to speculate that it might have been used to commune with spirits of the dead, or some chthonic deity of the underworld. This structure could be an early monument to a mystery religion, perhaps the earliest in these islands, predating Mithraism by hundreds, even thousands of years.

My thoughts were beginning to run away with me, when Bertie gave an odd little yelp. His torch had strayed onto a panel carved in low relief, just opposite him. The artist was skilled and the execution showed no signs of imprecision or crudity. The manner was vaguely reminiscent of those to be found on Babylonian and Assyrian monuments: precise, but stylised.

It showed a group of figures huddled together, one of which was wearing a kind of crown or diadem and seemed to be dominating the others. The figures were not human, nor recognisably animal. They looked like some strange miscegenation between a sea creature, of an octopoid kind, and a human or ape. One of them reminded me rather unpleasantly of the figure engraved on Felix Cutbirth's card.

"By Jove," said Bertie, "I wouldn't like to meet one of those on a dark night."

I told Bertie to stop making idiotic remarks, and we continued our descent. There were several more of these relief sculptures, each one stranger than the last. One depicted a group of human beings kneeling in homage, heads touching the ground like Moslems at prayer, before a strange lopsided creature with a head far too big for its body. In another further down, four man in profile were carrying a rigid human body horizontally. They appeared to be feeding it to one of the strange half-fish creatures; in fact most of the body's head had already entered the beast's vast open mouth.

Shortly after that my foot encountered not another stone step but soft, muddy soil. We were at the bottom of the well. I commanded Bertie to stop, and I tried the ground. I was afraid it was a quagmire into which we might sink, never to be recovered, but the soil, though moist and soft, appeared to be solidly founded.

I then noticed a strange thing. The aperture at the wellhead was almost exactly ten feet across, but the chamber at its base was wider. I measured it with the tape I had brought for the purpose and discovered that we were in a circular space slightly over twenty-three feet in diameter.

We must have been walking down a funnel that slowly tapered towards the top, but the widening (or narrowing, depending which way you look at it) had been done so gradually and with such cunning that we had never noticed.

The air at the bottom was not free of the odour of rotten fish, but it was not rank or stuffy, and it was almost as if a breeze was coming from somewhere. I noticed that at opposite ends of the circular wall were two black spaces with pointed arches, just wide and tall enough for a man of average height to walk through them. I shone my torch into one of them and it revealed a long, narrow tunnel leading into more blackness.

By this time Bertie had reached the bottom too, and was talking his usual nonsense. He had got it into his head that the whole thing was connected with King Arthur and Merlin, or some such twaddle. He said that he that the two apertures were bound to lead to "treasure chambers" and that we should explore them at once. I was resolved to do no such thing. We had had quite enough excitement for one day, but just then Bertie let out a cry.

"I say, look at this!" he said.

I prepared myself for yet another inanity, but Bertie had actually found something. He had been idly pushing his foot about in the mud and flashing his torch at it, when he had come across something shiny. He pulled it out of the mud, and we did our best to clean it up with our pocket handkerchiefs.

It shone still because it was made of some incorruptible metal or metals, pale yellow in colour. I suspected an alloy of gold and platinum, but this was highly improbable for such an obviously ancient artefact. The workmanship was very fine, but when I say fine, I do not exactly mean beautiful.

It was circular and in the shape of a coronet or diadem, but if it was a sort of crown, then the head it had enclosed was monstrous, at least twice the size of an ordinary adult human head. The pattern was one of intricately entwined whorls and concentric circles which, when you looked closely at them, resolved themselves into the coiling limbs of strange creatures whose bulging eyes were represented by some sort of milky white semiprecious stone. They were not pearls, but could have been white jade, though this seemed unlikely for England. The lowest band or border was composed of the interconnecting key pattern of swastikas that we had seen on the walls above us.

While Bertie was babbling on about how he had found King Arthur's crown, I took out the camera from my knapsack and put a flash bulb into the attachment. I only had a few bulbs so I had to choose my subjects carefully. I took one of the area we stood in as a whole to give an impression of the remarkable structure we had found. I took another, at

Bertie's earnest request, of him holding the giant diadem. I then decided that I should point the camera down the two tunnels that projected from our central chamber.

I took one without any effect, but when my camera flashed down the other tunnel I thought I saw through my viewfinder something move at the end of the passageway I was photographing: a pale grey-green something that was smooth and glistening. The next moment I heard a noise, halfway between a groan and a retching cough, but cavernous and hugely magnified. I turned sharply round to see if it was Bertie playing some stupid joke, but he was staring back at me, white and horrified.

The next minute we were storming up those spiral stairs as fast as we could go. Bertie, who was ahead of me, stumbled several times. Each time I picked him up and on we went. By the time we had reached the end of the steps and the rope ladder we were both gasping for breath. It was at least five minutes before we made the final ascent.

As we came out of the well the sun was setting in a clear evening sky, but for a few seconds it seemed impossibly bright to us. I ordered the rope ladder to be drawn up and the lid of the well to be replaced.

I had my camera with me. I turned and asked Bertie if he still had the crown with him but he said he had dropped it on the way up. I believed him; I think I believed him, but he had his arms folded across his jacket in an odd way.

Bertie had recovered from his fright amazingly quickly and was soon chattering away to the Clerk of Works about the well's "amazing archaeological importance." I noticed, though, that he was very unspecific about our discoveries and for that, I suppose, I should be grateful.

I returned to the Deanery exhausted, and at dinner, I am afraid, proved very unforthcoming about the day's events. Fortunately the Dean was in a very talkative mood. He was full of Mr. Chamberlain's flight to see "Mr. Hitler" and pacify him over the Sudetenland Crisis. He sees the Prime Minister's mission as the epitome of modern statesmanship and diplomacy. I am too weary and confused to agree or disagree openly, but I do not share his confidence in a peaceful outcome. Mrs. Dean remained entirely mute. and he barely looked at her.

The Dean then told me he had just heard the melancholy news that during the previous night the Archdeacon, the Venerable Thaddeus Hill, had died, of a "seizure." When the Dean said the word "seizure," I noticed that his wife looked at him very sharply indeed, and I think I saw the Dean's pale skin flush with embarrassment.

September 23rd

In the early hours of this morning I was rudely awakened by the Dean, No, not like the night before. He entered my room and shook me awake. There were intruders in the cathedral, he said: lights had been seen in the cloisters. I told him to alert the police; it was nothing to do with me, but he was insistent. I had never seen the Dean so animated.

I dressed rapidly and grabbed my torch. The Dean was waiting for me downstairs in the hall with a heavy old revolver and some cartridges. Handing me the gun, he said:

"Take this, my boy. My old service revolver from the Trenches. We have not a moment to lose." I thought he must be mad.

From the top of the stairs his wife in her night-gown stared down at us, wild and bewildered.

We gained access by the West Door, but finding nothing amiss in the cathedral itself, we hurried on to the cloisters. There, by the light of our torches, we could see that the lid had been removed from the well, and we could hear distant cries. Once we got to the well we could hear the cries clearly, albeit distorted by the well's weird echo. Someone was screaming for help, and I could swear the voice was Bertie's.

I loaded the revolver and put it in my pocket, then tucked the torch into my belt. The Dean helped me over the parapet and onto the rope ladder. So I began the descent into the well yet again. The cries from below had not stopped, but they seemed muffled and more distant than before.

I reached the steps and began to hurry down them far more rapidly than I would have wished. Once or twice I tripped and nearly fell into the black abyss. I reached the bottom and flashed my torch about. There was nobody, nothing.

I stood quite still, trying not to breathe too hard, the blood pounding in my head. Bertie—or whoever it was—must have gone through one of the two tunnels, but which one?

I decided to try the one where my flash photography had surprised something. I switched off my torch and entered the Stygian blackness of the narrow tunnel. Darkness and silence enveloped me. I felt my way, along smooth, slimed walls.

Then I began to hear something. It was like a chant, but the tune and the language were alien to me. I could see something red flicker against the glistening black walls of the tunnel. It was no more than a whisper of light, but it spoke terror to me.

The tunnel bent slightly, then suddenly debouched into a vast cavern over a hundred feet high. Naphtha flares, spurting naturally from the rock, lit the space with a pinkish glare from a thousand crevices. I was in an area at least as vast as the Cathedral somewhere far above me. Parts of the rock vault had been carved into strange shapes; parts had been left in their natural state, rugged and glistening.

Again I heard the chanting and, though clearer, it was sill alien to my ears:

Iä-R'lyeh! Cthulhu fhtagn! Iä! Iä!

About fifty feet from me across a smooth cyclopean pavement stood a naked man, his back to me. His hands were raised in the air, his almost hairless head thrown back in an ecstasy of adoration. At his feet lay a crumpled form in black. As I approached them across the pavement I recognised the fallen figure. It was Bertie Winship, still in his clerical cassock.

These two were between me and a third figure who stood, or crouched, some yards in front of them. Even now I cannot or will not describe it fully. Its colour was a greyish green and its form was stooped with a vast elephantine head on which reposed the coronet which Bertie had discovered at the bottom of the well. Its superabundant flesh, which seemed to disintegrate into a thousand liquid limbs, quivered with infernal energy. It appeared to sway and stoop to the naked man's chant—or was it the chant that swayed to its movement?

I drew and cocked the Dean's service revolver. The naked man must have heard this or my footsteps approaching because he turned and saw me.

"Get out, you damned fool!" he shrieked. "How dare you interfere?" It was Cutbirth, his evil-baby features contorted with rage.

"I have come to take Bertie back," I said.

"You cannot have him! He is already given to the gods. Go back, I tell you!"

At this, the creature let out a groaning screech which filled the cathedral cavern with hellish sound. Cutbirth turned his back on me and again addressed the monster:

Iä-R'lyeh! Cthulhu fhtagn! Iä! Iä!

Having uttered his cry, he stooped and picked up from the ground something shining and curved, like an oriental knife. Then, with his other hand he gathered up the unconscious form of Bertie by the collar. Bertie's head lolled back, unwittingly presenting his white throat to Cutbirth's blade.

"Put him down or I shoot," I said. Cutbirth laughed.

"You wouldn't dare, you damned sandal-wearing, psalm-singing socialist!"

I pulled the trigger, but the wretched gun jammed. It was a heavy, clumsy old thing. I pulled the trigger again and the gun fired, but the shot went wide and the recoil nearly threw me onto my back. The echoes of the shot filled the cavern with a clatter like machine-gun fire.

Then, gripping the gun in both hands, I steadied myself and took aim at Cutbirth's head. I fired again. The shot missed Cutbirth by quite a margin, but it hit the creature which loomed before him. The bullet went into one of its huge, milky eyes. The eye seemed to explode with the impact, spraying out torrents of green bile in the process. A hideous shriek filled the cavern.

Cutbirth dropped the knife and turned again towards me with rage and hatred in every knotted vein of his face. It was a fatal mistake. The beast, assuming that Cutbirth had been the perpetrator of the outrage against its eye, launched one of its great tentacle limbs against him, lashing him to the ground. Cutbirth scrambled to his feet and tried to make a run for it, but the beast was onto him with more of his limbs. A terrible, unequal struggle ensued.

Meanwhile I ran towards the unconscious form of Bertie. I was glad to find he was not dead, just heavily drugged from some hideous narcotic that Cutbirth had pumped into him. I picked him up in a fireman's lift and ran towards the little cavern entrance.

There I put Bertie down, because there was not room enough to carry him on my back through the tunnel. I would have to drag him by the feet.

I took one last look into the cavern. The creature had Cutbirth wrapped in his limbs and their two heads were very close together. It looked horribly like a lover's embrace. As the creature bent its head towards Cutbirth's, I saw the man's face for the last time. It was full of agonised fear, but also a wondering ecstasy, as if he half-welcomed the devouring kiss of his deity.

I heard a rustling and saw that the cavern was beginning to fill with other creatures, some bigger, some smaller than the one that was now feasting on Cutbirth. They were all piscine, shambling, unearthly, imbued with some sort of mind and power that was beyond my capacity to comprehend.

I took Bertie's feet and began to drag him through the passage. As I was doing so he started to groan. Consciousness of a kind was returning to him, but he was still impossibly weak.

We reached the bottom of the well, and then I had to half drag, half carry him up the spiral staircase. It took an age.

When we reached the rope ladder I was faced with a problem. He was still too doped and feeble to climb it himself and I could not carry him up it on my back. Then I remembered the rope that I had tied to the staple at the bottom of the rope ladder.

I detached the rope from the staple and tied one end

of the rope securely around Bertie's waist. Then, taking the other end of the rope, I climbed with it to the top of the rope ladder. Dawn was breaking over the Cathedral as I clambered over the well parapet. Fortunately the Dean was still there.

With much heaving on the rope we managed to pull young Bertie to the top. He was just revived enough by this time to scramble over the well enclosure and flop exhausted onto the dewy lawn of the cloister garth.

Over the next few hours I managed to get some sort of a story out of him. The silly young blighter had still got the coronet with him when we had came out of the well the previous evening. He had then done something that exceeded even my estimation of his fat-headedness. He had taken it to show Felix Cutbirth.

Apparently, Bertie had struck up a weird sort of friendship with Cutbirth, owing to a mutual interest in folklore and local legend. It was undoubtedly Bertie who had alerted him to our schemes with regard to the well.

To cut a long story short, Cutbirth, no doubt with promises of "treasure chambers" and the like, persuaded young Bertie to take him to the well and make another descent in the small hours. Bertie's memory collapses at this point but one can guess the remainder.

We are both in a state of shock and no doubt the reaction will hit us more heavily later on. Meanwhile the Dean has given orders that the lid is to be put back on the well and the padlocks restored. But has the genie been put back in the bottle? I doubt it.

October 5th 1938

This is the first time I have written in my journal for some days. I am recovering at Margate and my sister is with me. She takes me down to the seafront every day, puts me on a bench and tucks a plaid travelling rug around my knees, as if I were an elderly aunt with arthritis. I feel such a fool because there is really nothing wrong me, but every time I close my eyes they come. I can barely sleep, and when I do it is not long before I wake up screaming.

So I sit here watching the sea as it makes its slow gestures of advance and retreat upon the sand, like a sluggish invading army. Sometimes I fancy I see shapes forming themselves in the waves. I wait for them to resolve themselves into the monsters I once glimpsed, but mercifully they never do. One day beasts will come out of the waves, beasts of iron and steel, but not today.

I have just heard news of Bertie Winship. He had it worse than I did. He is in some sort of special Church of England nuthouse, but they tell me he makes a little progress. Bertie will recover, I feel sure of it, but he will never be the same Bertie he once was. Just as well, you may say, the perishing little pill! All the same, a part of me will regret the passing. By the end of it all we'll none of us be the same.

I know now what I am going to do. I am going to resign my lectureship at Wessex and enlist in the South Morsetshire. Chaos is coming; rivers of blood will flow, and I feel it is better to be in the midst of chaos than on the edge of it looking down into the black hole....

I must stop this.

It was St. Anselm himself who said: *credo ut intelligam,* "I believe in order than I may understand." I wish I did not believe. I wish to God I did not understand.

CHAPTER 10

*or we wrestle not against flesh and blood, but against princi-
palities, against powers, against the rulers of the darkness of this
world, against spiritual wickedness in high places.*

"My friends, those words of St. Paul, the patron saint of our church,
are more relevant here today, now, than at any time. We in Morchester
are facing a crisis, no less than a full assault by the Devil. The Antichrist
is abroad and the end times are approaching. And yet so many of our
brothers and sisters in Christ are sleepwalking towards disaster. Why?
Because they have not been truly baptised in the spirit; because they
have not been washed in the blood of the lamb; because they have not
been born again in the cross of Christ. And when the rapture comes
they will not be gathered up into the arms of Jesus. And they will say:
'Lord, we did not know.' And the Lord Christ will say: 'how was it that
these my brothers and sisters knew but you did not? Did you truly listen
to my Word and believe it? Were your churches living churches, or were
they whited sepulchres of dead traditions? Did you praise the Lord with
a joyful noise?' And they will look dismayed and a great wind will come
to sweep them into the endless corridors and caverns of Hell where the
fire burns endlessly but there is no light and the stench of scorched flesh
is everywhere, and the cries of the condemned dead eternally echo. My
friends, the hands of the Devil are on this town and his chosen instruments are a television crew who are searching out a blasphemous book,
not knowing what damnation is awaiting them, and worse—worse
still!—the representatives of God's Church who have let these people
in. I am going to ask you to stand with me in protest against the Devil
and his Book that you may be numbered with me among the faithful
and take your place among God's chosen ones."
For we wrestle not against flesh and blood, but against principalities,

against powers, against the rulers of the darkness of this world, against spiritual wickedness in high places.

Marie, from her vantage point in the church choir, was able to observe the reaction to her husband's sermon. She saw the moist, obedient look on the faces of the women and the indignantly heroic look on the faces of the men, and she hated them. There was something about Gary's power that made her sick. In the women there was always something sexual about their subservience: it was particularly evident in the young mothers. Then there was the way her husband pushed his passion beyond the limits of his real beliefs, so she thought. Then there was the fatuous glow of self-approval she saw in his face. He looked like a child gorging himself on a cake he has baked himself. And she knew that at the end of the day he would come to claim his reward on her body, fondly believing that she had been as enchanted as the dewy and makeup-less young mothers.

There was one face at the back of the congregation that she did not recognise and that seemed out of place. It stared stonily, while the rest of the congregation melted. A pair of fierce pale blue eyes stared out from beneath heavy white brows like an overhang of icicles on an ancient guttering. The old face with its shock of white hair was utterly uncompromising. It seemed faintly familiar.

Then it was gone. As the congregation rose to sing the next hymn, "Whatever shall we do, O Lord?"—with guitar and tambourine accompaniment—the face disappeared; and a few seconds later Marie saw the double doors at the back of the church swing, suggesting a brisk exit.

When Eastwood had seen out his worshippers and had coffee with them in the church hall and patted their babies and shared a few heartily innocuous jokes with his older parishioners and had a word with his church wardens about the collection, he retired for a brief while to the vestry, where a quiet moment of reflection and a half-bottle of whisky awaited him. There would be supper for him at home, prepared by Marie, but that could wait. His spirit, just like, everyone else's, needed its solitude.

In the drawer where he kept the half-finished manuscript of a book he was writing, called *Christ of the Concrete Jungle: Evangelism in the End Times*, was the half-bottle of Bell's of which he occasionally made use. He would allow himself an inch or so in his glass, no more. Officially, he abstained from drink altogether. He was reaching for the bottle in the drawer when he noticed that a folded sheet of white paper had been placed under it. He took it out and opened it. At the top was an embossed crest: that of a winged skull within a coronet. On the paper were scrawled the words.

I am on the tower. E. C.

Eastwood put the bottle back in the drawer and the paper in his pocket and left the vestry. He walked through the darkened church, his feet making no sound. Having made St. Paul's an evangelical haven, Eastwood had stripped out the pews and put down cheap carpet and stackable chairs, much to the indignation of the few die-hard ritualists who had once haunted St. Paul's. But all protest had been swept aside by the tide of ecstatic mums and dads with their children who came flooding into his church from the new housing estates around Morchester, to speak in tongues and sing endless choruses of "Shine, Jesus! Shine!" As a result, untenanted and without the speakers blaring, St. Paul's had curiously dead acoustics. It felt like the seminar room of a modern university, or a boardroom in a city tower block. Deadness was that quality which Eastwood often attributed to the Dean's kind of churchmanship, but it was present here. The irony escaped him.

Eastwood opened the little gothic doorway in the southwest corner of the church and began to climb the wooden staircase of the bell tower. This was a part of the church which had not been reconditioned; it still felt dusty and old.

A flight of spiral stone steps took him from the belfry to the roof of the tower where E.C would be waiting. Eastwood knew whom he would be meeting and did not like it.

By the time he reached the roof the sun was down. At one corner of the tower, looking out over the crenelated parapet at the city, stood a white-haired man, his back to him. He was gazing eastward, towards the dark crouching shape of the cathedral.

"Hi, Everard," said Eastwood.

The man turned to face him. "Sir Everard to you, little man," he said. The wild white hair and eyebrows gave his face a curious luminosity.

"I saw you in the congregation."

"I was there for a brief while to hear your sermon. Then, when your so-called congregation started to sing one of their appalling dirges, I had to leave. At least at the cathedral they make some effort to produce proper music."

"It is a matter of taste."

"It is indeed, and some people have bad taste, and some have good taste, and some, it would appear, have no taste at all and think that Palestrina is a kind of hair restorer. However, we are not met here to discuss the niceties of polyphony."

"What did you want, Sir Everard?"

"You're very abrupt this evening. Not your usual loquacious self. No, I wanted to commend your sermon. Very effective, especially if you do get your troops out against this ghastly television farrago about the book. If you manage to stop it altogether, then you will have achieved something worthwhile."

"That book is blasphemous. It must be destroyed."

"Perhaps it ought to be destroyed rather than fall into the wrong hands, but, above all, it must not be found. That is your job. You have to stop this ridiculous search. Only you and I seem to see the appalling damage it is inflicting. I mean, look at these disgusting murders."

"What! You think, they're connected?"

"Well, of course they're connected, you fool. I would have thought you of all people with your absurdly simplistic spirituality would have grasped that."

"But the victims—"

"The victims are irrelevant. They're just drabs, slags, pieces of meat in miniskirts. Their lives are not worth a note of my music, but they are part of the psychic disturbance over this book, and it must stop. And while we're about it, I want the ring."

"What are you talking about?"

"Don't play silly buggers with me, Eastwood. None of your arsehole antics here. I told you how to get hold of the ring, and you and your poxy church have been well paid for it. Now, I want it, please. It's a part of my inheritance."

"Why should I give you the ring? I risked a hell of a lot to get it, you know."

"Why should you give me that ring? Well, firstly because I paid you good money to get it. Secondly, because it is mine by right of inheritance, but you wouldn't understand that. Thirdly, because in the hands of a spiritual infant like you it could be bloody dangerous. Do I make myself clear?"

"How dare you talk to me like that!"

Sir Everard laughed. "Come here, Eastwood. Come! Come! I'm not going to do you any harm. I'm far too old and far too wise to do any such thing. Come to the battlements and look down with me. Now, what do you see?" Eastwood approached the parapet, and Sir Everard, who was nine inches taller than him, gently put his hand behind his head and bent Eastwood's gaze downwards. "Tell me what you see."

"What is all this?" Eastwood said irritably. His evangelical status had given him a natural liking for instructing others and a hatred of the reverse.

"Don't struggle with me, boy. Look!
See what a mass of gems the city wears
upon her broad live bosom! Row on row
Rubies and emeralds and amethysts glow.

"Look at the snakes of light swimming in her arteries, white this way, red the other. Increasingly you will become their Lord; you will dominate, not that dead cathedral over there. You will lead them in paths of righteousness to glory. Just two or three more steps and you are there. You can stop the traffic, set it in motion again, and have them singing to your tune. Think of it. You can almost do it now. Look!"

Eastwood looked; and saw, or thought he saw, the lines of traffic in St. Anselm's Street come to a halt. The cars began to hoot in protest, then something in his mind let go and the cars began to move again, white headlights approaching, red taillights retreating. He watched in fascination as the city began to look more and more like a great body stretched out before him, luminescent blood coursing through its veins.

"You see! It's all yours, Eastwood. Every dark path of its thoughts. Are you going to give me my ring?"

Eastwood tore his gaze away from the spectacle below. The action made him dizzy.

"Get out of my church, Cutbirth," he said. "Go away and never come back. I don't want you near the place again. Forget the ring. I got it. It's mine!"

Sir Everard stepped back from the parapet and studied Eastwood for a few moments. A kind of smile formed on his lips.

"Well," he said. "You're on your own now. You have been warned."

Eastwood watched Sir Everard as he walked away, opened the little door to the spiral staircase, and disappeared from view. He had hitherto found Sir Everard irascible and hard to deal with: this new mood of coolness troubled him. He turned from him to look again at the city.

Once again he was assailed by the illusion of a great body stretched out before him, breathing and pulsating, but sick. Men and women crept through it like microbes or conqueror worms infecting it with darkness, and he the surgeon ready to cauterise the wounds with a burning knife or squeeze out the diseased matter with a tourniquet. As he looked, he began to be at ease with himself and the path that God had laid before him. Then he remembered that Marie was waiting for him at the vicarage with a Lancashire Hotpot. He must fulfill her destiny too.

With every passing day the mystery of THE BOKE OF THE DIVILL deepens. In the course of my researches I have discovered a little known manuscript by the eccentric 17th-century antiquarian John Aubrey. It appears that THE BOKE OF THE DIVILL is not a myth. It was known about in the 1680s, having fallen into the hands of one Jeremiah Staveley, Canon of Morchester Cathedral. But it doesn't stop there. I have been able to ascertain—

"Blasphemy!"

"What the fuck!"

"Excuse me, would you mind not using that language? In case you hadn't noticed, there are children present."

"Well, what the hell are they doing here? You brought them, and presumably you made those stupid placards for them as well."

One of them read: MORCHESTER'S YOUNG CHRISTIANS SAY "DOWN WITH THE DEVIL AND ALL HIS WORKS!"

"Is that a 'cut,' Veronica?"

"No! Keep turning! This is great. We can use this footage."

They were filming (with the Dean's permission) on the green in front of the West Door of Morchester Cathedral. Huntley had just begun his piece to camera, which Emma and Veronica had worked on assiduously the night before. The day had dawned fine; they had set up easily; Huntley had been in a relatively benign mood. Then had come the invasion. The director and her crew had all been concentrating so hard on the shot that the protesters had seemed to appear from nowhere. Suddenly they were on them, mostly young mums and their kids, as they termed themselves, led by the Reverend Gary Eastwood and carrying placards that denounced the search for The Book as irreligious. Surrounding them, because Eastwood had alerted them, was a thin cordon of local reporters and photographers. Rapidly advancing in support was another film crew from the local television news.

"Are you responsible for this farce?" Huntley said, addressing Eastwood. Veronica, who could see the dispute might not go all their way, interposed herself and said: "All right, Dave, let me handle this."

"How many times do I have to tell you; it's David, not Dave."

"Oh, for Christ's sake, Dave!"

Eastwood, not inexperienced in such situations, stepped forward and addressed Huntley in his most unctuously emollient manner. He smiled as he turned his face so that the television news crew would give his features their best coverage.

"Hi, I'm Gary Eastwood, and I'm the rector of St. Paul's in Morchester and these are some concerned folk from my church. Can I say something here? Now, I'm not interested in causing trouble—"

"You could have fooled me."

"No, please! It's Dave Huntley, isn't it? Professor Dave Huntley? Look, let me say I'm a big admirer of your historical telly programmes, but I've got to ask in all honesty: what are you doing here, Dave? I'm just really disappointed that you should have sold out to some cheap sensationalist programme, trying to unearth this blasphemous book. Let me tell you something, I know a little about the ways of the Evil One; after all, it's my job. And let me tell you something; you're playing right into his hands."

"In what way?"

"I'm sorry, Dave?"

"And it's David to you, or perhaps Professor Huntley, actually. No; I mean I want you to tell me precisely how I am, as you put it, 'playing into the hands of the Evil One?'"

"Look, this is all very intellectually clever, no doubt, but unless you're prepared to listen I can't explain it to you."

"I'm listening, Gary."

"Look ... You see these folk here. They're just ordinary mums and kids. They haven't got college degrees or anything like that. They don't pretend to be incredibly intellectual or anything; they're just real, down-to-earth people. All they want to do is to lead a decent, godly life without having that decency threatened."

"And how precisely am I threatening it?"

"You don't get it, do you? You really do not get it."

"No, and I'm afraid I won't, unless your arguments become a little more coherent."

"That's great," said Veronica. "That's wonderful. Can we cut there? Have you got all that, Mick?"

"Got it."

"Right, now what I'd like is for each of you, Dave and—Gary, is it?—

to do a piece individually to camera. It needn't be very long: just a sort of overview of your respective positions."

"Veronica, darling, this is not some kind of circus."

"Right," said Eastwood. "As a matter of fact I agree with Dave here actually. We're not puppets, you know, performing for your squalid entertainment. There's more to us than just media fodder, you know."

"Excuse me," said Veronica. "I don't know who you are exactly, Gary, but I am offering you a platform for your somewhat squalid fundamentalist opinions. The least I could expect might be a little gratitude. Instead you throw it all back in my face."

"You can hardly expect him to be grateful to you for exploiting him, Veronica."

"Dave! Will you, for once in your life, shut the fuck up, you smug, self-satisfied, dreary little academic! Christ!"

"I'll thank you not to take my Lord's name in vain."

"Oh, and you bugger off too, you sanctimonious creep!"

It was at this moment that another figure made itself manifest, the large and strangely dignified one of Phyllis Tancock, the Dean's wife.

"What on earth is going on here? Do you realise that practically everyone in the close can hear you? When my husband the Dean gave you permission to film on the green, he did not licence shouting and profanity. This is not a bear garden! And you," she said, turning on Eastwood. "My husband has told me about you. You ought to be ashamed of yourself, dragging these women and their children about just to gratify your lust for publicity. Go home at once! My husband will see you in the morning."

"Look, Phyllis—"

"Phyllis? It's Mrs. Dean to you, Eastwood. I speak for my husband here. I'm not a nobody, you know. My father was Suffragan Bishop of Tunbridge Wells. Go along with you!"

And that, rather surprisingly, was that. The film crew and the protesters had dispersed. Phyllis was left surprised at herself and pleased, though her pleasure was diminished when she heard Veronica say to her sound man: "Did you get all that...? Great stuff!"

He liked to set out shortly after midnight, soon after his wife had fallen asleep. Hers was a deep sleep; it always had been, and, insofar as he loved anything, he loved her for it. It was a strange business, love. When he was really quite young he had succeeded in grasping intellectually what people meant by the word "love", and he managed very convincingly to simulate its effects, but from the beginning he had recognised it as an illusion. It was a pleasing invention, no more, like all the pretty poetry and music it spawned. The only reality was himself and the only God was himself. This must be the case for all human beings, naturally, but other human beings did not concern him, naturally also.

Once he was out of the bedroom and could move freely without the possibility of waking her, he felt the first rush of exhilaration. Now that was real, and no illusion. It was as if the blood flowed faster in his veins, and perhaps it did, because sometimes he could hear his heart beating. He went downstairs, opened the door quietly, stepped outside and shut it silently behind him. It was then that the second rush of adrenaline came, and it was so powerful that it almost lifted him into the air. With one more mental effort he could have taken off and flown over the city under the stars. One day, perhaps, he would. Almost he believed it; almost, but not quite because deep down he was a very hard-headed, rational sort of person.

As usual, he had parked his car some distance from his house. Women, in his view, had an almost psychic faculty of recognition. His wife would notice, even in her sleep, the sound of their vehicle starting up. He quickly ascertained that nobody was about before getting into his car and turning on the ignition. Dawkins Lane was his destination.

He remembered how it had all begun, but not why. The midnight walks around Morchester had at first been little more than acts of observation, surveying a city in its night-time mode, when all the cracks and fissures in the facade of its gentility opened up and the pus oozed out. He had watched the drunks, the vagrants, and the prostitutes with dispassionate interest. They were creatures not like him: they were driven by squalid needs and desires; they were puppets manipulated by monstrous idiots with huge doltish faces. He could almost see those mooncalf visages gloating over the city. He was no puppet; he was to be the puppet master; and it began with an act of almost-altruism.

Almost, but not quite, because he despised altruism, though he had a kind of respect for justice, or rather its exercise. He was watching, from the other side of the street, the entrance of a drinking club or bar called, for some idiotically humorous reason, The Archbishop's Well. He saw a couple coming out, he overweight in a Morchester Rovers strip and long, baggy shorts, she in a tight, thigh-length Lycra skirt and a turquoise bomber jacket. They staggered along the street, giggling, and he decided to follow them. As they rounded a corner, the woman stumbled against the man. One of her ridiculous high heels had given way. The man objected to this, and a quarrel began. The man started to hit the woman. She screeched. Nobody was about but he, the observer, and he was invisible to them in their rage.

The man by this time had knocked the woman down, so the observer crossed the road, seized him from behind, threw him down into the street and kicked him in the stomach. The man vomited; the woman was struggling to her feet and screaming at him, the observer, her saviour; so he aimed a punch at her throat, just below the jaw, and she went down again, lying in the gutter while he retired to a safe distance.

He watched the couple slowly recover their senses and get to their feet. To judge from their admittedly rather incoherent talk, they seemed to be quite unaware that a third party had contributed to their downfall. That was only just, he thought, as he left the scene silently.

A few nights later, he found an old male vagrant sleeping on a park bench in Morchester Park. He put one knee into the pit of the old man's stomach to incapacitate him and then put a plastic bag over his head until the thing stopped breathing and struggling. Finally, having ascertained that it was dead, he went on his way, disposing of the bag in a nearby waste bin thoughtfully provided by the authorities. That action had given him a quiet, proprietary sense of achievement, but he knew it to be a mere prelude. Women were to be his quarry.

He had looked in vain over the next few days in the local papers for some report of the vagrant's death. Its absence had mildly disappointed him at first, but then he felt pride. It was a death so insignificant that it had gone unrecorded. Presumably the body had been found, but no one had bothered to consider the possibility of murder. A life had simply vanished: only he, the observer, remained to contemplate a secret and perfect assassination.

Then had come the two girls. Of course, there was no escaping their being reported murdered, but even here he had been ingenious. Most commonplace serial killers—and he was neither commonplace nor, in his own estimation, a serial killer—usually betrayed themselves by repeating their M.O., as he had heard it called on the media; modus operandi, method of work. But he had deliberately varied his method. There was no obvious connection between the two, and the third would be different again.

Dawkins Lane was in the worst part of Morchester, in one of its oldest districts but on the very edge of the sprawling housing estates which had sprung up in the early 1950s to accommodate workers at the Morchester shoe factories. For some decades prostitutes had haunted its narrow streets, whose more permanent inhabitants had complained, but without result. All that, thought the Observer, was about to change. He was a man who believed, in a very abstract way, in doing good.

A light rain had begun to make pavements glisten under the yellow glare of the infrequent streetlights. The girls usually dwelt under these lights in order to be seen by the punters; now, in the rain, they trod on little golden shards of reflecting water.

He moved the car slowly to indicate that it meant business. Several women sidled towards it, anxious to be out of the rain, but the face within the car was obscure. The girl was eventually chosen because of her isolation from the others. The face and figure were barely examined; the door of the car was opened, but no word was spoken. When she climbed in she was smoking a cigarette.

"Would you mind? I don't like smoking in my car."

"All right, you're the boss," she said, throwing the cigarette out into the rain. "Where do you want to go?"

"We're going somewhere special."

"Right. If it's going to be a long time, you'll have to pay extra."

A sum was agreed upon. For a while they drove out of the city in silence.

"Here, where are we going?"

"You'll see."

"Mind if I take my shoes off? My feet are killing me."

"Go ahead."

"I bought them only yesterday. The shoes. I tried them on. Seemed all right. I liked the straps. I like them strappy shoes. I was buying them with my friend Tracey. She bought some too. We bought them in that new place, you know, Carter's, up the Mall. So we put them on and walked up the park. Then I said to Trace: 'I don't know about you, Trace, but my feet are killing me.' And she goes: 'So are mine.' So I said: 'Let's sit down.' So we sat down. And I said: 'It's nice to get the weight off.' And Trace said: 'You can say that again. I've been carrying this around all day.' So she took this thing like a book out of her bag. And I said: 'What's that?' And she said: 'It's a stamp album.' So I goes: 'What's that about, then?' And Trace goes: 'It's for putting stamps in that you collect.' So I go: 'I know that, you dozy muppet! I mean, what you want to go lugging a stamp album around for?' And Trace says: 'It's not mine; it's my boyfriend's. He collects stamps.' 'Well,' I said, 'if he's got a stamp album he would collect them, wouldn't he? So what are you doing with it, then?' And Trace said: 'I got fed up. With Darren'—that's her boyfriend—'it's stamps this, stamps that the whole time. I reckon he's not interested in me any more. It's just stamp, stamp, stamp day and night. So I took his album while he was down the greengrocers getting a jar of instant. We'd run out, see. I reckon it might be worth a bit. Some of these stamp collections are worth millions.' Do you know anything about stamps?"

"No," he said. The rain was coming down heavily, almost blinding the windscreen. The wipers waved frantically, giving off tiny shrieks as their rubber pads chafed against the glass.

""Anyway,' I said, 'you can't do that, Trace. Darren's all right. He may collect stamps and that, but he's not bad. There are worse things to collect than stamps, I can tell you, and I should know. I knew a bloke once who collected pickle jars, and it wasn't just the pickle jars, neither; it was the things he kept in them.' So anyway we were gabbing like that and then this bloke comes up, big bloke, like, official. And he says: 'You can't sit there on that bench.' And I goes: 'Why not? It's a free country.' And he says: 'Don't you know somebody died on that bench only a week ago.' I said: 'No; who was he, anyway?' And he goes: 'I don't know, do I? Just show a little respect, that's all I'm saying. Just show a little respect.' He says: 'How would you like it, if you'd died on that bench.' I says: 'Well, I didn't, so I'm not bothered.' And then Trace pipes up—that girl kills me sometimes—and she goes: 'Excuse me, mister, you don't collect stamps, by any chance?' Laugh? I nearly died—"

"Shut the fuck up."

"All right! No need to be rude. Are we nearly there yet?"

"Oh, yes. Nearly there."

"Well, thank God for that. My feet are killing me." She looked at him. "It's like weird. I can't see your face properly. My eyes must have gone funny. Have you got a name?"

"Jeremiah."

"Funny sort of name."

"And yours?"

"Sharon."

The man laughed.

"What's so funny about that?"

The rain stopped. He let the wipers squeak on for a while, then switched them off. They turned into a drive. About halfway up he turned the car off the gravel and onto a green verge.

"Here we are."

"Where are we going?"

"For a little walk. Out of the car!"

"All right! I'm coming."

When they were out of the car he switched on a torch and indicated a path through some shrubbery.

"Where the hell are we?"

"You're going to find out."

They were surrounded by high hedges that glistened in the sudden illumination of torch light and dripped from the recent rain. He led the way, occasionally looking behind to see that she was keeping up. She had taken off her shoes and was feeling the wet grass under her feet, not an unpleasant sensation. He was leading her down paths flanked on either side by high yew hedges. The smell of indeterminate greenness was heavy in the air. Occasionally he would turn an unexpected corner and then he would take her wrist to guide her through.

"Fuck me, what's that?"

His torch had suddenly illumined a grey, grinning face surmounted by curling grey hair through which two stumpy horns emerged. The neck and armless torso on which the head rested were muscular, but equally corpselike in hue.

"It's a faun."

"No it's not, it's a fucking stone statue. What's this all about?"

"We're nearly there."

"Where?"

"Here! This is the place."

"What place?"

"We are in the centre of the maze at Bartonstone Hall."

He shone the torch round an ellipse formed by high yew hedges. The grass at their feet was clipped and there was a curved stone bench at one apex of the oval.

"Is this where you want to do it?"

"This is where I want to do it."

"Well, thank Christ for that!"

She sat down on the stone bench and began idly to pick fragments of grass off her bare feet. Above them the sky had cleared and a few stars were out, but no moon. He shone the torch at her. She shaded her eyes against the glare.

"Let's see you for a change," she said.

"That's not the deal."

"All right. You're the boss."

He switched off the torch and for a few moments she saw nothing before her eyes accustomed themselves to the absence of its glare. By this time she was conscious that he was behind her breathing hard. A leather-clad arm encircled her neck and the torch was on again, this time so close to her face that she could feel the warmth from the bulb. Then something sharp entered her lower abdomen and tore its way up inside her. The pain she knew was terrible, but more terrible still was the un-healable havoc that was being created within. Her last sensations were of an explosion of blood somewhere in the middle of herself, an internal ocean of agony into which she sank with barely a gasp.

From his point of view it had been an exquisite moment. Her illuminated face had revealed every twitching moment of pain and horror until a kind of shutter had fallen over the staring eyes and they were no longer conscious. It had been good and deeply fulfilling, but all too brief. He wished now he had brought his digital camera with him, to record the incident, to make it everlastingly real to him. Perhaps he would, next time, but then, photographs have a habit of being found—and that would have been the end of his career.

As these thoughts came to him, slowly, dreamily, in the hour of his triumph, something in the outer reaches of his brain told him that he might not be alone with his prey. There was a rustling behind him, then he felt a sickening thud on the back of his neck.

Consciousness came to him in slow waves of pain. There was of course the ache of his bludgeoned skull; then there was the fact that he appeared to be lying in the wet grass on his stomach with his legs securely tied together at the ankles and his arms trussed up behind him. He tried to roll over onto his back, but a weight on his legs prevented him, and something dreadful was being done to his hands.

It was the worst of his agonies, but it was a long time before he could locate it. Besides the weight, there was some sort of grunting and snuffling going on behind him. Besides the pain, something warm and living was close to his hands. He felt tepid spittle on his palms. At last he understood: something was trying to bite off one of his fingers—the third finger of his left hand, to be precise. It was then that he began to scream.

He screamed and struggled long and hard, but the more he struggled the more the weight bore down on his back, and the more he screamed the more the teeth of the beast mangled his finger until, with a hideous sinew-tugging wrench, the thing came off.

His screams had blotted out all other sound, but by now he had become hoarse and his cries of pain had diminished to a sobbing whimper. Still the weight was on his back, and throughout the confusion he heard the identifiable sound of a man gasping to catch his breath. It was that sound which made him start to scream again, but he was stopped.

His head was jerked back, and a balled-up handkerchief was stuffed into his mouth; then another handkerchief was tied across his mouth to stop the first handkerchief escaping. His gorge rose, and he wanted to vomit, but he could not. There was a pause, with more heavy breathing from behind him. Finally, a heavy kick from a leather shoe rolled him over onto his back, and he could see again.

He lay facing the stone bench upon which rested two old-fashioned lanterns with lighted candles inside them. To his right lay the body of the murdered prostitute, Sharon, in a similar position to his. Above and in front of him stood a man in a greenish tweed three-piece suit spattered with blood. He had a wild shock of white hair, and the eyes beneath the bushy white brows were impenetrable. In one hand he held the severed finger.

"Hello, Eastwood," said Sir Everard Cutbirth.

Eastwood tried to make a sound but the gag prevented him. He simply had to watch while Sir Everard pulled something off the finger, then, with a lazy, careless flick, cast the mangled appendage into the nearby darkness of the yew hedge.

"I tried to pull the ring off but it wouldn't come, and I had somehow forgotten to bring a knife with me, so I had to remove your finger by mastication. Luckily I had on my spare set of artificial gnashers." He took out his false teeth to show Eastwood, then returned them to his mouth. "You see, I told you you should have given me the ring. It is now returned to its rightful owner." And he put it in his waistcoat pocket.

Then he sat down on the stone bench between the two lanterns and contemplated Eastwood. His expression was mild, even a little concerned.

"I was following you tonight from the start. You're not hard to read. I had no difficulty in manipulating you from the very beginning, and your obvious dislike of me was a positive advantage. It put you off your guard, you see, when you found that I was not even attempting to charm you. You have always been a psychopath, but with all psychopaths there is a trigger that sets them on the path to becoming a banker, a politician, or a killer. With you it was the ring. You thought it gave you some sort of immunity, didn't you? Typical magical thinking of the low-grade psychopath. And the murder of prostitutes? With its spurious moral justifications? It's so very old hat: been done to death, you might say. I followed you because I was curious about your psychology, only to discover it was very commonplace. However, the fact that you are a minister of the church may lend your case a certain spurious psychological depth. Imagine my outrage when you turned into my drive and took your to-be-disembowelled drab into my maze in my park. Only conceive of my disgust, as that dreary old maid Jane Austen might have said. But no; you haven't the imagination to conceive of anything but your own egotistical gratifications. Well, now you are going to have the inestimable privilege of experiencing the torments of eternal damnation, even while you still live, thanks to my imagination. This may take some time. I am an old man now, and, though robust for my age, I find lifting heavy weights a problem, and I have to watch out for my dicky back."

Using his feet, he rolled Sharon's corpse towards Eastwood until she lay beside him, exactly parallel with his own recumbent body. Then, kneeling down on the grass and taking a length of rope from his pocket, he ran it under Eastwood's back. After several abortive attempts and with much swearing, he managed to roll Sharon's corpse onto Eastwood's body so that her dead face touched his. This position he secured by tying the rope he had slipped under Eastwood around both bodies, so that they were bound securely together in a parcel, the one on top of the other, the dead on the living, a two-backed beast.

When he had finished his work he lifted himself up, brushing damp grass from his knees. He took a lantern from the stone bench and held it over their two heads to look into Eastwood's eyes. As he had hoped, they were full of the terror of ultimate despair and the beginnings of madness. It was some time before he could tear himself away from the spectacle.

Finally it was time to go. The stars were fading, giving way to a still grey dawn. An early bird began to sing in one of the trees of his park. Sir Everard blew out the candles in both his lanterns and made his way to the exit of the maze's epicentre.

Before leaving he turned back for a last look at his strangely godlike achievement and murmured something. Though he spoke softly, Eastwood's sensitised ears heard every word, and the phrase lodged like a mantra in his brain.

"Joined through all eternity in one long kiss!"

CHAPTER 11

I'm very sorry, Veronica," the Dean was saying, "I'm going to have to ask you to stop filming. I can't have any more disturbances like yesterday's."

"Who put you up to this? That wife of yours?"

The Dean was shocked. Even today, in the twenty-first century, this sort of blatant questioning of his position, these personal references—and in the Deanery too!—should not occur. He had summoned Veronica that morning for what he hoped would be a dignified if distressing interview. It was not going to plan, but then, life seldom did. He walked to the window of the sitting room where, rather than his study, he had chosen to receive her and stared out onto the close, the great grey cathedral and the rooks in their immemorial elms. The view consoled him a little: some things did not change.

"Suppose I were to tell you that we actually may be on the verge of finding this book for you. This very valuable book."

"No! I really am very sorry, Veronica, but I am adamant." The Dean was vaguely conscious of sounding pompous, but he didn't mind that much. Phyllis had said to him in bed that morning, "You must be firm, Geoffrey!" And he was being firm.

"Well, I'm sorry, Geoff," said Veronica, asserting her ascendancy by means of this abbreviation, "but we can proceed without you, and we will. My company has very influential backing. This isn't going out on some cheap media channel. The BBC has expressed interest. It could be difficult for you when it is shown."

"I could prevent it."

"Get real, matey."

"Then, as the Duke of Wellington might have said, 'publish and be damned'!" The Dean was proud of that. He felt stronger by the minute.

"I don't think you would like it generally known that the book was stolen from under your very nose. From your study, in fact."

"What!"

Veronica leaned back with the satisfaction of a bridge player who has just played an ace and knows that her opponent has no trumps left in his hand. Quietly, she explained what Emma had told her the previous evening.

The Dean listened with mounting agitation and embarrassment. Finally he said, "But you have no absolute proof that Sir Everard stole the book from the Bishop's Box."

"No, but it's a fair conjecture. And we soon will have proof."

"How?"

"There is no need for you to know, Dean," said Veronica. The truth was she didn't know, either. "So do we continue to have your blessing, Dr. Tancock?" The Dean was too flustered to notice the rather coarse vein of mockery in Veronica's tone. Absolute victory makes vulgarians of us all.

"Yes, yes. I suppose so. Yes, yes."

"Right. Thanks. I'll see myself out." As Veronica was opening the study door to leave she encountered Phyllis Tancock in the doorway with a tray of coffee and comestibles.

"So sorry," said Veronica, "can't stay for coffee; I've got to be in a meeting." As she slipped past the Dean's wife, she was already taking her mobile from a pocket and dialling a number.

"Hello? Emma, love? My room at the White Lion, fifteen minutes. And try to bring this Valentine bloke with you. He might be useful. I'll get hold of Dave Huntley. Ciao."

The Dean and his wife heard the door of the Deanery slam.

Phyllis set down her tray. "I made some of my rock cakes," she said. "I thought they might soften the blow."

"Unlikely," said the Dean, who had experience of his wife's rock cakes. "Highly unlikely."

"You did tell her?"

"Oh, yes."

"And—?"

"They're going to carry on."

"But you did ban them from filming or shooting, or whatever it is they do on cathedral premises ... Geoffrey...? Oh, really!" She turned from him and trotted indignantly towards the door. The Dean, enraged, followed, seized her by the wrist and hurled her onto an old sofa by the window.

They stared at each other, panting, then Phyllis said: "Geoffrey, if you are going to rape me again, at least let me take off my shoes. My feet are killing me."

The Dean looked at his wife in amazement. A slight smile and something in the eyes betrayed that she was making fun of him. The laughing girl that he had married had not altogether vanished. Slowly, reverently, he knelt down and began to untie the laces of her sensible brogues.

"I'm bored," said Davies to Aston as they came out of choir practice.

Aston knew the reason. Once more, he and not Davies had been given the treble solo in the anthem for the Sunday matins. Aston had not wanted it, but he understood vaguely why he had been chosen. Music came to him as naturally as song to a nightingale. He felt he should console Davies for his loss.

As they passed the Deanery they saw the Dean closing the curtains of his sitting room window.

"What's he doing?"

"Something disgusting," said Davies. "Did you see the way he looks at you at evensong?"

"No. I've got other things on my mind."

"Oh, yeah! All old men that age are revolting. Matheson's another."

"Is that bicycle of yours still working?"

"'Course! Why?"

"You said you were bored, Davies. I'm going to take you on an adventure."

When Veronica returned to the White Lion, she found Emma and Valentine waiting for her in her room. The tall elderly man who rose to greet her and studied her with an intense, humorous gaze was disconcerting. Veronica liked to place her fellow human beings in safe, impermeable categories, and she could tell at once that this man belonged to none of them. What did he want out of all this? That was the question she needed to ask, but couldn't.

"So what do we do?" she said after the polite preliminaries had been dispensed with. "We believe this man Cutbirth has stolen this book, which, according to him, belongs to his family. I'm having a bit of an existential crisis here. I'm not sure what I'm doing, why we're looking for this book in the first place, what we do if we find it except make a lot of money for the cathedral, who will probably sell it to pay for their stupid roof. I mean, will this make good television, or what?"

As soon as she had spoken she regretted it. She had spoken her mind, aired her doubts, made herself vulnerable. Interestingly, neither Emma nor Valentine seemed interested in taking advantage of her confession: they were merely letting silence fill the room. It was curiously soothing.

Finally Valentine spoke, and it was as if he were talking to himself. "'If the fool would persist in his folly he would become wise.' The can of worms has been opened. You have set out to find the book. You have raised the sleeping giant. If you halt the pursuit now, the consequences could be far more dangerous."

"Dangerous? What do you mean, dangerous?"

Valentine merely looked at her.

"You think that … things have happened because we have been looking for this book? That's rubbish."

"That is not quite what I said."

"All right, but what do we do?"

"We go and see Cutbirth," said Emma.

"When?"

"Tonight."

"Do we bring a camera crew?"

"Not to doorstep him," said Valentine.

"And—?"

"We see what we shall see."

At that moment Huntley burst into the room.

"Look here, Veronica: I thought I'd made it clear that I was to be consulted on any developments that occurred."

"That's why I asked you here, Dave darling," said Veronica.

But Huntley paid no attention; he was staring at Valentine. "Good God, Nightfall, what the hell are you doing here?"

"Hello, David," said Valentine. He was smiling, but otherwise motionless.

"Excuse me," said Veronica, "what's going on here?" Emma gave her the details in her ear, sotto voce, at the end of which she said to Emma, "Why didn't you tell me this before?"

"More importantly," said Huntley, "why wasn't I told?"

"I think I'm beginning to see daylight," said Veronica, "This Valentine, or Nightfall, or whatever his name is, helped Emma out because he knew about Dave Huntley and wanted to get his own back. Now I understand."

"So everything he says could be bollocks because he wants to shaft me because I exposed him as a fraud," said Huntley. "Don't believe a word he says."

"It's not like that, and you didn't expose him as a fraud," said Emma with a fierceness that surprised even her.

"Revenge is a dish best eaten not at all, cold or hot," said Valentine. "It contains poison. That's why it doesn't interest me. If you decide to believe that I am actuated by a desire for revenge, David, you will be wasting a great deal of time, and a great deal of Veronica's time, and, presumably, money. And I'm sure none of us would want to do that."

Veronica looked at Valentine suspiciously. Having little sense of humour herself she was unusually sensitive to the possibilities of mockery. Valentine's expression gave nothing away.

"What I don't understand, Valentine, is why you should want to recover this book."

"Because it's very dangerous."

"You don't seriously believe in all that witchcraft-and-curses stuff, do you?"

"It's dangerous precisely because it's believed to be dangerous. Objects acquire the energy that people across the centuries have bestowed on them, a force field for good or evil. Things have started to happen; we need to neutralise the force field, and a populist historical television programme is as good a neutralising agent as any other."

After staring at Valentine for a while with a rather theatrical expression of contempt, Veronica said, "God, you are a smug, self-righteous creep, aren't you, Valentine? I don't blame Dave for manipulating you out of your job. He may be a louse, but he's not a sanctimonious louse."

Valentine laughed. That annoyed her even more.

Huntley said: "I did not manipulate—"

"Never mind that now," said Veronica. "Tonight we go up and confront this Sir Everard Cutbirth. You'd better come with us, Valentine. Much as I dislike you, you seem to be the only person who is clued up about this affair."

"I object," said Huntley.

"You have no right to do any such thing, Dave. We go tonight in my car, and the crew can follow in the van and await my instructions. Agreed?"

One of Veronica's strengths was that she never minded being disliked; most of the time she barely noticed the antagonism with which she surrounded herself.

It was a mild early-autumn afternoon. Mists gathered fleetingly in the hollows of the Morsetshire countryside. The soft light endowed the yellowing leaves with a special opulence. It was good bicycling weather, and Davies was enjoying himself, despite the frustration of not knowing where Aston was leading him.

"Where are we going?" he asked for the tenth time as they raced through the picturesque village of Morton Episcopi.

And for the tenth time Aston answered: "You'll see. Just follow me."

Just outside Morton Episcopi Aston turned right, following the signpost to Bartonstone, and they began the slow but arduous climb up Cutberrow Hill. It was a struggle, but cool air and the inexhaustion of youth sustained them. And just as they were beginning to feel the strain, the road levelled and began to dip again as they came over the southern flank of Cutberrow Hill.

Almost at the bottom of the dip stood the entrance to the drive leading to Bartonstone Hall. Without any indication other than a perfunctory hand signal Aston turned left up the drive. Davies abruptly changed direction to follow him, nearly coming off his bike in the process.

"Bloody hell, Aston, you might have warned me!"

Aston turned his head towards Davies briefly, smiling impishly, then, a few yards further on he skidded to a halt.

"We park our bikes here," he said indicating a bush just off the drive. "Behind here where they won't be seen."

"Aren't we trespassing or something?"

"Duh! Yeah! I thought you said you were bored."

Davies said no more in case he offended Aston. Insofar as he could explain anything about his friendship with Aston, he liked the dominance. It gave him reassurance, and the courage occasionally to transgress. Having mentally submitted, he felt permitted to show a little aggression.

"Okay, Aston. So what's the big secret adventure, then?"

Aston noted the artificiality of his friend's bravado and did not even look round, but gestured him to follow.

There was a sort of path running through rhododendron shrubberies and under tall coniferous trees. The grass beneath was damp where the sun had not penetrated, and the air was moist and silent: dark green was the predominant colour. Oppression was faint, but distinctly present.

They came to a long grassy clearing that luxuriated in sunlight. Directly ahead of them was a dark yew hedge, kept and clipped as the surrounding vegetation had not been. In this dark wall of greenery an arch had been carved and a path led inside. Beyond the arch could be seen more walls of clipped yew, rising to a height of some twelve feet, roughly flat-topped but with some shaggy excrescences.

"Welcome to the famous Bartonstone maze."

"Bloody hell, Aston. We're not going in there, are we? We could get lost."

"No, we couldn't. I know it like the back of my hand. My pa used to be head gardener here until he had an argument with that bloody bastard Sir Everard Cutbirth."

Davies as usual was impressed with Aston's aggressive maturity.

"Come on! Let me show you the Mysteries of the Maze. Whoo!" And Aston was back being a child again.

"Whoo!" said Davies to encourage him, and they ran into the maze.

Soon they were walking again. There was something about the Bartonstone maze that discouraged running. The atmosphere between the high hedge walls was close, almost like that of a stuffy room; the heavy, funereal smell of yew seemed to hinder their breath. Aston led the way, occasionally pausing to consult his memory, less confident of his expertise than he had been, but trying hard to disguise it.

"Keep going left," he said, "That's the secret." But one or two left turns had brought them round in a circle. As they became more involved in the dark corridors, sounds from the outer world vanished; the sky above was white, uncrossed by so much as a single bird.

They turned a corner where, in a niche clipped out in the yew, they came face to face with the statue of a grinning faun. Its head and armless torso were set on a plinth decorated in relief with swags of fruit and flowers between bucrania, the carved skulls of cattle, their eyes hollow and dark. The whole was sculpted from a dark grey limestone, which gave it a sepulchral feel.

"Christ," said Davies.

"No. Pan," said Aston, authoritatively but inaccurately. "That's good. I remember it now. That means we're near the centre of the maze."

"So what's in the centre of the maze?"

"Duh! It's the centre of the maze, dummy. We'll have reached it."

"Big deal!"

"You can tell your children about it. That is, if your balls drop and you have any."

"Ha, ha! You can talk, Mr. Head Eunuch of Morchester Choir!"

"Shut it! What's that?"

In the silence that followed, both very distinctly heard a faint whimpering sound. It was hard in this stuffy plethora of leafage to tell from what direction it came.

"Let's get out of here," said Davies.

"No. Come on. It might be a girl or something that's got lost," said Aston, who was acquiring a romantic streak.

They turned right at the limestone faun and came by a series of twists and turns into the centre of the maze. There, as Aston remembered it, was the oval amphitheatre with its grass arena and, at one apex, the curved stone bench with its supports carved in the shape of gryphons. On the grass just in front of the stone bench was a strange object, which looked at first like a giant chrysalis. It seemed to twitch feebly and then emit a sound like the high-pitched whimper that they had heard before. Around it were scattered little fragments of bloodstained cloth.

Horror is all the more terrible for growing slowly and both boys experienced its gradual efflorescence as they began to understand what they were looking at. A man and a woman were tied together facing each other. The woman wore a short leather skirt that was stretched tightly across her buttocks and the legs that emerged from it were fat and very white. She wore a pink fake fur jacket somewhat stained with a dark reddish brown substance and she was motionless.

The man to whom she was tied wore a leather jacket. His mouth was caked with bloody spittle and there were shards of ensanguined linen adhering to it as if, perhaps, he had managed to bite through and expel a gag made from a handkerchief. His lips moved slightly; his breath came in gasps, and the eyes rolled senselessly in their sockets. He did not seem to see them, and perhaps he was barely alive, but something in him still stirred.

His face and figure were those of a young man, but his hair was as white as the moon. For this reason it was some time before the two boys recognised that they were looking at the Reverend Gary Eastwood, rector of St, Paul's, Morchester. His swivelling eyes began to focus on the two boys and he mouthed something that at first they could not hear. Aston tentatively approached to within a few feet of the bodies and could now distinguish what Eastwood, in a high reedy falsetto, was saying. Between gasps of breath, he repeated a phrase:

Praise the Lord! Praise the Lord! Praise the Lord!

Aston studied the body of the woman to which he was tied. There was something about her that he did not understand. She was so utterly motionless. Davies crept up to Aston's side to stare. They had never seen such a thing before.

"Bloody, hell, she's a corpse!"

They knew she was no longer alive because of the loll of the head, the blank stare of the open eyes and the fact that her nose had been bitten off. It fell from Eastwood's dying mouth as he piped again:

Praise the Lord!

In an almost simultaneous movement Aston and Davies turned and began to run. Their exit from the maze was long delayed by the fact that they took several wrong turnings that led to dead ends. Once, to their horror, they found themselves returning to the centre of the maze. Once, in his furious panic, Aston crashed his way right through one of the yew walls, nearly scratching his eyes out in the process. When at last they were out of the maze, they found their bicycles and pedalled furiously down the drive and into the little dip before the ascent of Cutberrow Hill.

It was as they were toiling up the hill that exhaustion overtook their terror. They got off their bicycles and wheeled them slowly to the hill's crest.

"What are we going to do?" asked Davies. "We can't just leave them there. I mean, shouldn't we phone someone?"

"All right. Yeah. I suppose we should."

"Well, go on then. You've got your mobile, haven't you?"

"Oh, right! Thanks a million! And get the call traced back to my mobile? No way."

"Well, what?"

"I've got a better idea. Did you notice as we went through Morton Episcopi, they've still got a working phone box on the village green? The dozy yokels."

"Bloody Hell."

"Yeah, well, that just might come in useful."

They rode on to Morton Episcopi and stopped by the phone box on the green. Davies was told to watch out to see if anyone was observing them while Aston went into the box. Davies could not hear what Aston was saying in the phone booth but he seemed very animated and there was a curious expression on his face. When he had come out, Aston said: "Come on! Quick, or we'll be late for evensong," and they rode off.

In a narrow part of the road just outside Morton Episcopi they were nearly driven off the road by a car with four people in it, closely followed by the film company van that they had seen around Morchester. When they had passed, the two cyclists stopped to recover from the shock.

"What did you say on the phone?" Davies asked.

"I rang the police. I said: 'Something perfectly dreadful has happened in the maze at Bartonstone Hall. I think they're dead. You must come at once!'"

"Bloody hell! Did you know, you sounded exactly like Mrs. Tancock, the Dean's wife, just then?"

"Of course, I did, you dozy prat. That's who I said I was!"

"Bloody Hell!"

Davies's admiration of Aston's genius was immeasurably increased, but so also was his fear of him.

"Aston! Davies! *J'ai failli attendre.* Do you know who said that?"

"You, sir?"

"Don't try to be clever with me, Aston," said Mr. Matheson, the Precentor, as they were robing in the vestry for evensong. "No, boy. It was Louis XIV."

"French, was he, sir?"

"He was indeed, Davies, and do you know what he meant by that remark?"

"Are you going to tell us, sir?"

"I am, Aston. The Sun King, as Louis was popularly known, was speaking to one of his courtiers who had only just arrived in his presence on time. And he was saying—an approximate translation—'I very nearly had to wait.' What do you mean by coming into the cathedral all of a fluster like this? And what are those scratches on your cheek, Aston?"

"Fell over on my bike into a bush, sir. Hurrying to get to evensong on time. Which we did, sir."

"Yes. Well, next time, boy, don't cut it so fine; then you won't run the risk of doing irreparable damage to your famously cherubic complexion, will you, Aston?"

"No, sir. What's 'cherubic', sir?"

The Dean watched this interchange with some amusement. He had always found Matheson's sarcastic pedagogue act something of a cliché and therefore irksome. He managed a conspiratorial wink at Aston, who responded with a look of shock and consternation. The Dean would not try that again. It was time to lead the choir into the cathedral.

It was an unusually small congregation that evening, and his wife was not among them. The Dean noted it, but was not dismayed. As sometimes happens, the very poverty of the attendance gave the service an unusual intensity. The Dean found himself freed from the usual concerns about accessibility and "relevance" that troubled him when a larger group of worshippers were concerned. In one of those sudden and tantalisingly evanescent moments of revelation, he understood that relevance was irrelevant: the moment was itself and required no justification. The archaic words of the Book of Common Prayer were what they were and were one with the echoes and the silence of the cathedral.

And yet, there was something not right, something which troubled the stillness and it did not come for once from the Dean himself. Nervously he glanced over at the Bishop's stall opposite him, but though he detected a few irrational shadows clustered in that area, he saw nothing definite. It was only when the anthem began that he looked again.

Matheson had chosen something comparatively safe and conventional for this evening: Wesley's six-part setting of Psalm 51, "Cast me not away," with no heart-melting treble solos, no polyphonic fireworks. But its beauty was not less potent for being everyday and unadventurous; in fact, the Dean, who was, after all, an unusual man, found it all the more thrilling for that very reason.

> *Cast me not away from thy presence*
> *And take not Thy Holy Spirit from me …*

He looked at the vacant stalls opposite him and saw, to his surprise, that there were three people staring back at him. There, in the Bishop's stall, was Hartley, his red and raddled face twisted into its customary expression of wistful malignity; next to him sat Staveley, aloof, haughty, contemptuous, lost in his own fiery self-absorption. The third figure was new. He sat next to Staveley and furthest away from the Bishop, wearing a modern suit and a dog-collar. The Dean would have recognised him sooner as the Reverend Gary Eastwood had it not been for the unexpected shock of white hair. His eyes met the Dean's: there was a look of utter bewilderment in them, a mute appeal.

Some movement in the choir distracted the Dean from this spectacle.

One boy on his side (*decani*) was swaying almost drunkenly, his usually rubicund complexion dead white. He was staring directly at where Eastwood was in the stalls opposite. It was Aston. Quite suddenly he vomited and collapsed onto the music desk in front of him. There was a commotion and he was led out by Davies and one of the tenors.

The Dean looked again at the three. They were still visible to him, but something about them had changed. Their poses seemed more fixed and rigid; not as if they were dead, but as if an image-maker had frozen them in their characteristic moment. The Dean puzzled over this, until he realised that the change was not so much in them as in him. He accepted them: they were what they were; he no longer wished them away, and therefore they had no power over him.

The anthem came to an end, and he rose to give the prayers. That evening his voice seemed to sing them. It was as if he were an instrument being played. A detached part of himself wondered at it. For a brief moment the thought occurred to him that it was a pity more people were not present to hear his magnificent intonations, but the thought itself was not part of him, and he let it go. And then he came to the words which nearly always suffused his being with a kind of glow:

> *Lighten our darkness we beseech thee, O Lord, and by thy great mercy, defend us from all the perils and dangers of this night, for the love of thine only Son, Our Lord and Saviour, Jesus Christ.*

They answered—*Amen!* And it was as if all eternity were in attendance.

The Dean looked again towards the Bishop's stall and saw nothing more than a faint miasma of greyish smoke hovering where the three clerics had been. It reminded him of the layer of cigarette smoke that used to accumulate in rooms at the end of a long ecclesiastical sherry party. No one smoked indoors in company any longer: those days were happily over.

When the service was ended and the celebrants were back in the vestry the Dean made enquiries after Aston's well-being. It turned out that it was nothing serious—"probably something he ate"—and that in the manner of young adolescent boys he had made a complete and rapid recovery. The Dean might have tried to interrogate Aston himself, but he was prevented by the unexpected intrusion into the vestry of his wife. Mrs. Tancock was in an unusually indignant mood and the Dean wondered if he had done something else to offend her.

"Phyllis," he said. "You weren't at evensong just now."

"Well, of course not! I've just been detained by the police!"

The rest of the vestry fell silent. The Dean turned round to see the whole choir, frozen in various stages of disrobement, staring at him and his wife. Aston was staring particularly hard, his complexion having turned from its previous sepulchral white to a deep carmine red.

"Come outside," said the Dean to his wife, "let us discuss this further, out of the range of little prying ears."

When they had found a place to be alone, under the great Rose Window in the South Transept, Phyllis explained that she had been visited by the police because they had received a call purporting to be from her from a call box in Morton Episcopi. It had told of terrible goings-on up at Bartonstone Manor. She had explained to the police that she couldn't possibly have been at Morton Episcopi as she had only just returned to the Deanery from an important meeting of the Morchester Ladies Sewing Circle. Her presence there could be vouched for by any number of impeccable witnesses.

"The police then told me that whoever had phoned from Morton Episcopi had, as they rather vulgarly put it, 'got my voice down to a T.' Isn't that extraordinary?"

"Most. And are the police going to investigate these dark doings at Bartonstone?"

"Well, I suppose so! I don't know! But look here, Geoffrey, what are we going to do about this? We can't have people rushing about, impersonating me all over Morsetshire."

"Phyllis, dear, I doubt if anyone is going to make a habit of it. What on earth would be the point? I think we shall just have to put it down to one of those strange random occurrences with which we in this mortal existence are occasionally beset."

"Sometimes, you know, Geoffrey," said Mrs. Tancock, "your philosophical approach to life can be really rather offensive."

CHAPTER 12

Mrs. Milsom, the housekeeper, opened the dining room door of Bartonstone to cross the wide entrance hall in the direction of the library. It was invariably her worst moment of the day. She did not particularly like arriving in the mornings to cook and clean for a man who lived alone in a vast and slowly disintegrating mansion; but it was the end of the day that was most dispiriting. There was never a sense that she had achieved anything, because the house was so vast and there was always more to do, and because no gratitude was ever expressed by its owner; there was barely even an acknowledgement of her presence. And yet, if she did not go at that hour to the library to tell Sir Everard that she was leaving and that his supper was ready for him in the microwave, his rage would be unspeakable.

She had experienced enough of his rages to dread them. She particularly remembered the first really horrible one when she had told him that she no longer wished to live in Bartonstone Hall as his housekeeper, but was prepared to continue to come in on a daily basis to cook and clean. His rages were not explosive; they were cold and hard, and articulated with venomous eloquence.

Of course, leaving him might have been an option for a younger, more strong-willed person with better prospects for re-employment, but long service had made her unfitted for any other occupation. He paid her adequately, that was all that could be said.

Of late a new torture had been added to her servitude. By himself Sir Everard had rigged up a system of speakers and amplifiers all over Bartonstone Hall, and at odd moments he would play recordings of his music through them—always his own, never anyone else's—very loudly, so that the whole house seemed to tremble under the assault of his symphonies, quartets and concertos. Mrs. Milsom's musical tastes were not educated; she liked a nice tune, and Sir Everard, though accomplished in many musical skills, was not a specialist in nice tunes. If asked to de-scribe her employer's music Mrs. Milsom would always say, with studied neutrality, that it was "very modern", which of course it wasn't any lon-ger. Hints of unfashionable tonality persistently hovered; but above all it was recognisably his music and no one else's.

As yet on that evening, silence prevailed. The Hall was as clean and tidy as Mrs. Milsom could make it, she had seen to that, but there was no way she could dispel the prevailing atmosphere of decay: the smell of damp, the threadbare upholstery, the paintings that were nearly black from age and neglect. Mrs. Milsom knocked on the library door and, not receiving the usual immediate and peremptory "Come!", she de-cided to enter anyway.

Sir Everard was crouched over the great bureau in the middle of the library. The desk lamp in the shape of a gilded Corinthian column with a parchment shade perched over its capital was the only illumination in the room. Sir Everard continued to ignore his housekeeper, intent on something—a book or document that Mrs. Milsom could not see—that lay open on his desk.

Mrs. Milsom coughed.

Sir Everard leapt up and turned to face her. His face was as white as his hair, and he was shaking with fury.

"The Devil damn you, woman, don't you know how to knock?"

"I did knock, Sir Everard."

"Then you have the common courtesy to wait until you are asked to enter."

"Very sorry, Sir Everard," she said in her dreariest voice. The nearest Mrs. Milsom could get to insolence with him was a certain sullenness of manner. "I'm finished for the day, Sir Everard. Your supper is downstairs in the microwave."

"Well? And what is it?"

"Chicken pie, Sir Everard."

"Chicken pie, eh? Chicken pie!" Sir Everard enunciated the words as if he were going to make something of it. He was immaculately dressed in a pale grey three-piece suit with a white shirt and a thin tie of silvery silk. The ensemble gave him a curiously spectral appearance. Mrs. Mil-som wondered what had become of his usual tweeds. She had looked for them in his dressing room in order to take them to the cleaners, but they were nowhere to be found.

Sir Everard suddenly seemed to lose all interest in Mrs. Milsom and walked across to his music system, the pinpoints of whose coloured lights glittered under one of the bookcases. He took a CD from its jewel case and said, "All right, get out! Unless you want to stay and listen to my third symphony."

Mrs. Milsom fled. She felt a sudden irrational need to make it outside the front door before the music started, and she almost succeeded. The result was that she was somewhat breathless when she emerged and paused for a few moments under the front entrance's grandiose classical portico. Behind her she heard the groan of strings and the crash of symbols that announced the first movement (andante con moto) of Cutbirth's Third Symphony, and the sharp metallic scrape as Sir Everard slid in the bolts of the front door, which he did every evening after she had left. Mrs. Milsom always felt vaguely insulted by his action.

She had descended the steps of the portico and was just embarking on the gravel drive when a car drew up in front of her.

"Excuse me," said Veronica lowering the driver's window. "We're here to see Sir Everard Cutbirth."

"Have you got an appointment?"

"No, but—"

"Sir Everard doesn't see no one. Not even with an appointment."

"And who are you, may I ask?" Veronica asked.

"I'm Mrs. Milsom to you. Sir Everard's housekeeper. And who are you? Something the cat's brought in?"

By this time all four of the car's occupants had emerged. Though some inches shorter than any of them, Mrs. Milsom, unintimidated, scrutinised their faces boldly; fear of Sir Everard had immunised her against all other terrors.

"Perhaps you could let us in, Mrs. Milsom," said Emma.

"Sir Everard bolts the front door at night, and it's no use ringing or knocking because he won't hear, not when he's got his music on. And anyway Sir Everard will probably be eating his chicken pie by now. I made him a chicken pie because I don't live here, see. I live in the next village, Bartonstone Parva, with my husband." There was a pause while everyone digested this largely redundant information.

"Actually, we need to see Sir Everard rather urgently," said Huntley.

"Well, you can't," snapped Mrs. Milsom. Then, having scrutinised him for a while, "Here, don't I know you? Aren't you that man off the telly?"

This was more hopeful. "Well, as a matter of fact—"

"Doing those historical thingys? My husband likes them. I don't.

He's disabled, you see. Oh, yes. I know you. You're one of these media personalities, aren't you?"

Huntley gave her his most engaging smile. "I suppose you might say—"

"Well, you're not very good, are you? No. Some people have it, but you haven't. It's the charisma. You haven't got any. You're not tellygenic, as they say. My husband agrees. He can't stand you. He likes the programmes, mind, but he thinks you're no good.

"Now, you," she said addressing Valentine. "It's Mr. Valentine, isn't it?" He nodded in agreement. "You run that nice shop in Morchester that sells all those books and art and that. Not that I go in there. I don't go in for all that arty business. But they all speak very highly of you. You've got it, you see. You've got the charisma. You could be one of those personalities off the telly if you wanted. A proper one."

"I'm afraid I don't want, Mrs. Milsom," said Valentine. "In fact there is nothing I should like to be less." This answer seemed to give Mrs. Milsom peculiar satisfaction. She nodded several times, as if he had just confirmed her most entrenched prejudice.

"Well, there you are," she said, "That's just the way, isn't it? Just like life. Those that want to be can't, and those that can, don't want to be. It's a vicious circle." Mrs. Milsom set off again down the drive, then stopped. She turned. "Mr. Valentine, if you really want to see that nasty old man, you go round the back and through the metal gate down the basement steps. You'll come in through the scullery into the kitchen. I always leave the door there unlocked, just in case." And, turning again, she trotted away from them into the gathering dusk.

"Do you really think we should be doing all this?" said Huntley.

Veronica studied Huntley with some amusement. There was pleasure to be had from the crushing of his vanity, even by a nobody like Mrs. Milsom. "Of course we should. Emma, get the torches out of the car. Where is the van with the crew? They should be here by now." She got out her mobile and dialled. "Mick …? Where are you ….? A flat tire ….? Oh, God in heaven, that's all we need … Well, when you've fixed it come on here at once … No, on second thoughts, wait till I ring you…. Right. Come on, you lot. What are we waiting for?"

Bartonstone Hall was huge and seemed even more huge in the falling dark. It had been built in the eighteenth century at the height of the Cutbirth's family fortunes, by Sir Cuthbert Cutbirth, an amateur architect of severely neo-classical tastes. The result was a vast, ponderous and relentlessly symmetrical building. Sir Cuthbert had particularly favoured Italy during his Grand Tour and had embraced Palladio without truly understanding him. This lack of aesthetic judgement also accounted for the number of dubiously attributed Italian Old Masters and "school of" Salvator Rosas and Canalettos which Sir Cuthbert had bought while on tour to adorn his mansion. When subsequent Cutbirths had tried to sell them to pay off their gambling debts, they had found them to be almost worthless, and the pictures remained at the hall, unloved, becoming more tarnished by the decade.

They found the metal gate to the steps that led down to the Hall's cellarage. There, as promised, was the scullery door and it opened onto a passage with various utility and store rooms to one side of it. At the end of the passage was a further door with a frosted glass panel in it through which they could see yellow light shining and from which came the sound of music, as yet indefinable.

Emma, Huntley and Valentine moved rather tentatively towards this goal, but Veronica became impatient. She strode ahead of them and opened the glass-panelled door.

What met their eyes was a large old-fashioned kitchen with a low, vaulted ceiling, painted all over in cream, now somewhat stained from years of culinary use. Against one wall was an ancient cast-iron kitchen range with copper pans hanging in rows it. In the middle of it all was a long scrubbed deal kitchen table at one end of which, facing the door, sat Sir Everard Cutbirth eating chicken pie. The music they had heard in the passage was now almost deafeningly loud, coming as it did from a huge speaker, of rock-concert proportions, on top of a refrigerator.

The moment he saw them, Sir Everard's entire face became contorted with rage.

"Who the Devil are you?"

"Hello, I'm Veronica Boyd. I'm a freelance film director. I do apologise for—"

"Oh, yes! I remember you! Well, get out, you hideous old harridan, and the rest of you too!" But his expression softened slightly when he saw Emma.

Impervious to his insult, Veronica said: "Sir Everard, if you could just turn down the music for a moment, perhaps I might explain—"

"Certainly not! You will at least have the common courtesy to wait till the end of the movement. And listen!"

And so they waited and listened until the end of the symphony's second movement. It seemed to them a very long five minutes. While they were doing so, Sir Everard paid no attention to them but addressed himself to the finishing of his chicken pie. The movement over, Sir Everard turned down the volume from a remote control at his elbow, so that the third and final movement (allegro con brio) could still be heard but did not bar all rational communication. He walked to the sink with his cutlery and empty plate to deposit them there. He seemed in a marginally more tranquil mood.

"Well, what did you think?"

"Of the music?"

"Well, of course of the music! What did you think?"

"Yes, very impressive," said Huntley emolliently. "Your own?"

Sir Everard nodded.

Huntley was pleased with himself for having grasped that what they had heard was one of Cutbirth's own compositions, so he added, "It reminded me a little of Benjamin Britten."

Sir Everard Cutbirth's face once more writhed in fury. The words were barely out of Huntley's mouth before he knew he had said the wrong thing.

"Benjamin Britten! Benjamin Britten! That syphilitic sissy! That neurasthenic nancy boy! That conshie catamite who scampered off to the States with his whining pansy pal Peter Pears when we were facing Hitler and then scuttled back to England when the coast was clear to dodge the American draft. The man had no guts, no heart, no balls. All he had on offer was a thin drizzle of creepy piss—technically very accomplished piss, I grant you, but that only makes it worse. How can you respect a man who writes practically all his operas about child abuse? Listen to that!" He paused to hear the sound of a great brazen climax in the finale of his own symphony. "There's passion! There's pain! There's heart! You won't hear that in bum-boy Britten."

"No indeed," said Valentine in a very neutral tone.

Sir Everard gave him a searching look, but decided to let it pass. "Well, what do you want?" He was addressing the four of them, but his eyes lingered on Emma. It was a prying, fingering gaze.

"We would like to talk to you about the book," said Valentine, the one person of the four who felt immune either to Sir Everard's loathing or his lust.

"What book? I have no idea what you are talking about."

"Oh, yes, you do, Sir Everard. We're talking about *The Boke of the Di-*

vill. We know you stole it from the Deanery."

"Prove it!" There was a pause. The music, sinuous and brass-heavy, droned on. "Anyway, it's mine! It belongs to my family. It has done for centuries. How dare you?"

"Sir Everard," said Huntley, "we don't want to take the book off you. In fact, as an historian, I very much favour your claim to it. All we want to do is make a programme about it. That could very much enhance its value should you want to sell it—"

"Sell it? Who says I want to sell it?"

"I'm not saying that necessarily—"

"Well, how much? How much d'you think it would fetch?" Sir Everard's rage had dissipated into a nervous edginess. He was fidgeting with a gold ring on the little finger of his left hand.

"Of course," said Huntley, his confidence increasing, "I would need to authenticate it, but if it really is what we believe it to be, an ancient grimoire, it could go for millions—"

"Grimoire! Huh! Do you think I believe all that metaphysical mumbo jumbo? I've looked at it. It's all rubbish. A lot of gibberish, diagrams, and crude drawings. Like that absurd Voynich manuscript, which a lot of idiots have wasted their lives trying to decode. It's probably some elaborate hoax, but it's ancient all right. However, if you can guarantee me a few million, no questions asked, I might be prepared to …"

"We would need to see it first," said Veronica.

"Very well," said Sir Everard, smiling for once. The last notes of his third symphony were sounding, a series of brass chords and timpani crashes. Several seconds elapsed while the music found its conclusion. When it was over, he said: "Follow me."

They mounted a flight of uncarpeted stone steps, designed in earlier times to be used only by servants, and came into the great hall of the house. It was an impressive cube the height of two floors, with a grand marble staircase and a coffered dome ceiling modelled on the Pantheon in Rome. Illumined now only with a single lamp on the cassone by the library door, the great space was draped in shadow, so that it resembled a mausoleum. Classical marble busts on plinths enhanced the effect. Through the two tall windows that flanked the front door, they could see the shapes of Cutbirth's landscaped park, deep blue against an indigo sky. A sliver of moon was out and stars were beginning to show.

"Well, there you are," said Sir Everard, indicating the library door. "It's in there, on the desk. Yes, you can take it away with you for tests or examination or whatever it is, but I'll want a document signed by all of you to say that you have taken charge temporarily of my property until such time as it should be sold." Valentine noticed that Sir Everard was once again fidgeting compulsively with his ring. They agreed to his terms.

"Well, go on, then;" said Sir Everard, "you can go in there and get it if you like."

"Emma, fetch the book for us, will you," said Valentine. The rest all stared at him. "Emma, I am right in thinking that you are a virgin, are you not?"

Emma blushed unseen in the gloom. It was her greatest, her most carefully guarded secret. She was not ashamed at all of the fact, but she would never have mentioned it. She had once compared it to being the possessor of a valuable but now distinctly unfashionable work of art, like a Leighton or an Alma-Tadema. She nodded assent.

"What bloody nonsense is this?" Sir Everard's usually composed rage had deserted him. He was now practically screaming. "What cretinously superstitious rubbish are you spouting? How dare you come into my house and—who are you anyway? I will not have you fouling my family seat with this asinine idiocy. You're all mad. Get out! Get out!" He stamped on the marble flags in his rage and tore at his left hand so that the gold ring he was wearing flew off and bounced on the floor with a tinkling sound like that of a tiny bell. Sir Everard stared about him wildly, half amazed at his own paroxysm.

At that moment a strange thing happened. A blue light flashed through the shadows of the hall and then vanished. Huntley and Valentine who were facing the windows and the front door could see that it came from the park.

Sir Everard screamed: "Jesus in Hell, what's that?" He turned round to face the window and saw the blue light flash again.

"It looks like the police," said Valentine.

"Then what in the name of the Devil are they doing trespassing on my property?" Sir Everard rushed to the front door and tried in vain to wrench it open, bolted as it was. Breathing hard, he recovered himself a little, then attacked the bolts. As he began to scrabble with them, he uttered little inarticulate screams of rage and frustration. Finally he had slid them back, pulled open the heavy oaken door and rushed out into the night.

"Emma," said Valentine quietly, "Go into the library, get the book and

200

bring it out. If you can, try to find a cloth to wrap it in." Emma obeyed.

"What is this bollocks, Basil? I mean—" said Huntley, momentarily at a loss for words, "you don't believe in this … bollocks, do you?"

"What bollocks would that be?"

"Exactly," said Veronica. "It's ridiculous. All that rubbish about virgins went out with the Middle Ages, didn't it?"

"But then, you forget—so did *The Boke of the Divill*," said Valentine.

Emma emerged from the library carrying an object encased in a red velvet cushion-cover. Even Veronica noticed that there was a new serenity and purposefulness about her.

"I think we had better get out of here," said Valentine. "No, not by the front door. We're bound to be held up by the police."

"Back through the kitchen, then," said Huntley.

Valentine shone his torch on the floor until he had found the ring. Pulling out a handkerchief, he picked it up and put it in his pocket, then turned to follow the others who were making for a doorway at the back of the hall. It was not the way they had come.

The steps down were of stone and very like the ones that had led up from the kitchen, so that all four of them believed, or hoped, that they were bound in the same direction. A single naked bulb at the top of the steps showed them the way downwards, but the steps continued until it became a distant point of light. Emma and Veronica switched on their torches.

"This is not the way to the kitchen," said Huntley.

"Yes, Dave, we know that," said Veronica.

"Shouldn't we go back?"

There was a distant bang. Valentine, who was the last of the four, said, "I don't think that's possible. The door at the top of the stairs has slammed shut. The police may be there by now."

At that moment the light went out. They had only three torches.

They seemed to be going down into the earth. The walls were no longer lined with brick but rough-hewn rock. Still they went down. All of them in their different ways became possessed by an entirely irrational fear that the descent would never end, they would simply continue to go down forever into the depths of the earth. No one spoke this fear out loud because they knew it was absurd, but the knowledge in no way dissipated their terror. The air felt thick and old; a prevailing dampness infected their clothes and crawled over their skin.

Then Veronica, who was leading, shined her torch ahead of her and this time saw that the steps came to an end. Beyond them stretched a narrow tunnel whose floor was impacted earth, but she could see only a very little way ahead. Something had happened to her torch. To her it appeared as bright as ever, but the light did not seem to penetrate; the beam it should have exuded did not illumine more than a few feet in front of her. All the same, she shouted back to the others that there were no more steps; they had "touched bottom." The phrase—indeed, the whole situation—struck her as absurd.

She was followed by Huntley, then by Emma, carrying the book and the second torch, with Valentine a little way behind the others, bringing up the rear. The first three had reached the bottom of the steps when they heard a cry. Valentine had tripped and fallen down the last remaining steps, landing painfully. The torch he was carrying had flown out of his hand and smashed itself against a wall. Emma shined her torch back at him.

"Are you all right?"

"Fine. Just a little ..."

"What happened?"

"We must move. We must move on quickly."

"At least let me help you up."

Emma helped Valentine to his feet. He was clutching his knee and he was bleeding.

"Can you walk?"

Valentine nodded.

"Let me help you."

Valentine smiled and put his hand gently on her shoulder. Emma was conscious that he was not putting as much weight on her as he might want to. It touched and annoyed her in about equal measure.

Veronica said from the front, "Can we get on, please! I think these stupid torch batteries are giving out." She had also noticed that her own voice seemed distant and faint, as if it came from a few feet away and not from herself.

"You're right," said Emma looking at her torch. It was as bright as it ever was, and yet it only illuminated a small area a few inches around itself. It was as if they were walking through a black fog, but there appeared to be no smoke.

"What the hell's going on?" whispered Emma to Valentine.

"It has begun."

"What?"

"The attack."

"What attack?"

Valentine gently put his finger to her lips. "Keep going. Give me the torch. With your free hand take hold of Huntley's. Don't let it go, however much he protests. Tell him to do the same with Veronica. Keep moving."

When it came, each of them felt it in a different way, but to all of them its physical attributes were unimportant. It was the abstract qualities that were predominant, those of isolation and fear—above all, fear.

For Veronica, it was as if weights had been put on her feet, or as if she were wading through a swamp. Something was trying to stop her, slow her body, and slow her mind by pushing bits of black cotton wool into her head. Huntley heard whispers: he could not tell exactly what they said, but they condemned him, mockingly, like a million sarcastic schoolmasters. Above all, they emphasised, with painful honesty, the utter futility of his achievements, or rather—because what they said was not audible—they forced him to contemplate it. Emma felt a thousand fingers travel over her body, lustful and enquiring, poring over every crevice and every thought. All of herself was exposed; incursion and destruction were waiting, and in that was the terror. It was the threat more than the fact that scared her. Valentine felt the wound in his leg take over every thought in his head, every nerve in his body: the wound threatened to engulf him. He would become the wound. And there was nothing beyond them that they could cling to except each other.

Veronica said: "What the hell is going on? This is ridiculous." She said it to no one in particular. It was simply a way of shrugging off her terror.

"It is fear you all feel," said Valentine. The others could all hear him, but his voice came to them over a great distance. "Do not deny it. Accept its presence. It exists. It is not an illusion. Hold on to each other and try to carry a little of the fear that others are feeling. It is the same."

"This is bollocks," said Huntley.

"It isn't," said Emma.

"It exists. Don't try to possess it. Don't let it possess you. Simply recognise it for what it is, and don't give it command. You know Hume was wrong. Absurdly wrong."

"This is no time for philosophical ramblings, Valentine," said Veronica.

"On the contrary, this is one of those moments when they might come in useful. Hume said that when he looked inside himself all he discovered was a bundle of sensations, passions and so on. All he discovered … But what was the he that discovered it? That was real, too. So he was wrong by his own unconscious admission. Remember that: you are not your passions and your fears, you are the he and the she. Hold on to that he and she, and don't let the fear mask it. That self is the living spirit, the minute sand grain of freedom on the floor of compulsion's vast ocean. Don't let it go. It is ultimately all you are."

"But why? Why now? Why us? What the hell's going on?" Huntley was shouting, barely in control.

"We are in the fourth dimension. The book opened it. The discovery of the book; the theft of it. And for the first, but perhaps not the last time in our lives, the gates of Heaven and Hell are open for our inspection."

"Well, I can't see a damned thing!"

"That's just as well. What we are experiencing is enough. Hold onto each other. It is vital that we remember that we are not alone. We are all under attack. Move forward."

And they did, though without any sense of progress. All of them felt in their different ways that time and space had been pierced by something else. Call it the fourth dimension, if you like, thought Huntley, it's just metaphysical mumbo jumbo. Yet all around him he felt, as did the others, the invisible flight of multitudes, as if he were trapped in a cave with a million whirling bats, or inside the weaving pattern of a flock of starlings as evening falls. They brushed past him, almost as close as he was to himself, almost … He held on to that piece of counsel from Valentine, however reluctantly. These things, they were not exactly thoughts or beings or even sensations, but they were there; and he held on—just—to the idea that they were not, in the end, him. He grasped Veronica's hand in one of his own and Emma's in the other, and just at the moment when he thought he might give up the struggle, he felt a squeeze from both of them simultaneously. He recognised himself as a self among selves. And Veronica, of all people, to be giving him reassurance! Just then, he felt her hand almost release his, as she stumbled.

"Hang on," she said. "Steps again! And we're going up at last, thank God." The thanks were almost meant, as was the acknowledgement of divinity. Almost.

As they climbed, whatever had attacked them began to fall away.

Valentine's leg was still as painful as ever, though, and he needed help from both Huntley and Emma—still clutching the book in its cushion-cover—to mount the steps. A profound weariness began to make itself felt. Ahead Veronica could see a greyish aperture that gave her some hope. She was light-headed, her mind for once singularly free of thoughts, preoccupations, ambitions. It reminded her of something in her childhood, not so much a memory as a state of mind, that she had somehow lost over the years: the open heart—what Keats called negative capability. It was a long time since Keats had come into her mind; not since Cambridge.

The steps climbed up towards an arched entrance into an area which was obviously above ground, but which their bewildered minds could not at first determine was interior or exterior. The floor was of smooth, knapped flints, and the structure that surrounded them was roughly dome-like, with a round aperture at its apex open to the stars. The walls, which enclosed a nearly circular space about fifteen feet in diameter, were composed of cement into which, while still wet, had been placed countless shells of infinite variety, pieces of coloured ceramic shards and fragments of mirror glass which sparkled like stars when their torch beams passed across them. In among this reckless and exotic confusion some genuine antiquities had been set: the occasional fragment of Roman relief sculpture or stone inscription, usually of a funerary nature. Around the wall at eye level a double row of skulls had been set. Emma counted a hundred and twenty of them. Below this, a narrow stone bench encircled the space. The entrance to the open air was composed of large rough-hewn slabs of rock cemented together in an apparently random fashion, evidently made to look like the mouth of a cave. Outside the entrance and to their left was a mirror-like sheet of water, which darkly reflected the stars and the curved silver knife of the moon.

"Evidently we are still in the grounds of Bartonstone Hall," said Valentine lowering himself painfully onto the stone seating. "This place looks like a grotto, perhaps even an ornamental hermitage, certainly a folly of some kind, built at the same time as the house."

"More like a catacomb, with those skulls," said Huntley.

Valentine shifted uneasily on the bench. Emma watched him, concerned, wondering what she could do to help him. When Valentine spoke it was some of the verses that she had first read in the chapbook he had given her:

"Yet those that may may seek its secrets well
Who know no guile and broache the House of Lies
And find where four times thirty sorrowes dwell
In shelly cavern under starrie skies.

—four times thirty is one hundred and twenty. One hundred and twenty skulls, and the 'shelly cavern' must be our grotto. We seem, by some strange chance, to have come to the right place."

"Well, right or not," said Veronica, "we can't stay here all night. I'd better see where Mick and the boys in the van have got to." She took out her mobile and switched it on.

"Blast and buggery, no signal! Look, you lot stay here. I'll go and reconnoitre, see if the coast is clear, find out where the hell we are. I'll be back when I've found my bearings and got a signal." For once, she sounded reassuring. "Keep your peckers up," she added.

This was not like Veronica at all, and there was something a little embarrassing about its denial of her customarily abrasive nature. On the other hand, it seemed to mark a pleasant new departure. With that, she left them.

Valentine was now slumped on the bench in a stupor of exhaustion. Emma put the damaged leg up and did what she could to bind the wound with her handkerchief. She made a pillow for his head with her sweater so as to let the anaesthetic of sleep offer its temporary relief.

"Well, are we going to look at this famous book?" Huntley said.

"What! Do you really want to?"

"Of course! It'll be hours before Veronica gets back. We may as well pass the time somehow. You're not superstitious, are you? All that stuff that happened down there—" he indicated the arched entrance to the steps that gaped like a Hell Mouth "—that was just lack of oxygen. It wasn't real."

"The fact that it was due to lack of oxygen doesn't necessarily make it unreal."

Huntley shook his head and laughed condescendingly. "Come along, young Emma. Let's have a look."

She hesitated. It was strange. For all his affected superiority and scepticism, Huntley seemed to want her to give him permission to inspect it.

"Right you are, then," she said eventually. She handed him her torch and took the book to the cave mouth of the grotto, where she removed it from its temporary velvet sleeve and set it down on a convenient ledge of rock.

"Hmm," said Huntley examining the black leather binding. "Genuinely old. Perhaps even medieval. Wait a minute; there's something scratched on the front board." He shone his torch aslant the binding so as to pick up the lettering more distinctly. "*Ubi enim thesaurus vester est ibi et cor vestrum erit.* Latin: 'for where your—'"

"'Where your treasure is, there will your heart be also.' It's from the Latin Vulgate translation of Luke's gospel."

"Harmless enough. Thank you, young Emma. You appear to have your uses after all, virgin though you be."

In other circumstances Emma might have taken offence; but she saw in his sneer the feeble bid to maintain dominance. She merely sighed. Huntley did not hear her; he had opened the book.

The first three pages were black. They were made of some thick paper that looked as if they had been dyed or painted that colour. Huntley stared at them, shining his torch at various angles to see if anything could be made of it. Slowly he began to realise that the darkness was not uniform but consisted of infinitely subtle gradations of black, some marginally lighter or darker, some parts matte, some glossy, one area looking as if it was composed of closely cropped black hair or fur. As he continued to stare, he began to see things in the blackness, in particular a pair of eyes which appeared to move and then fix themselves upon him. Suddenly a hand from behind Huntley stretched across and flicked the pages over so that the black ones were obscured. It was Valentine. He had woken from a brief and troubled sleep.

"For God's sake don't stare at that!" he said.

"What the hell is it?"

"It's what's called a *Speculum Caliginis*, a Mirror of Darkness. It's just a sort of conjuring trick really, but a pretty nasty and clever one. They're rare things because there were only about three or four artists in the medieval period who could make them; all of them monks, I believe. They used these different blends of black inks and pigments to create the illusion, if you looked at it for too long, that there were things moving about in the darkness. Nobody knows how to make them anymore, thank God."

"What were they used for?"

"Divination, I believe. Fortune telling. A variation on 'skrying in the stone.' But mostly they were just used to frighten unsuspecting people like you and me."

"Reminds me of those black pages in Tristram Shandy."

"That's not a coincidence. The Reverend Laurence Sterne, who wrote it, was no mean occultist."

"How come you know all about this and I don't?"

"That is a mystery."

"Shall I go on looking?"

"Of course. If you wish. But I will stand behind you just in case, if you have no objections."

Huntley had many, and violent ones, but for some reason he did not voice them. He turned the pages.

"Aha! Canon Alberic's scrapbook," he murmured, chiefly to impress Valentine, at the same time wondering why he should be so anxious to impress him.

It was indeed a kind of scrapbook. There was paper, parchment, vellum and a fragment or two of papyrus gummed onto the pages. The papyrus was inscribed with Egyptian hieroglyphs, and a Greek inscription at the top of the page proclaimed them to be the work of the legendary Hermes Trismegistus.

"Highly unlikely, seeing as how he never existed," said Huntley who enjoyed being quietly dismissive in a scholarly way.

Many pages in the body of the book were written on vellum in Latin in a clear late-uncial script. Huntley was reluctantly impressed: this indicated that at least some of the text dated back to as early as the eighth century, and possibly even earlier. The writing was clear and hardly faded at all and Huntley was able to translate with ease. Most of the pages had titles like: "To Discover a Murderer by gazing into a Crystal" or "To Obtain the Love of a Woman or a young Boy," and the writing that followed contained detailed instructions accompanied by diagrams and, in some cases, drawings. These were exquisitely drawn and coloured, reminding Huntley of the Book of Kells, that high-water mark in pre-medieval manuscripts. The only difference was that the designs, far from being religious or Biblical in subject matter, depicted strange, sometimes obscene events. The illustration accompanying "To Obtain the Love of a Woman or a young Boy" showed a mature bearded man in a long red gown, but with wings for arms, hovering directly above the cowering naked body of a pubescent girl lying on a stone slab. Through the man's rich gown could just be seen the tip of an erect penis. In another, a group of demons were holding an elderly man down in a great cauldron, which was suspended over a riot of curling red and yellow flames. At the head of the page in large illuminated letters was the legend, which he translated as:

To obtain domination over one's enemies, and to extract the last scintilla of humiliation from one's persecutors

"Handy, I suppose," commented Huntley, glancing with a smirk at Valentine who was staring blankly at the pages and did not respond. Huntley was now definitely enjoying himself. He turned the page.

What he next saw froze him into a kind of paralysis of disbelief. The page contained no text, but was arranged very much like one of the illustrations in the Book of Kells. There was an elaborate frame of an intricate Celtic design painted in many subtle colours and enlivened with little flashes of gold leaf, but it was the picture within the frame that arrested him. It showed a man in a blue gown embroidered with silver stars seated at a high writing desk or scrinium of the kind used in monks' scriptoria. The picture resembled superficially those early representations of the Evangelists at work on their gospels that preface their texts in early manuscripts, but this was not quite the same. In the first place the background was dingy and seemed to represent the walls of a chamber hung with a variety of disagreeable objects: hacked-off arms and legs, a grinning skull with a grotesquely extended cranium, a baby in a bulbous glass vessel who appeared to be screaming in agony, and, suspended on a peg, what looked like the complete flayed skin of an old man. But this was not the worst, as far as Huntley was concerned. The fact was that the face of the scribe, though executed in a style consistent with eighth or ninth-century Saxon or Celtic work, was unmistakably his own. Huntley had to blink several times before he could acknowledge that what he saw was not an illusion.

He could say nothing, in case he gave away his alarm. He deliberately avoided looking at that page and stared at the page opposite which seemed to contain the usual rows of discreet Latin uncials: no more than a text, but as he continued to look the letters began to turn and dance before his eyes, then form themselves into phrases:

Quis es? Cujus es? Quid petis?

And then the letters danced again and formed themselves into their English equivalent:

Who are you? To whom do you belong? What do you seek?

And now his head was spinning, and he really could not tell what was in his brain and what was in the book, or even if he was in himself or the book.

He was in a lecture hall, explaining the book to an enraptured audience; he was in a bookshop on a book tour, signing innumerable copies of his book *The Boke of the Divill*, a book about the book. The admiring faces, the attentive audiences at dinners, lectures, seminars, television studios became a blur. The faces all seemed the same; then he found that he could change the faces at will, but that was no more satisfactory. Then a change. He was in his study at Oxford conducting a tutorial and opposite him on the sofa was an attractive undergraduate—male or female? Sometimes it looked like Emma, but he could not be sure, and that too was unsatisfactory, nevertheless the pressure was great. Blood thumped in his head. He rose and advanced on the young girl—yes, it was a girl—no! A young man. Definitely a man. But it did not matter. Then he was being thrown down face first on the sofa and he felt a weight on him and clawing hands. He struggled to be free, or at least to turn round to face his oppressor, but when he did, he saw whose face it was pressing close to his, filling his lungs with greasy breath, panting with unfulfilled longing. It was his own face, but horribly transformed: old now and grey and jowled, thin haired and bag-eyed, but still his own face. It was straining after something, but not a person, not even a body, just an idea, an illusion that he knew was empty, but that he still pursued, until all the blood vessels broke in his head. Summoning every effort Huntley closed his eyes, covering them with his hands to stop the smallest taint of light from penetrating, then threw his head sickeningly back away from the book.

A voice beside him was shouting in his ear. "You've seen enough!"

Huntley started violently, then took his hands from his face. It was Valentine, and Huntley was back with him in the grotto. Huntley turned his back on the book, not daring to look at it again. He gave a little nervous laugh, in an unsuccessful attempt to make light of it all, but he was shaking uncontrollably.

"Well," he said. "I don't think that will go down well on prime-time television! Can you close the book now, Basil?"

"You don't want to close it yourself?"

"Rather not. Don't know why. Go on. You do it!"

Basil obeyed.

"Bloody Hell! Did you see what I saw?"

"I doubt it."

"So what did you see?"

"That is another story," said Basil Valentine.

Emma, who had been looking on, said, "Shall I take charge of it now?"

"If you would, Emma," said Valentine. "Thank you."

"Don't you want to see for yourself?" Huntley asked, the tremor in his voice still evident.

Emma looked at Valentine, who gave her an almost-imperceptible shake of the head.

"No, I don't think so," she said, taking the book and returning it to its cushion-cover.

A few minutes later Veronica returned. "All right. The coast is now clear. Most of the police have gone, but the drive up to the house is still cordoned off, so we can't get to our car. I've found a way to get through the grounds and onto the road where the van with Mick and the boys will be waiting to take us back to safety. All ready?"

The three murmured their assent.

"Anything happen while I was away?"

"Not really," said Huntley.

Veronica subjected him to a brief, searching stare, but decided to let it go. "Let's be on our way, then!"

Just before they left the lake behind, Valentine took something from his pocket and threw it high over the still water. It fell with the smallest of splashes, and slow glassy ripples swelled outwards from where it had fallen. The Morchester Cathedral Museum had lost its ring forever.

CHAPTER 13

The constable looked through the window into the police cell. An old man with a shock of white hair sat and stared at the wall opposite. The expression was remote and unfathomable.

"Has he said anything?" the constable asked when he became conscious that the station sergeant was standing behind him.

"He asked for his solicitor, that was all. Arrogant bastard, if you ask me."

"Is he guilty?"

"As hell. Have you heard what he did with those two bodies? And one of them a vicar."

"Is he going to be any trouble?"

"Shouldn't think so, but keep an eye on him. He'll be in for the night, if not longer." The sergeant left him, but the constable continued to stare at the object of his reluctant fascination.

Slowly Sir Everard turned his head towards the door. For a moment the constable and he looked into each other's eyes, until the constable turned away, unable to take it any longer.

"Bloody hell," he muttered and went in search of tea.

It was not long after their confrontation that Sir Everard found himself descending a rope in the dark. The rope was silver in colour and faintly luminescent, the only thing that could be seen apart from his hands, which grasped it. He stared at the hands, wondering if they were really his, because he could not see the rest of his body, even though he could feel its weight. Around him the dark was close, muffling, and yet somehow infinite, as if he were in a vast chamber full of pillows and quilts. The sensation was both claustrophobic and agoraphobic at the same time. He was slipping gradually downwards. Surrounding him was a faint smell, the familiar yet frightening smell of himself and his own old age.

He was becoming acutely aware of his situation, which baffled him rather. One thing he knew: that he had a choice. He could haul himself, hand over hand, up the silver rope, or he could slip downwards, carried by his own weight. Yes, he had a choice, but he also understood that he was not going to avail himself of that choice. He would slide downwards: because he was angry, because he had ceased to care, because he was not going to be told what to do, even by himself. He would inhabit his own world and nobody else's—and so he let himself go.

There was no sensation of falling, just a gentle downwards motion with the bright silver rope between his hands. Then his feet touched the ground, a slightly yielding surface like that of a deep pile carpet. He was surrounded by darkness, but the silver cord remained, the only visible thing and still within his grasp. Or perhaps not. Yes, it was still within his grasp if he jumped and made an effort; but he was not going to jump: his jumping days were over.

He turned his back on the rope and began to walk away from it for a few yards, pausing and then looking back. A thin streak of silver still gleamed, in the black air above him, but it was now far beyond his reach. He told himself that the climb upwards had never been a feasible alternative—and where would it have led?

He began to walk down a gentle incline that with every move seemed to him increasingly inevitable. The atmosphere around him smelt of himself, now perhaps a little oppressively so. Ahead of him a grey speck began to widen into an entrance. This was his destination, inevitable now and fated. He walked into it.

Sir Everard found himself in a vast hall of classical decoration and proportions, like a gigantic auditorium, domed, bounded by tiers and galleries and boxes. There was a raised stage flanked by dull red velvet curtains, encrusted with gilded thread, ruched and swagged with ropes of gold. The seating in the stalls was red plush, and far above him were gigantic chandeliers, their showers of grey crystals shimmering in the dull half-light. He was alone in the great auditorium, but on stage some vague figures were moving about, taking their places at music desks. There was a conductor's podium too, onto which climbed a crooked, rather simian figure, but in white tie and tails and carrying a conductor's baton. Sir Everard found a seat—there were so many to choose from!—and sat down.

The conductor, his back to Sir Everard, his head so stooped that the shaggy top of it could barely be seen above the collar, raised his baton.

The musicians sat upright, attentive to him, their instruments poised, and then the music began.

For a few moments Sir Everard could not tell what it was that they were playing. The realisation slowly came upon him, not exactly with pleasure or delight, but with a kind of reassurance. It was a piece of his own. In fact it was the first major orchestral work he had composed, done while he was still at the Royal College, an overture called, rather portentously, *The Atom Age* (Opus 1). It had won some sort of prize, he recalled, and had been played at the Proms and once or twice subsequently. Though youthful and perhaps immature, the music was recognisably his own: those strident brass fanfares, the long sinuous half-melodies on the strings, the impish woodwind figures. The music filled the vast auditorium thrillingly: the orchestra played well. And yet he, Sir Everard, was not thrilled, and it was hard at first to understand why not. It was only after the overture had ended and the orchestra had almost immediately embarked on a second piece, his first symphony, that he began to understand. He was the only hearer, and, in whatever world he now existed, he was alone. In the darkness beyond, there were no other listeners; he and his work had been long forgotten. Nothing would respond to him with acclaim, nor even with malediction: his creations had become his gigantic echoing tomb, his grandiose and empty sepulchre. He knew the infinite horror of survival without existence. And even then, he was damned if he would leave....

By the time the officer looked again into the cell, it was too late. He sounded the alarm and resuscitation was attempted but failed. Somehow, that thin, silver-coloured silk tie Sir Everard had been wearing had been secreted and had not been removed from him. One end had been attached to one of the window bars, the other in a ligature around Sir Everard's throat. He had made a neat job of it.

Marie was surrounded by love. She was assured of that. But it was the kind of love that is exercised without imagination or empathy and is really a form of self-indulgence. She was sitting on the front row of chairs facing the choir in St. Paul's Church in the midst of a large and emotional congregation. She did not want to be in the front row; she did not want to be in church at all, but to have refused would have been to cause a lot of boring offence. The people who professed to love her so much were surprisingly quick to take offence if she ever acted or spoke in a way that they disliked.

On either side of Marie two middle-aged women—"sisters", they called themselves, but only "in the sight of God," not in reality—were holding her hands and generally pawing at her with unwelcome solicitude. In the chancel was a group of people who had come over from a fellow Evangelical church in Brighthaven to "lead the worship." They were there, they said, "to hold up our brothers and sisters in Christ in their hour of tribulation." At their head was Pastor Tom Haddock, a big man in a shiny suit, with a shiny hairless face that beamed with enthusiasm. He was the pastor of several churches in Brighthaven, a popular and charismatic figure, whom Marie's husband Gary had always, albeit privately, regarded with the utmost suspicion.

The last few days had been the worst in Marie's life. It had begun with her becoming terribly worried when Gary did not return from "a healing service" in someone's home that he had said he was going to. She knew that these impromptu "healing services" could last an unconscionably long time, but when midnight came and went, then one, two and three, she became fearful. She could not sleep. She brooded because lately she had noticed a change in Gary. It was not that he had become less loving or generous—if anything he was more demonstrative than ever; it was that she had become conscious that he was playing a part. He was not being a good and loving Man of God, but assuming the role of one, and giving a splendid performance, but still a performance. This she had at first put down to what is called "professional deformity," the way an occupation bends some people into a shape that is not altogether natural to them. But, increasingly, she had wondered if it went deeper than that—or perhaps shallower. She had started to wonder if there was anything beneath the façade at all.

Then, at six in the morning, the doorbell had rung—and it was the police. The few details which they had given her had been horrific, and all the more horrific for being utterly baffling. This had been compounded when she was at last permitted to see the body. That shock of white hair! Those staring eyes!

Very soon Gary's church took over. Its members, relying on an even more incomplete grasp of the events surrounding Eastwood's death than Marie had, concluded that he had died heroically combating the forces of evil headed by Sir Everard Cutbirth, whose suicide in custody had confirmed his guilt. Marie had accepted this version of Gary's end because of its convenience, and kept any reservations to herself. The only unpleasant consequence was that she was now being fêted as a kind of martyr-by-association and was being compelled to take part in all the pious junketings attendant on an unofficial canonisation. Hence the great festival of mourning and celebration that was held that Sunday afternoon.

Only one consolation had emerged from this nightmare. The previous day she had, with her supporters' reluctant permission, gone to the doctor to get something to help her sleep. While she was there, the doctor had conducted a number of tests, and Marie had found, not greatly to her surprise, that she was pregnant. It was a secret that she was determined to keep very closely to herself. She knew how happy it would have made her brothers and sisters in Christ (particularly the latter) to know this fact, and it gave her a certain malicious satisfaction to deny them that joy. But the malice was only slight; her reticence was mainly motivated by the knowledge that, if these people knew, there would be no getting away from them. Their kindness would be overwhelming and unbearable.

Throughout that interminable service of mourning and worship, the resolution had grown in her that, at all costs, she must get away from Morchester. A fierce desire had become a conviction, an article of faith that, to save herself, she must escape from this fervent and closely knit coven of loving Christians. She had to remove herself from all those people who wanted her to be what she was not, and the even greater number who simply assumed that she was what she would never be. Even in the midst of the endless choruses and the orgies of extempore and verbose prayer—"we simply really just do praise you, Lord!"—she hugged the thought of flight to her with a warmth that she would one day feel for her child.

Some kind of disturbance was occurring in the chancel where Pastor Tom Haddock was leading the worship. Against a discordant background of strumming guitars and shimmering tambourines, Pastor Tom was delivering an impromptu eulogy of Marie's husband. "My good friend and fellow warrior in Christ," he was calling him, now associating himself with him in the unspecified spiritual battle that had laid low the Reverend Gary. His eloquence on that point had called forth a good deal of gesticulation, but this, it seemed to Marie, was now becoming extravagant. Moreover, the others surrounding Haddock in the chancel, musicians, singers, pious hangers-on of all kinds, also seemed to be performing the same wild gestures.

Marie wondered if they had become possessed by the kind of charismatic fever that sometimes descended on churches like St. Paul's. She had read about the "Toronto Blessing," but this looked more like a curse. Haddock had stopped orating and was concentrating all his energies on fending off a physical torment in the air around him. Others looked equally troubled and the disturbance was beginning to manifest itself in the body of the church. A woman screamed. Marie's two "sisters" fell to their knees, dragging her with them, and began to pray fervently for deliverance. It was then that Marie saw them.

It looked like a plague of flies, except that they, whatever "they" were, were bigger than flies. They swayed and swooped over the congregation like flocks of migrating birds, turning their victims into angry and confused maniacs. The air was now full of cries of pain. The creatures seemed to sting as well as harass. Several people fell to the ground in convulsions, shouting out for assistance but receiving none. The rest were too busy looking round in astonishment and trying to avoid the next onslaught.

There were now several swarms in action all over the church. One came very close to Marie, knocking over her kneeling "sisters" and pinning them face down to the ground. Above the screams and expostulations of the assembled worshippers, Marie heard a high-pitched whining sound halfway between a mosquito and a coffee machine. Close to, the flying things looked like insects; flies, probably, albeit unnaturally large ones, with black bodies and black semi-translucent wings like the black lace on sexy underwear. Marie thought that they had tiny white faces and sharp, protuberant mouth parts, but she could not be sure— they flew so fast.

Still on her knees, Marie began to crawl to the side of the church. The sisters tried to stop her, grabbing hold of her legs, but she kicked them off. She noticed that those at the very edges of the church were less subject to assault than those in the body of the nave. She reached the south wall of the church and began to feel her way along it, skirting the tables and stands loaded with books and refreshments, and the hideous displays of children's paintings with which it was beset. Surprisingly few people were following her example. The chaos was now universal and complete. As Marie reached the door at the back of the church she turned round to see Pastor Tom Haddock in the middle of the chancel steps, whirling round and round like a dervish. He opened his mouth to cry out, and a swarm engulfed it. He fell to the floor, choking, his gaping jaws black and alive with multitude. Marie passed through the church door and out into the clear air beyond.

She had half expected the confusion to follow her, but it did not. The autumn afternoon was mild; there was a little sun and much cloud. The city was quieter than usual, even quieter than it generally was on a Sunday afternoon in September. Marie began walking in no particular direction. Her mind was full of plans. She would pack and leave that very night. She would go and stay with her sister, her real one, in Bromley. She would find a job as a science teacher again. She would have her child.

Instinct had directed her steps into St. Anselm's Street, through the great medieval gateway, and into the close. On either side, surrounding the great enclosed space, were the ancient houses of the close, serene, with their classical porticoes and their walls of mellow red brick. A plume of white and yellow smoke was rising from behind the Deanery. Odd. A little too early for a bonfire of leaves.

She crossed the road and onto the green. Ahead stood the massive, intricate facade of St. Anselm's Cathedral, its details faintly gilded by the pale sunlight. It was as if Marie had not seen that great house of God before. There were no flies on St. Anselm's.

CHAPTER 14

It was in the Deanery garden on the same Sunday afternoon that the final act was played out. After lengthy consultations and debates it had been decided, in the end unanimously, and the Dean had invited Veronica, Emma, Huntley and Valentine to witness the event. Veronica had insisted that Mick and the film crew should come too, to record it all. After some demur, the Dean had agreed, provided they leave immediately after it was all over.

Phyllis had fretted about what sort of refreshment would be appropriate for such an occasion, and the Dean had said: "Tea for the crew, and fruit cup for the rest of us." For once Phyllis had not argued.

In the middle of the Deanery lawn Dr. Tancock had set up his barbecue, an instrument that he only made use of once or twice a year when the choir were invited to partake of a celebratory meal of burgers and sausages as a return for all their hard work. The barbecue generally made the Dean nervous. He did not use it often enough to have become accustomed to its ways, and was always afraid of being found out as an inadequate barbecuer, a purveyor of meat that was both charred and raw. On this occasion at least, no such anxieties were involved.

Into the tray of the barbecue he placed three fire-lighters—no expense would be spared—and covered them with kindling wood. Once he had got the fire going he would overlay the kindling, not with charcoal, his usual practice, but with actual lumps of smokeless coal.

The Dean lit the fire-lighters and stood back to admire the effect. The flames began to lick and devour the kindling in a perfectly normal and satisfactory way. It was absurd to have expected otherwise, but somehow he had. He gazed at the sunlight on the lawn and the willows beyond, between which the fleet waters of the Wyven, tributary of the mighty River Orr, flashed and chattered. His wife came into the garden from the French windows with a watering can.

"Phyllis! What on earth are you doing with that?"

"I'm just watering the azaleas, Geoffrey. If we're having a film crew here, I want them to be looking their best."

"But nobody's going to be filming your azaleas, darling. We will be concentrating on the main event."

The use of "darling" had come as much of a surprise to Dr. Tancock as it had to his wife. She raised her eyebrows, smiled faintly and made her way to the flower borders.

The others soon began to arrive, first Veronica and Huntley, then Valentine, limping slightly, with a walking stick and leaning on Emma's arm. Then came the camera crew and the sound man. Once they were all gathered on the lawn with their fruit cup and their tea, the Dean said: "Shall we?"

"Hold on," said Veronica. "Just need to check the equipment."

When she had confirmed that the camera was properly focussed and the sound man was not falling asleep and all was in order, she nodded to the Dean. He went indoors and a minute later emerged carrying *The Boke of the Divill* in a supermarket plastic bag. Somewhere in a tree not far distant a bird began to sing.

"You're not going to regret this?" said Huntley.

"Oh, no. Thanks to your discovery of the Norman silver crucifix under the lid of the well, I shall have more than enough to pay for the chancel roof."

"You're not going to sell it, are you?"

"Oh, dear me, no! But I am going to say we're going to sell it. Then all kinds of art lovers and Cathedral enthusiasts will become very indignant and get up a petition and raise a lot of money so that we won't have to sell it after all."

Phyllis gave her husband an admiring glance.

"Are we ready?" said the Dean. The rest nodded.

"Turn camera, and action!" said Veronica. "Rolling?"

"Rolling," said Mick.

"Sound on?"

"Sound on."

"And cue Dean!"

The Dean frowned at Veronica but she did not react: her mind had withdrawn into filming technicalities. He removed the book from the plastic bag and approached the barbecue. The coals on the fire were by now glowing red. Opening the book with its pages facing downward, the Dean placed it on the coals and immediately stepped away to avoid the sudden blast of heat he felt.

For a long moment nothing seemed to happen, then the flames began to curl round the vellum pages in a sinuous orange embrace.

"I wonder if Hitler would have approved of this," said the Dean, but nobody reacted. The joke, if it was a joke, died stillborn.

Suddenly the flames themselves were engulfed in great billows of white and yellow smoke that remained solid and shapely as they rose in the windless air. Tiny particles of colour—red, green, blue—flickered through the little clouds and were gone. The smoke darkened and assumed the colour of flesh—not living flesh, but dead. Faces seemed to form, then vanish, then reappear. Emma saw Cutbirth, white and enraged; Phyllis saw Eastwood. The lean yellow mask of Canon Jeremiah Staveley appeared, then turned upside down and split apart. The Dean noted the red and raddled visage of Bishop Hartley, a look of furious concentration on his brow as if he were desperately trying to keep his head together, but it blew apart like all the rest. There were other faces, ancient and wicked, which none of them recognised. For a brief moment Huntley even saw his own features, old and tired, as if close to a despairing conclusion. But this was only for a second, if that; or so he told himself.

Veronica was staring at the spectacle enraptured, a light of pure enthusiasm in her eyes. "Bloody Hell," she muttered to herself. "Just wait. Just you wait!"

There was another rush of flame and the smoke began to diminish. Some of them thought they heard a thousand tiny cries coming out of the flames, like sonic sparks in a night sky, but it may only have been the crackling of the fire and the birds in the trees.

When the conflagration died down, they saw that every page had been consumed and only a few tattered shards of the black leather cover remained. These the Dean idly stirred into the coals, then added a little more fuel.

"Did you get that, Mick?" asked Veronica. Mick put his thumb up.

"Brilliant," she said. "Just run it back. Let's have a look."

Mick wound back the recording in the camera; then Veronica peered through the lens and pressed replay. But there was nothing recorded on the camera, absolutely nothing, not even shots of the garden: nothing. The same applied to the sound: nothing. Various possible remedies were tried, but without success. Mick shook his head in disbelief.

"Damn!" Veronica said. She would have liked to use a stronger word, but for once in her life she felt constrained.

"We live in an age of unbelief," said Valentine. "Even our machines are sceptics."

Portrait by Anthony Christian

ABOUT THE AUTHOR

REGGIE OLIVER was, like M. R. James, a Newcastle Scholar at Eton. He took an honours degree in classics at Oxford and then went on the stage. Since 1975 he has been a professional playwright, actor, and theatre director. Besides plays, his publications include the authorised biography of Stella Gibbons, *Out of the Woodshed*, published by Bloomsbury in 1998, and six collections of stories of supernatural terror, of which the fifth, *Mrs Midnight* (Tartarus 2011) won the Children of the Night Award for "best work of supernatural fiction in 2011" and was nominated for two other awards. Tartarus has also reissued his first and second collections *The Dreams of Cardinal Vittorini* and *The Complete Symphonies of Adolf Hitler*, in new editions with new illustrations by the author, as well as his latest and sixth collection *Flowers of the Sea*, which was nominated for a World Fantasy Award. His novel *The Dracula Papers I—The Scholar's Tale* (Chomu 2011), is the first of a projected four. Another novel, *Virtue in Danger*, was published in 2013 by Zagava Books. An omnibus edition of his stories entitled *Dramas from the Depths* is published by Centipede as part of its Masters of the Weird Tale series. His stories have appeared in over fifty anthologies.

THE CONSCRIPT

They told me I must write my name
Upon a scroll of death;
That some day I should rise to fame
By giving up my breath.

I do not know what I have done
That I should thus be bound
To wait for tortures one by one,
And then an unmark'd mound.

Made in the USA
Columbia, SC
01 December 2017